MURDER IN THE MOON WHEN THE LEAVES FALL

A Spotted Tongue Comanche Mystery

By D. R. Meredith

TABLE OF CONTENTS

ACKNOWLEDGMENTS

For those authentic touches that make a historical setting immediate to the reader, I must thank that master of arcane Texas facts and nineteenth-century firearms: C. F. Eckhardt. You passed on before I finished Spotted Tongue's story, but without your help and advice, Charley, I would have made many more mistakes than I have, and any errors concerning firearms are my fault, not yours. Thanks again, Charley, wherever you are.

Another person who helped more than she can know is Barbara Goodin of the Comanche Language and Cultural Preservation Committee. Thanks, Barbara, for recommending the *Comanche Dictionary and Grammar* by Lila Wistrand-Robinson and James Armagost. I may never learn to speak Comanche, but studying the language, along with the linguistic, historical, or cultural information often included with the translation, gave me some sense of the Nermernuh, The People.

My thanks also to Jason D. Stratman and the dedicated people at the Missouri History Museum Library Archives who provided copies of newspaper articles by William Fayel on the treaty council at Medicine Lodge. Many thanks to those unheralded individuals responsible for making so much archived material housed in public libraries and university and historical society archives available on the Web. It saved much wear and tear for the author.

Others I owe for advice are Richard S. Wheeler, who knows a bit about firearms himself. One individual who said he was nearly as invested in Spotted Tongue's story as myself is Scott Erwin, owner of Scott's Custom Computer and my guru of all things tech and computers. Every time my computer went down, my software failed to perform, and I was generally in desperate straits and falling further behind my arbitrary writing schedule, Scott arrived with his expertise that I lack and probably always will. For the past three years, Scott kept me up and running and generally sane. Thanks, Scott, my tech hero. Your name belongs on the title page beside mine.

Finally, the person to acknowledge is my husband, Mike Meredith, who kept the coffers filled but otherwise kept his demands minor so I could afford to tell stories about a people who, for nearly 200 years, ruled the Southern Plains of the United States. Yet, apart from those who grew up in Oklahoma and the American Southwest or are somewhat familiar with the life of Quanah Parker, very few people know much about The People. Welcome to Spotted Tongue's world.

GLOSSARY

Awl	A piece of bone sharpened to a point and used to poke holes in tanned hide.
Bow and Arrows	Made by each warrior or by old men beyond the age of fighting or hunting. Arrowheads were originally flint, but Comanche later used iron obtained by trade or theft. The wood of the Osage Orange tree was preferred for bows, while the young shoots of the dogwood were used for arrows.
Breechclout	A broad strip of cloth of finely tanned hide, generally six feet in length, drawn between the legs and looped over a belt. The flaps might extend to the knees.
Cannibal Owl	The owl was considered a harbinger of bad luck.
Comancheria	A region controlled by the Comanche and to a much lesser degree, their occasional allies, the Kiowa, that included southeastern Colorado, southwestern Kansas, the western half of Oklahoma, eastern New Mexico, and Texas from the Panhandle south to the Edwards Plateau, east to near present-day Waco, and west to the New Mexico border. This was the area considered the Comancheria by the Mexicans, Texans, and the United States. Truthfully, the Comanche would raid into East Texas and south into Mexico.

Council Chief

Sometimes called Peace Chief, he was usually an older man who no longer went on raids, but who offered counsel to male band members. He chose when and where to move camp and organized buffalo hunts but had little other authority. Each individual male band member was free to accept or reject his advice on other matters. Therefore, a council chief's mark on a treaty was virtually meaningless.

Division

A word often used by historians and anthropologists to designate major units of the Comanche. Within each division were numerous autonomous bands. Originally, there may have been thirteen divisions, although present-day Comanche claim perhaps as many as thirty-five, but by 1867, many of these became extinct or may have merged into other divisions. By Spotted Tongue's time, there were five major divisions, each having several bands operating independently of one another. Those divisions were the Penateka, or Honey Easters; Nakoni, Those Who Turned Back, later called Wanderers; Yampirika, or Root Eaters; Kotsoteka, or Buffalo Eaters; and Kwahadi, or Antelope Eaters. The Kwahadi were the most fierce and aloof of all Comanche divisions.

Leggings

Made of buckskin and close fitting, they would extend as far as the hip and be heavily fringed along the seam, with the fringe at the heel being six to eight inches long.

| **Medicine Bag** | A small pouch carrying objects sacred to a warrior and worn under the breechclout next to the genitals. |

| **Moccasins** | Distinctive from those of other Plains Indians because of the heavy fringe along the seam, Comanche footwear was made of buckskin uppers and soles of tanned buffalo hide. They were frequently decorated with strings of beads sewn from the toe to the lace, along the seam, and around the top of the moccasin. |

| **Nermernuh** | The name the Comanche called themselves, roughly translated as "People." |

| **Nerm** | The name an individual Comanche called himself, translated as "Human Being." |

| **Paint** | Made from clay and various weed and berry juices. Black was only used when going to war or on raids. |

| **Parfleche Bags** | Large intestines, most often of the buffalo, are cleaned and used for storage of pemmican or other dried food, other goods, and extra clothes, but not ceremonial clothing. |

| **Pemmican** | Wild berries, cherries, plums, or grapes that are ground and mixed with dried meat and tallow or marrow and stored in a parfleche bag. Pecans and other nuts are often added. |

Quiver

Fastened to a band worn over the right shoulder. In wet weather, the bowstring was carried under the armpit.

Scalp Lock

A small, braided section of hair at the crown of the head. A red or yellow feather was often tied to the scalp lock for decoration. Otherwise, the hair was parted from the forehead to the crown to form a braid on each side of the face. Women wore their hair cropped beneath the ears.

Shirt

Made of the skin of deer or antelope and heavily fringed around the neck and down the sleeve. It was generally worn only in cold weather; otherwise, the men were bare-chested.

Smoking Lodge

A tipi or lodge in which the male members of the band met with the council chief to perform a smoking ritual. These meetings, claimed by some historians to occur daily, served to mediate personal disagreements and controversy among members. It was also used by men too old to raid or hunt as a place to socialize. Women were not allowed.

Tipi or Lodge

Made of tanned buffalo skins sewn together and sometimes painted with magical symbols and stretched over a framework of from twelve to thirty poles. It is also referred to as a lodge.

Tweezers
Made of bone or shell and used by men to pluck out all facial hair, including eyebrows.

War-Bonnet Bag
A tubular-shaped bag holding feathers, war paint, hairbrush and mirror, and worn hanging from the waist.

War Chief
Often called the Trail Chief, he was the leader of a raiding party or war party. Selected by consensus of the members of the raiding or war party, he had absolute authority for the duration of the raid or battle.

War Club
A chunk of flint weighing around two pounds shaped roughly like an ax head but with one end tapering to a width of one to two inches. The head was fastened to a handle usually fourteen to sixteen inches long.

War Lance
A fourteen-foot pole with a projectile point of flint or, later, iron, and decorated with scalps.

War Shield
A round, slightly convex shield of laminated buffalo hide stuffed with fur or pages of books stolen during raids, decorated with animal fur, bear teeth, and scalps, and carried using two bands around the left arm. Magical symbols were often painted on the surface. They would deflect a lance or arrow and beyond fifty yards, a musket ball. They were considered powerful magic and

stored in a rawhide covering outside the tipi when not in use. Women were not permitted to touch them.

Wardrobe Case

Made of rawhide in the shape of an envelope with a tied-down, fold-over flap, the wardrobe case carried extra clothes, most particularly ceremonial clothes.

Wrist Band

A rawhide band worn on the left wrist to protect it from the reverberation of the bow strings.

HISTORICAL NOTES

It is always a risk to write a historical novel because no one knows absolutely what the truth is. Writing of the Comanche in pre-reservation times is doubly risky. The Comanche had little oral history and, as a nomadic people, left almost no archaeological record. All we know of their days as a free, nomadic people are old records of the Spanish Colonial, Mexican, the Republic of Texas, and the United States governments, along with captive narratives and a few diaries and journals of traders, explorers, and military men who recorded a brief glimpse of these mysterious beings referred to as "Lords of the South Plains" by one historian. The rest of our knowledge rests on myth, legend, and hearsay.

The first mention of the Comanche in the South Plains, according to Spanish Colonial archives, is in 1705, when a band of Mountain Utes appeared in New Mexico accompanied by a band of short, dark-skinned men they called *"Kahmahts,"* later translated as "Those Who Are Always Against Us." Comanche is a Spanish corruption of the Ute word. They are believed to have once been Northern Shoshone who, for whatever reason and many are cited, broke away and migrated from the mountains to the Great Plains and south to the lands of Kansas, Oklahoma, Texas, southeastern Colorado, and eastern New Mexico. They had few myths, folklore, or rituals. Remembered tribal lore said they sprang from a mating of the animals, primarily the wolf, whom they revered. Therefore, there was a taboo against killing the wolf and its four-legged cousins, the coyote and the dog.

The Comanche called themselves Nermernuh, which means "true human beings," or "People." All tribes had their own name for themselves, and most loosely translated as "People." Each tribe of "People" believed themselves to be more human than any other. It is a form of ethnocentric behavior that arose during a time when small populations lived isolated from other tribes in a vast, empty continent. When one lives separately from other human beings, one tends to believe that your ways are best. It is a trait of all human cultures regardless of race.

Whatever their history may have been, there are a few facts that are indisputable. They were the finest light cavalry among the Plains Indians. They were a warrior culture whose style of fighting is closely akin to that of modern-day guerrillas in that they used the tactics of hit and run. They seemed to rise from nowhere, strike at an isolated cabin, pueblo village, or other Indian encampments, then disappear into the Comancheria. To citizens of Mexico and the settlers of Texas and New Mexico, the Comanche, in their traditional black and white war paint applied in horizontal stripes across their faces and wearing buffalo scalp headdresses with the curved horns still attached, were the stuff of nightmares.

The Peace Commissioners at Medicine Lodge Creek seemed unaware of the threat posed by the Comanche to the settlers of Texas and New Mexico, as well as the residents of Mexico, despite the vocal warnings. They ignored the absence of the Kwahadi Comanche, the most warlike of all Comanche bands, and disregarded the warnings of all the chiefs of the five tribes that they could not speak for or control their young warriors.

Although Quanah Parker of the Kwahadi said much later he was at Medicine Lodge, I could find no independent verification of his presence that I trusted. All other historical figures who appear in my novel are mentioned multiple times in multiple contemporaneous sources. Quanah Parker was not mentioned until decades later by people who had not been at Medicine Lodge but accepted his claim at face value without researching further or at all. He was not listed as having "touched the pen," an Indian expression meaning signing a treaty. If he was there, he stayed well in the background, perhaps for the very reason I attributed to him in Spotted Tongue's story. Certainly, the white commissioners, the journalists, and the Army were unaware that the son of a famous white captive and a Comanche chief, soon to be known as the fiercest war chief of the Comanche, who was never defeated in a face-to-face battle by the United States Army, was lurking in the shadows at the Council. Although I use the name Quanah Parker in my book, he was not actually called that until the early days of the Reservation.

When you meet Spotted Tongue, Fat Belly, Shaking Hand, Wild Horse, and the other Comanche, do not judge them by today's standards. They were warriors and lived by the warrior's code. They were a stone-age, nomadic people whose culture was as different from that of twenty-first-century Americans as can be imagined. Stealing horses, raiding settlements and isolated cabins, rape, murder, and the taking of captives were not crimes to them but acceptable behavior. Their behavior differs very little from that of any army of any conqueror in history: the Egyptian Pharaohs, Alexander the Great, the Roman Caesars, Genghis Khan, William the Conqueror, the Christians and the Moslems during the Crusades, and the Spanish Conquistadores, to name a few. Many an enemy village was put to the torch--after being looted, of course, and the maidens ravished--during the endless European wars of past centuries. Where the Old World and the New World differed radically was what historian T.H. Fehrenbach calls the Amerindians' worldview. The Amerindians, including the Comanche, saw the world as ruled by random chance and magic. They did not recognize cause and effect. When Spotted Tongue loses his ability to "make medicine, to call his spirit animal for aid," he believes he loses the ability to protect himself against bad luck. His perception changes when he learns that medicine, or the lack of it, doesn't alter events. This knowledge makes him different, and in a society as conservative as the Comanche, being different could be as dangerous as being a Quaker in Puritan New England. His belief system is shaken to its very core.

The Comanche spoke a dialect of the Uto-Aztekan language group, which is rendered as English in the narrative. Sprinkling random Comanche phrases that require lengthy translation needlessly interrupts both the narrative flow and the suspension of disbelief and adds nothing to either the verisimilitude of the story or the reader's ability to identify with the characters. The only Comanche words used are the names of the various divisions of the tribe, such as "Kwahadi." "Nermernuh," "People," and "Comanche" are used interchangeably in the narrative. Otherwise, only a few single Comanche words are used and translated by the next word, and hopefully, they do not interrupt the narrative flow.

To create believable characters placed in the context of their culture and society set against the larger white society that surrounded them was a task that was almost overwhelming at times. I owe much to scholars without whose books and articles I would have floundered in a morass of misinformation, disinformation, inconsistent and contradictory information, and careless research presented as accurate. Those interested will find a suggested reading list at the end of the book, and yes, there will be some books that will contradict information in other books. If you are a glutton for information, consult the bibliographies of those volumes for further references and sources. If you read everything listed in all the bibliographies, will you know the truth? Probably not. Only tantalizing glimpses, varied perspectives, inconsistencies, and limited verifiable facts. History is not an exact science, and the historical novelist can only fill in the gaps with her best logical guess based on the facts she knows and trusts. That is why it is called fiction.

With the exception of historical figures whose personalities are based on historical research, all other characters are a product of my imagination. The Treaty Council at Medicine Lodge Creek actually happened; the murder I describe is loosely---very loosely---based on an actual altercation, although the names of those involved are not in the historical record, and the ultimate outcome of the altercation is mentioned in two different sources which contradict each other. As with other instances of contradictory information, I picked the version that best suited the plot.

What is the only absolute truth I can state without a disclaimer? If I had been Spotted Tongue, I wouldn't have signed the Treaty of Medicine Lodge either.

PROLOGUE

*"You can no more stop this than you can stop the sun or moon;
you must submit and do the best you can."*

- General William Tecumseh Sherman

Near Cache, Oklahoma, 1925

Spotted Tongue peered through milky eyes at his youngest granddaughter, a light-skinned young woman of some twenty-five winters. Daughter of his daughter by his third wife, a Tejano he had captured during a raid in the summer after the council at Medicine Lodge, Mary Riley looked more like her white father than her mixed blood mother. Spotted Tongue called her Little Fawn because of her large, pale brown eyes and narrow face that reminded him of a baby deer. Her eyes always held such a curious and innocent expression, again like a newborn deer.

She was his favorite of his many grandchildren, perhaps because she had defied her mother and grandmother to seek him out. Her grandmother, his third wife, may the Cannibal Owl take her, had abandoned him when he surrendered at Fort Sill more winters ago than he cared to remember. His third wife had returned to her Tejano family, taking his young daughter with her. He would have hunted her down if he had not been locked up at the time by the soldiers. Had it not been for Quanah Parker speaking for him, Spotted Tongue might have been put on an iron horse for some faraway place to be locked up for many winters. He pledged his word to Quanah not to search for his third wife but to let her go. Quanah's heart was always soft toward captive women because his mother had been a captive Tejano. Of course, Quanah had never lived with Spotted Tongue's third wife.

From what few stories Mary told him, his third wife and daughter had not been treated well in the white lodges. Her white Tejano family felt his third wife was shamed for marrying a Comanche warrior, and she and his daughter lived as outcasts in a cabin on her family's land. Naturally, his third wife blamed him, and because she did, so did his daughter. His third wife had always had a contrary personality. His lodge had been a more peaceful place after she fled back to her family. If she had not taken his daughter, he would have felt well rid of her.

He had met his daughter once after her mother took her. She had come to take Mary back to Texas, but the girl refused to go. His daughter blamed him. His daughter looked like him, with high, broad cheekbones and dark skin. She blamed him for that, too. He could not deny she was his blood, but her bitter tongue and ugly temper belonged to her mother. She did not even speak Comanche but cursed him in English. Spotted Tongue spoke English better than he let on, but answering her in Comanche left her red-faced and sputtering. Her husband, Mary's father, looked embarrassed by his wife's behavior. He should have been embarrassed for himself. No Comanche husband would have allowed such behavior by a daughter toward her father. But there was much Spotted Tongue still did not understand about white men despite nearly fifty years of observing them.

Sometimes, he wondered how the white men, who could not rule their own families, ever defeated the People. Except there were so many white men, more than the blades of grass on the prairie. Still, Spotted Tongue's surrender with Quanah Parker's *Kwah-heeher Kehnuh,* or Kwahadi as the white man called them, remained a burning hurt in his chest even after so many winters. That Spotted Tongue, proud Comanche warrior and war chief, had been forced to strip himself of his lance, knife, bow and arrows, war club, shield, and guns, which still took away his appetite if he thought too long on it. It was that memory of the shame of surrender that exploded into fury at his daughter. He was Spotted Tongue! No woman, even if she was Comanche and his daughter, would despise him in his own lodge. That had been nearly six winters ago, and his back had still been straight, and the strength had not yet left his legs. He laid hands on his daughter's shoulders and pushed her through the door. Her white husband hesitated a moment to look at his daughter's face before following his wife. Mary Riley, his Little Fawn, stayed inside the lodge, tears leaking from her eyes.

When Spotted Tongue saw Little Fawn crying, he felt even angrier that her mother had broken the blood bond between them. A Comanche was true to his kin to the death unless your kin dishonored the People, like fleeing from battle or stealing your wife. Then, it was different. Spotted Tongue forced out thoughts of his daughter from his mind where she no longer owned a place. Her dishonor made her an outcast.

No doubt she would blame him for that, too.

"*Toko?*"

The sound of the Comanche word for grandfather pulled Spotted Tongue from his memories. Mary Riley, his Little Fawn, spoke his tongue after these many winters visiting his lodge or house, as she always reminded him it was called by the white man.

"It's a house, *Toko.* A lodge is a tipi made of tanned buffalo hide."

"House, lodge, all the same thing, both keep out rain and cold wind," he answered in English, which he spoke better than she spoke Comanche. Sometimes, she did not say the words the right way; sometimes, she put the words together wrong. She would learn better.

He leaned forward in his chair to rub his knees.

Little Fawn frowned in concern. "Do your legs hurt, *Toko?* Do you want me to call the doctor?"

"Legs ache all the time. I do not want the white doctor. His medicine is no good."

"Do you want me to call the medicine man?" Little Fawn frowned even harder. She was raised a white woman and believed in the white doctors' pills and potions, not the Comanche way of chants and rubs.

"Medicine man no good, either. White or Comanche, neither keep many winters from stealing a man's strength. No reason to listen to Red Feather's chants. He sounds like the frog croaking anyway. I want to hear a frog croak, so I go down and sit by the creek. Better you tell me why you came to visit so soon after you go back to school at the big medicine lodge."

Little Fawn sat down on the footstool next to where his feet rested. Her big eyes sparkled even in his cloudy vision. "It's a university, *Toko,* the University of Oklahoma. And I am studying anthropology. That means I learn about the origins, behavior, and culture of humans, in my case, the Comanche. You're one of the oldest living Comanche; you remember the way the People lived before they settled on the reservation."

Spotted Tongue reared up straight, his knees forgotten. "We did not settle on the reservation! The white man and his soldiers forced us! Quanah Parker said he would go to the reservation when the white men came and made him. And they did. And we went because the children were starving, the old people were sick and dying, and the soldiers chased us all the time. We could not hunt the buffalo, those the white hunters had not killed already."

He sank back in his chair, enjoying its softness. That was one good thing about the white man's world: stuffed chairs that hugged an old man's body.

Little Fawn patted his leg. "I'm sorry, *Toko,* I know you didn't surrender because you wanted to. I didn't mean to insult you."

Spotted Tongue waved away her words, feeling the old ache of shame settling in his chest. Surrender! Its hurt never went away. "It is all gone now. My friends and brothers are gone, even Quanah Parker, these many winters. My wives are gone. Some of my children are gone. The lodges along the rivers and in the Palo Duro Canyon are gone. The buffalo is gone. My pony herd is gone. No point in talking about what is gone. I live in a house now, sit in a white man's chair, and I own land, much land, and cattle. I am one rich Indian, just like Quanah was. Not what the white man expected. Quanah Parker and I were two smart Indians who played the white man's game of land and cattle and trains. But I played better than Quanah. I am still rich, but he died poor, five hundred dollars, more or less left. I don't know why or what he did with his money."

"But *Toko,* you only own 320 acres, your allotment and your first wife's allotment that you inherited. The rest belongs to your children and grandchildren."

Spotted Tongue frowned. Little Fawn's words were true ones in the white man's way. He did not own all the land he claimed. In the old days, a Comanche commanded the respect of the People as long as he could hunt and fight, but when old age darkened his eyes and stole his strength, the young braves no longer listened to his counsel. Old men owned too many ponies, had too many wives, and talked too much of peace treaties and no more raids. But how else would a young brave get ponies and wives and respect if not by raiding? The young men picked their own trail, and it was most often the trail of war.

In the old days, if he had as many winters as he did now, he would control little influence on a few of the young men. But it was not the old days. There were no more buffalo hunts, no more raids, no more war. Now, a man earned respect by outsmarting the white man, and he and Quanah had learned the skills to win the white man's game of money, land and power. Age did not steal away those skills; age gave a warrior more knowledge of the enemy and more patience to defeat him. So Spotted Tongue held the respect of his young men, even if some of his sons were not so young anymore. They listened to his counsel and followed it. He did not have to own the land himself to control it.

"All the same family, all the same land. I don't want to talk about the old times," he finally said.

"But I need you to talk about it. I need to write it down on paper for my teacher so I can receive my degree. I can't be a real anthropologist without a degree. Please, *Toko,* I need your help."

"Explain what this paper is you need to write," said Spotted Tongue, his heart going soft inside his chest as it always did when Little Fawn asked him for a favor. He listened as his granddaughter tried to explain what the paper was and how it would help her. It made as little sense to him as much else the white man demanded. The People never worried about what happened in the past; they had enough to worry about providing their families with buffalo meat to eat and hides to make clothes and lodges. Unless others wronged them. Then they remembered for many winters and taught their sons and grandsons to remember. Just ask the Lipan Apaches, the Tonkawa, the Mexicans, and Tejanos how long the memory of the Comanche was.

Spotted Tongue settled back in his chair, wincing as he shifted to find the most comfortable position for his sore back. "What do you want to know?" he asked. "How we hunted buffalo? How did we choose our camping sites? How did we go on raids? How did we make our weapons?"

"No, other Comanche have already told the anthropologists about all that."

Spotted Tongue laughed. "Other Comanche only tell the white men what they want them to know. Then the white men go away happy and leave the Comanche alone."

"You mean the other Comanche lied?" asked Little Fawn, her big eyes looking even bigger with shock.

Spotted Tongue shrugged. So trusting was his Little Fawn. Every man lied at one time or another. "Just not tell everything. None of the white man's business how the Comanche lived. But I tell you the truth, Little Fawn, so you can write it down on paper. First, I tell you how we hunted the buffalo."

"I'd rather you tell me about *Oru hoiaitu kish'wat,*" said Little Fawn, reaching for her pen and paper.

Spotted Tongue felt his mouth fall open. Even if Little Fawn's words were an awkward translation, he understood what she meant. "How did you hear of He Who Hunts Down a Bad Person? All who called me that are dead and those born on the reservation know only rumors of me if their fathers talked of me at all. The People, those who did not die of hunger and sickness, worked too hard trying to survive on the reservation to bother telling stories of a man who walked such a strange trail. Many of the People did not understand a man who hunted other Comanche, and they distrusted me. Some even feared me. I was like the Cannibal Owl; I brought bad luck if I came to your lodge to ask questions."

"Green Willow told me," said Little Fawn, looking more like a Mary Riley with her paper and pen and her spectacles sitting on her narrow nose. "You know, your first wife. She told me before she died."

"I know who Green Willow was," said Spotted Tongue. "That woman always talked too much. Sometimes, I wanted to trade her back to her father for the ten ponies I paid for her."

"She said you were a manhunter, that you hunted down Comanche who wronged other Comanche. Wrongs like murder and theft. You were a detective, *Toko?* That's an English word that means-----"

"I know what it means. Someone called me that many, many winters ago. He wrote stories on paper, too," said Spotted Tongue, his mind flying back to that camp on Medicine Lodge Creek and the tall, thin white man. "But those times are gone. I am no longer the man who hunted men so evil they would kill others of the People. Now there is the white man's police and the white man's law, hangings and the stone lodges they call prisons. There is no place for an old Indian. Why talk of those times?"

"Because I'll learn so much about Comanche society, about how peace was kept within the band." She smiled at him, that smile that made her eyes crinkle at the corners and made him weak inside. "And because you want to remember, *Toko*."

He heard the teasing in her voice, and her smile made her a dangerous woman. He hoped her white boyfriend, whom he had met and approved of a little, knew how dangerous she was. Probably not. A man never knew about a woman like Little Fawn until she was already in his lodge choosing where to put the cooking pot.

"*Toko?*" she repeated.

He pondered. Perhaps it was time to tell of those times. Now that his eyes grew dim and the world around him was as dark as when night approached, his memories would be light and their colors strong. To remember would be like living again when the Comanche was free, and the land was his.

"It was the Moon When the Leaves Fall, what the white man calls October," he began slowly, and the room faded away into a wide valley lined with lodges and the white man's tents, and his chair turned into a pure white pony. . . .

CHAPTER ONE

"I believe, however, religiously, that the only ultimate solution of this whole question is, that the Indian shall take his place among other men and accept the march of civilization, as he must ultimately, or there is nothing except his destiny that awaits him, which is extinction."

-Remarks by Senator Samuel C. Pomeroy of
Kansas during a debate in the U.S. Senate, July 17, 1867

The Great Treaty Council at Medicine Lodge Creek, Kansas - October 1867

The mounted horsemen, ominous, black silhouettes against the setting sun, rose over the low hills to the west like levitating ghosts and halted to gaze on the encampments below before riding down the slopes in two loosely formed columns. Spotted Tongue, Comanche warrior and war chief of his band, studied the encampments as he would an isolated settlement to be raided.

The shallow valley of Medicine Lodge Creek, rimmed on either side by low, sandy hills covered with thick grasses seared brown by the hot, dry season now ending as the coming winter approached, curved in a half-circle from west to east. A hundred or so buffalo skin lodges of the Arapaho, along with a few of the Cheyenne, sat at the bottom of a thickly timbered hill on the western end of the narrow stream, while next to them was a small encampment of white men and Indian interpreters in their canvas tents. The encampments of Kiowa-Apache, Kiowa, and the Comanche bands were on the eastern end of Medicine Lodge Creek.

A mile away from the Arapaho and on the south side of the stream, the tents of the Peace Commission were pitched on a small bluff and circled by army ambulances. Army pickets patrolled the perimeter, watching the Indian camps while the Indians watched the pickets, neither quite trusting the other. The army encampment was pitched nearly a quarter of a mile away, close enough to prevent the Commission from being murdered in their beds should the fragile peace break but far enough away to pacify the Indians.

Below the Peace Commissioners' encampment, the supply wagons formed a semi-circle around the teamsters' camp, more wagons than Spotted Tongue had ever seen at one time in one place, more wagons than warriors in his band. There were wagons of presents for the tribes after touching the pen to agree to the treaties, but most carried food, for the white chiefs must feed the tribes who came to the Council.

The jingle of the chains of the picket lines, the occasional braying of the teamsters' mules, the distant, high-pitched yipping of packs of dogs in the Indian camps, and the banging of cooking pots as Negro orderlies began their mess duties intermingled with the sounds of voices and laughter in the Peace Commissioners' encampment. On the banks of Medicine Lodge Creek, the low hum of different languages and the frequent shouts of children lent an aura of peaceful co-existence between the Indian camps.

The pony herds of the tribes grazed on the thick buffalo grass, burned brown by the past summer's sun, that grew on the hill slopes on the other side of the creek. Young boys watched over their individual tribes' ponies, driving them to water in the early morning, then herding them back to graze and warning away any stranger, white or Indian, who came too close or showed too much interest. The five Indian tribes had not fought one another for some little time, but a fine, strong, well-trained war pony could prove a temptation to any man. All knew the peace between them was like morning mist by a river: it could melt away with the coming of Father Sun—or with the theft of a fine pony.

Women clustered in the front of lodges, tending to fires and cooking food outside rather than inside their lodges as they commonly did. Cooking outside meant the women could both watch the children and gossip with one another about all the exciting happenings at the Peace Council.

Meanwhile, naked small boys, many not more than three or four winters old, darted around the squaws' feet, racing one another or playing the kicking game. Young girls, wearing nothing but breechclouts, played with dolls made of stuffed buckskin or helped their mothers tend to the cooking.

At the far end, at the greatest distance from the white men's camp and next to the Kiowa, were the buffalo hide lodges of the *Nawkohnee,* the "Nokoni" or Wanderers, and the *Kuhtsoo-ehkuh,* the "Kotsoteka or Buffalo-eaters, as the two bands are called by the white man. Their lodges were mostly soot-stained, but a few were covered by newly tanned buffalo hide with wide bands of medicine symbols painted in red and yellow, blue and ochre. Spotted Tongue's band sometimes joined a raid with the Nakoni and sometimes with Kotsoteka but consider themselves free men who ride where and with whom they please.

Spotted Tongue shook his head in disapproval at the location. No Comanche should raise his lodge surrounded by the camps of other tribes, even if the other tribes were Kiowa, and so close to the tents of the white men. Always stay on the edge of such an encampment as this so that the band could flee to the open prairies if an enemy too numerous to fight appeared. It was where he would have ordered the lodges raised if he had been one of the council chiefs of those other bands.

The air smelled of dust, pony and mule dung, the burning wood of cooking fires, the acrid smoke of distant prairie fires, an aroma of boiled buffalo meat, the white man's coffee, and the pungent odor of over five thousand Indians and white men gathered for the Great Treaty Council. It was a peaceful encampment, unaware of over forty Comanche warriors on their best war ponies, carrying their decorated war shields and armed with lances, war clubs, knives, and guns, although Spotted Tongue's revolver rested at the bottom of his war bonnet bag. He had little use for it and didn't understand why the white man did. The gun was inaccurate any further away than a warrior could spit. Spotted Tongue would rather depend on his iron-tipped arrows and bow made of the finest Osage orange wood. He could send an arrow through a buffalo at thirty paces and through a man at a hundred paces or more. And he could send his arrows, one after the other, nearly as fast as the white man's guns could fire, faster if the gun could only fire one shot before reloading. He could deflect most bullets with his war shield if he was skillful enough---and he was.

His war shield also had power. It was decorated with bear teeth to show he was a great hunter; the scalp proved he was a mighty warrior, and the horsetail proved he was a clever trader. These decorations were not painted on his shield, as were many warriors. The teeth were from a bear he had killed himself; the scalps were those he had taken during raids or battles; and the horse's tail was from a favorite pony killed during the war with the Arapahos. No one else could claim a war shield as powerful as that of Spotted Tongue.

But new long guns were appearing, ones that could fire many bullets before reloading. Spotted Tongue felt a quiver of uneasiness as he thought of these new long guns. They were accurate over hundreds of paces, and sometimes the bullets would pierce a war shield, even his, although it was padded with the white man's paper between the layers of hardened buffalo hide. Paper was a better padding than animal fur, and most Comanche raiding parties stole however much they could find in the isolated cabins and settlements they attacked. Spotted Tongue often looked at the black marks on the paper and wondered if it was a form of white man's magic that he should learn. One could never know too much about an enemy---and the white man was the enemy of his blood.

Spotted Tongue felt the war fever rise in his belly. For a moment, despite the promises to lay aside their lances and war clubs for the Treaty Council, he wanted to lead his band and all others who would join him and attack the encampments below. He wanted to scream his war cry and send his arrows through the white men's breasts, smell the scent of spilled blood, and hear the popping sound of scalps pulled from their heads to decorate war lances, war shields, and lodges.

He sucked in several breaths to cool his fever. There were the white soldiers and their guns, and the Arapahos might not join him. If the Cheyenne Dog Soldiers were present below, they would join to avenge the massacre at Sand Creek and the burning of another Cheyenne village in the Smoking Hills only a few moons ago, but the Dog Soldiers were camped along the Cimarron nearly fifty miles away. Only Black Kettle, the old Cheyenne chief, and his followers were at the encampment below, and Black Kettle wanted peace with the white man. The Kiowa would join; they enjoyed a good fight, but old Chief Satank might counsel against it. As for Santana of the Kiowa, who knew what he might do? Besides, there were the presents promised to the tribes. No Comanche turned down presents when he didn't have to trade his ponies to get them. No, decided on Spotted Tongue. He would not lead his warriors into a risky fight he had little chance to win, especially since he had lost his power to make medicine. The spirit of the wolf had abandoned him. He had no protection against bad luck.

"Spotted Tongue," whispered Fat Belly, the son of Spotted Tongue's father's brother. "Look at the white man's camp on the little bluff. See how they have no place to run? We could circle the camp and crawl up to the top of the bluff. They would never hear us, only the sound of their own death cries when our arrows pierced them."

"What about the soldiers? What about their guns with many barrels? I see at least two of those. They spit out many bullets at once when the soldiers turn the handles."

Fat Belly frowned as he thought, his broad forehead wrinkling up in a series of furrows under the red and yellow paint that divided his head and body down to his breechclout. Most Comanche had only painted their faces with maybe a few magical symbols on their bare chests, but Fat Belly believed that if a little paint was good, then more was better.

"We could kill the soldiers first. Besides, the guns with many barrels are pointed toward the Indian encampment, and no soldiers are near them," said Fat Belly, still frowning as he tried to follow Spotted Tongue's words. "You have strong medicine, Spotted Tongue. Your medicine will protect us."

Spotted Tongue felt fear tighten his belly. While not a council chief of his band, he is chosen most often as a war chief to lead raids, thus earning respect, and wielding great influence. But he knows he is not worthy of respect or influence. He had told no one that he could not make medicine. The spirit of the wolf would not answer his need for protection and strength while he led raiding parties. He was alone

He had tried to confide in Fat Belly, but the plump-bellied warrior did not understand his words. Worse, Fat Belly had looked frightened. If Fat Belly, who was his brother, was frightened, what would the other warriors do? Coyote Dung and his friends would call him bad luck and demand he be cast out on the prairie alone. No other band would accept him. A man alone on the prairie would die.

"My medicine will not stop the bullets of the gun with many barrels, Fat Belly. I would lose many warriors, and I would not listen to their women's mourning cries. Besides, by attending the peace treaty council, we are bound to put aside our lances and arrows when we arrive. To do otherwise would be dishonorable."

Fat Belly shifted the war shield he wore on his left arm. "How do you know all that?"

Spotted Tongue felt his isolation from Fat Belly and the other Comanche warriors. They no longer understood him. He did not understand himself. He only knew that he could observe and visualize what would happen given the obstacles before him. He did not understand why the other warriors could not do likewise. But they depended on their medicine, and he could not. He could only depend upon himself. What frightened him most of all was that the loss of his medicine made no difference to the success of his raiding parties. How could that be? Was all that he believed wrong? Just stories to tell children around the campfire?

"I just know," he replied, impatient with his friend.

"It's his medicine, Fat Belly," said Wild Horse, a son of Spotted Tongue's mother's brother and the finest maker of arrows in the band. Spotted Tongue had traded a fine pony for two quivers. "No one has a medicine like Spotted Tongue. Remember how he captured the white pony he rode on the last raid? And the woman, Little Flower, his second wife that he captured on that same raid? Would that we had a woman like that to warm our blankets on cold nights."

"It's not his blanket she warms," said Fat Belly, a chuckle rumbling from his throat.

Spotted Tongue turned his face away from his brothers and toward the encampments again, glad that they knew little about what went on in his blankets. Beautiful Little Flower with her black hair that curled around his fingers, her eyes the color of a pale summer sky, and her skin the color of the summer moon when young men rode the war trail made his stomach tighten every time he looked at her. She also made him guard his male organ. He should have named her *po? aya?eetu*, Thistle, because when she fought him, it was with nails and teeth, biting and scratching, until he pinned her under his body and tied her hands.

Other times, when he returned from a raid with captives and fresh scalps on his war lance, she hid in his arms but cried when he took her. He did not understand. The scalps were not of her people; the captives were white, but not her people. There were many other Indians besides the Comanche, but they were not his people. He didn't care about the Cheyenne at Sand Creek except as another example of the perfidy of the white man. Why should Little Flower care about white men she did not know, who were not her kin? He did not understand white women. He smiled to himself. Sometimes, he did not understand Green Willow, his Comanche wife, either. Women, whether Comanche or white, were strange creatures. It probably had something to do with their bleeding every moon. It made them a little crazy.

"Think of all the guns and goods we could take, Spotted Tongue," said Shaking Hand, another son of his father's kin. Named for the tremors in his left hand that had afflicted him since birth, he could still loose an arrow with the best warriors in the band.

"Look, Spotted Tongue, who is that riding toward us from the Comanche lodges? He still sits straight on his pony, but I think he is old," said Fat Belly, shading his eyes to squint at the rider. "What do you think he wants?"

Spotted Tongue watched as the rider approached. Fat Belly was right; the rider was not young but not very old either. He rode his pony with a dignity not seen in an excitable young warrior, but he also slumped just a little, like a man whose back is tired from many winters spent on horseback. As the rider drew closer, Spotted Tongue recognized him and straightened himself to sit tall and dignified on his own pony. He and the rider had chosen different trails two winters ago, and neither could ride side by side again.

CHAPTER TWO

"...THE Commanding officer of Fort Arbuckle, may in his own way convey notice to the tribes that this boy must be Surrendered or else war to the death will be ordered. There must be no ransom paid."

-Note on the end of a letter, dated June 25, 1867,
by General William Tecumseh Sherman,
in regard to the practice of paying ransom to the
Indians for the return of white captives.

"There will be no fight with the white man," said the older man as he pulled up his pony in front of Spotted Tongue. At least the older Comanche was dressed as one: his leathery face painted in blue and green and yellow stripes with white dots on each cheek and wearing tanned buckskin leggings and moccasins with long fringe on the seams of both. Spotted Tongue had seen him wear white man's clothes.

Spotted Tongue heard his friends mutter in disapproval. "Horse's Back, you are not council chief of our band. We no longer camp with the Nakoni but ride with the Kotsoteka, as it is our right to leave one band and choose another. You have no authority to give us counsel."

"My heart still hurts that you left us and that so many of our young warriors and their families followed you, Spotted Tongue."

"Two winters ago, near the Arkansas River, you touched the pen and agreed to a treaty. My band of warriors did not agree with the treaty—as is our right, so it was best to choose another path to follow. You have no authority to give us counsel. Besides, as a war chief of my band, I have already said there will be no fight."

Horse's Back looked at the encampments at the bottom of the low hill, his face solemn. "Then you are wise and your medicine strong. The white man would ride against us if we broke our word and attacked this camp. The whites are as many as the snowflakes in a blizzard, but they do not melt with the coming of the sun. The white father would send as many soldiers as the leaves on the trees in spring to punish us. The prairie would turn red with the blood of Co-manche warriors."

"The white soldiers could not find us," stated Fat Belly, absolute belief in his voice. "We will ambush them, then disappear before they can take to their horses. Better yet, we will steal their horses."

"The Cannibal Owl has stolen your wits," said Horse's Back. The white soldiers have not found us because they have not yet tried. If our medicine remains strong, maybe they will not think to send many soldiers in many bands."

"So, you will touch the pen to the treaty?" Spotted Tongue asked the old chief. "How will this treaty be different from the one of two winters ago? Will you go to the reservation to be penned up like ponies?"

Horse's Back clinched his fist that rested on his legging. "The Nakoni are growing fewer. We have fewer warriors since you left with your band. Our women do not bear many children, so there are fewer lodges. We are disappearing, Spotted Tongue! I must save the People any way I can, and that means we must leave the Comancheria and hope to prosper on the white man's path. The Nakoni cannot lose any more young men to the warpath."

"You cannot speak for your warriors," Spotted Tongue reminded him, feeling guilty about leaving the Nakoni, but like Horse's Back, he had to do what he did. "Each Comanche speaks for himself."

"Does the buffalo calf teach wisdom to the bull buffalo?" said the old warrior, his voice sharp with wounded pride. "But the white man believes the council chiefs speak for their bands. They do not hear us when we tell them otherwise. I will do what I must. Besides, if I don't touch the pen, the white man might withhold his gifts."

Spotted Tongue smiled at the old chief's words but was still not certain if Horse's Back meant to touch the pen for life on a reservation or if he would do so to fool the white man.

Wild Horse, Shaking Hand, and Fat Belly laughed. They heard what they wanted to hear. "Why waste good ponies in trade when the white man will give us presents for nothing," said Fat Belly, patting his large stomach.

Spotted Tongue didn't know why his friend had such a large belly. He didn't eat more than the other warriors or not much more. Shaking Hand said the fat warrior was like a bear who stored food in his body for his long winter sleep. Spotted Tongue didn't care. As long as Fat Belly stayed on his pony, he was the equal to any warrior. On foot, he was slow and awkward. He took fewer scalps than the rest of the band because they were faster reaching a body and could make the circular cut, pop off the scalp, and be back on their ponies before Fat Belly could pull his knife and squat down. Spotted Tongue would rather have Fat Belly at his side in a fight than any other warrior---as long as Fat Belly stayed on his pony.

Spotted Tongue motioned with his arm, and the two columns started down the slope toward the encampments. Horse's Back rode beside him, his words resting like a stone in Spotted Tongue's chest. Since he lost his medicine, he felt like a man trapped in front of a buffalo herd with nowhere to run. He would be trampled to death—like the Comanche would be trampled by the white soldiers. Still, he could not force himself to submit.

He would fight. It was the Comanche way.

His warriors made no sound, but he doubted they would be heard over the eruption of screams and shouted commands from the camps below as one, then another, and another saw them. White soldiers scurried like squirrels from campfires to grab their long guns. Two other groups ran to the guns with many barrels, frantically hauling them around to face the Comanche columns. Women and children from the Cheyenne and Arapaho lodges fled into the heavy timber while their men seized their lances, bows, and arrows. The men of the Kiowa and Kiowa-Apache camps also grabbed weapons and splashed across Medicine Lodge Creek toward their horse herds. The Comanche camp stirred with warriors taking up their lances, then stopping, waving their arms and shouting.

"Like ants when a pony steps on an anthill," said Wild Horse, laughing at the confusion and shouts in six different languages.

"These ants have guns with many barrels," said Spotted Tongue, wondering if there would be a fight after all.

Suddenly, a horse broke out of the dusty confusion of shouts and running feet, ridden by a figure in tanned buckskin trousers and shirt.

"Is that Phillip McCusker?" asked Shaking Hand, peering downslope. "I heard he would be here as an interpreter."

Phillip McCusker, the only white man Spotted Tongue knew of who had been allowed to marry a Comanche woman and the only white man he trusted. Well, as much as he could trust a man of two halves: Comanche and white man.

McCusker lived with his wife's band some of the year and always joined buffalo hunts. He was careful not to learn of any raids on Tejano settlers but often tried to mediate for the release of captive women and children. Spotted Tongue vowed to keep silent about Little Flower. He had no intention of returning her to her people.

"Spotted Tongue! Horse's Back! Don't you know better than to ride in the dark? We couldn't see who you were. The Peace Commissioners, the army, and the teamsters figured they were about to get their hair lifted. We thought you might be the Cheyenne Dog Soldiers riding in to start a fight like Black Kettle has been warning us about. The Peace Commissioners are damn near shitting their pants just thinking about the Dog Soldiers, then you ride in all painted up and your buffalo scalp headdresses on. The newspaper reporters are hiding under their bedrolls saying their prayers, well, some of them anyway. There are a couple of them that the Devil himself couldn't scare."

He looked over their shoulders. "Where are the women and children? White soldiers get mighty suspicious when they see Indians without their women and children because it generally means they have come for a fight. The white war chiefs, like old General Harney, are strutting around and barking out orders like they're expecting arrows to start flying. And speaking of a fight, you men don't have any white captives, do you, Spotted Tongue? Horse's Back? Better turn them over if you do. General Sherman is threatening to wipe out any band that has white captives, and you can count on that red-headed devil to do just that. And the General said no ransom."

"The women and children are behind us with the lodges, including Spotted Tongue's two wives," said Fat Belly, his usual good humor restored after his anger at Horse's Back. "Spotted Tongue won't sleep without his second wife to warm him up."

"When did you take another wife, Spotted Tongue?" asked McCusker. "What did your first wife say about it?"

"He took her on---yiii!" yelled Fat Belly when Spotted Tongue poked him in the ribs with the end of his lance.

"I took a second wife a few moons ago," said Spotted Tongue over the grumbling of Fat Belly. Trust the fat warrior to say the wrong thing at the wrong time. All his wits must reside in his big belly.

"And we didn't hear of the peace council in time to arrive sooner, so we are late. Also, because we stopped to put on our paint and our best leggings and moccasins," explained Spotted Tongue, talking fast and loud to cover any more comments from Fat Belly.

"Well, you missed the first round of gifts and food. The Peace Commissioners gave out rations of flour, sugar, and coffee, poured it all on a blanket, and then measured out portions for each lodge. Santana of the Kiowa watched over the distribution to make sure nobody got more than his share, blowing that damn bugle of his every other breath until most of the whites wanted to tear it from around his neck and stuff it down his throat. I felt the same."

"The white Commissioners gave some clothes as presents, too, but I can see you are all dressed like dandies, so I guess you didn't need any white men's britches," said McCusker. "Fat Belly, did you leave any paint for anybody else? And your hair shines like silver. What did you use on it, bear grease or buffalo dung?"

"Buffalo dung. There's more of it than bear grease, and you don't have to kill the buffalo to get it."

"Well, nobody will overlook you, Fat Belly, but be careful you don't trip over the fringe on your moccasins. It's got to be longer than your feet."

"He doesn't need to fall over his moccasin fringe," said Wild Horse with a grin. He can fall over a blade of grass." Fat Belly swiped at Wild Horse with the end of his lance but hit his shield instead.

"Well, come on down, and I'll introduce you to the peace commissioners, or at least the ones who changed their pants. And I want to meet your new wife, Spotted Tongue. I want to see the woman you'd risk Green Willow's temper over. I'm surprised that woman didn't take a cook pot to your head."

Spotted Tongue clenched his teeth to keep ugly words from escaping his mouth. Sometimes, other men's teasing stung like the prairie's nettles. "A Comanche warrior may take as many wives as he is willing to trade ponies to gain. Green Willow has no say in the matter."

Phillip McCusker guffawed. "Unless you cut out her tongue, I bet she had a lot to say."

"Let us meet these commissioners with the dirty breechclouts," said Spotted Tongue through his still-clenched teeth. He would have to warn his friends not to say anything about Little Flower. He didn't want the commissioners or soldiers to hear that he had a white captive in his lodge. Green Willow warned him not to bring her along, but he did not trust that she would not escape if he left her behind with no one to guard her but a few boys too young to be warriors and men too old. Now, he had to worry that the white men would learn about her and demand her back. When a warrior lost his medicine, bad luck was sure to follow.

"So, the Council has started already?" asked Spotted Tongue just to change the subject.

"Sort of," replied Phillip McCusker. "The Cheyenne Dog Soldiers rode away after they scared the piss out of the whites. They're camped up on the Cimarron about 50 miles away. Except for Black Kettle and his band, of course. The Council agreed to wait four days to start talks, but old Satana of the Kiowa said his people and the Comanche would not wait because they needed to return to the Comancheria to prepare for winter, so business starts tomorrow with the Kiowa, the Kiowa-Apache, and the Comanche. Both sides will make speeches to impress the other side, and of course, the whites won't understand the Indians, and the Indians won't understand the whites."

"But won't you interpret? How can whites and the People not understand?" asked Spotted Tongue.

Phillip McCusker spits on the ground. "There's more to understanding than knowing what the words mean, Spotted Tongue. The whites want us to live like they do and don't understand why we won't. We want to be left alone, and the Council insists they can't do that."

"So, there will be no peace," said Spotted Tongue.

"Don't seem likely, but we'll see what happens tomorrow when the chiefs speak. Maybe both sides will listen to the other. Can't ever tell what people will do, but if you ask me, I think the deck is stacked against the Indian. Gotta build the railroad and safe roads for travelers and stagecoaches and protect settlers on their farms... You're in the way, Spotted Tongue."

CHAPTER THREE

"Captured—Mrs. Rachel Plummer, daughter of James W. Parker, and her son, James Pratt Plummer, two years of age; Mrs. Elizabeth Kellogg; Cynthia Ann Parker, nine years old, and her little brother, John Parker, aged six years..."

-Attack on Parker's Fort, 1836,
Indian Depredations in Texas by J. W. Wilbarger;
A Facsimile Reproduction of the Original, Eakin Press—
Statehouse Press, 1985, Page 306

"What were the white chiefs like?" asked Green Willow.

"The Commissioners?" said Spotted Tongue, slowly pronouncing the strange-sounding English word. He was not sure what the word meant exactly in the white man's language, but in Comanche, he suspected it meant trouble.

"Quit showing off and tell me," his first wife demanded.

Spotted Tongue hesitated a moment as if picking his words carefully just to watch Green Willow glower with impatience. His first wife suffered from too much curiosity and too little patience. Both traits could make life uncomfortable at times in his lodge, but he admitted her curiosity helped keep him abreast of what his warriors were thinking. Wives were incurable gossips, never keeping anything to themselves. If a husband farted, everyone in camp knew it before the stink went away. It was embarrassing sometimes.

It was not that women had nothing else to do. They butchered buffalo, dried the meat for the cold months, scraped the hides to make clothes and lodges, gathered berries and nuts to make pemmican, watched the children, put up and took down the lodges, packed household goods when the band moved camp, and cooked food to eat. In short, they did everything but hunt, make weapons, go on raids, and go on the warpath. Still, they wanted to know everything that happened in camp. Women were strange. They never seemed to recognize when something was man's business. At least, Green Willow didn't.

"Spotted Tongue! Tell me!"

"And if I don't, what will you do?"

"Go talk to Fat Belly's first wife, Slow Like a Turtle. She can always make him tell her everything. But I would rather you tell me what you think. You see more than he does. Sometimes, he sees like a child."

Pleased at her comment, Spotted Tongue nodded. Green Willow never wove words to entrap a man into doing what she wanted. Her words always went straight to the belly like an enemy's lance, so he did not feel she flattered him. She always told the truth as she saw it. He was proud that she knew his worth.

"They all had hair under their noses, and most had hair on their cheeks and chin. The old ones had eyebrows like furry worms. The white men don't pluck out the hair on their faces like the Comanche do." He stroked his face, which was smooth and hairless, even his forehead, where he had plucked his eyebrows. He found the white men's facial hair repulsive, but it was only one more thing that he didn't understand about them.

"Old Chief Satank has hair under his nose," said Green Willow.

Spotted Tongue shrugged in distaste and dismissal. "He is a Kiowa, not like a Comanche. Kiowas are not Nermernuh." He didn't need to say more. The Comanche allowed the Kiowa to share the Comancheria, and they joined one another's raiding parties and war parties and married one another's women, which made them almost family, or at least distant kin, but the Kiowa were not the equal of the Nermernuh. Everyone knew that---except maybe the Kiowa.

Green Willow nodded in agreement. "Tell me more about these white chiefs. What do they wear, and how tall are they? Do they walk with dignity like the Comanche?"

"Why don't you wait until Father Sun rises from the east? Then you can see for yourself without wearing me out with your questions?"

"I want to know now, Spotted Tongue," Green Willow insisted.

He sighed with resignation. That impatience again. One day, his first wife would choke on it. But it was easier to answer her questions than to ignore her. On reflection, short of beating her out of her senses, it was impossible to ignore her. And he never hit a woman. It would make him feel less than a warrior to beat someone weaker than himself---if that someone was one of the Nermernuh. Mexicans, Tejanos, other Indians, and whites were another matter. They were not kin; they were not of the Nermernuh.

His friends, Fat Belly, Wild Horse, and Shaking Hand, felt the same; they never beat their wives either. Maybe a slap sometimes when a woman came close to driving a man mad, but never a beating. Not Coyote Dung, though. Coyote Dung beat his first wife so badly that she ran off with another warrior and took all their kin with them to join one of the Kwahadi bands. Coyote Dung's plight caused much laughter in the smoking lodge, but not even Coyote Dung, the foul stench that he was, suggested hunting down his wife and her kin. Comanche did not fight other Comanche---most of the time. But sometimes they did, and it left bitter feelings.

"They are white, but not all the same white. Some had much red on their faces, and others' skin was the color of tanned buckskin. White men turn brown if Father Sun shines on them all day like Comanche warriors turn darker in the hot moons. Some had white hair, some had hair the color of the buffalo, and some had no hair. Some had hair that curls like Little Flower's." He broke off speaking and looked around the camp for his second wife. "Where is she, Green Willow? Have you been watching her?"

"She's in the lodge. She was trying to wipe off her face paint, so I tied her hands behind her back."

Spotted Tongue dropped his piece of boiled buffalo meat back in the cooking pot, wiped his hand on his breechclout, and jumped to his feet in one continuous motion. "Her shoulders will hurt tied up like that," he said, leaning over to enter the lodge.

Green Willow grasped his arm. "Wait, Spotted Tongue! We must talk about Little Flower."

He shook her off and ducked into the lodge. The cook fire outside lent enough light for Spotted Tongue to see his second wife sitting hunched over in the dark shadows opposite the entrance to the lodge, her pale eyes a contrast to the orange, yellow, and red face paint Green Willow had applied only after he had pinned her down and held her head still. Little Flower had not wanted her face painted or her long hair chopped off below her ears in the style of Nermernuh women. Even in a soft buckskin poncho top and skirt, she did not look much like a Nerm. But Spotted Tongue knew the white men would only see what they expected to see: a Comanche woman in buckskin and face paint.

"See, Spotted Tongue," said his first wife as she followed him inside. "She is sitting in your place where women are not to sit. She does everything wrong. She leaves pieces of flesh when she scrapes the buffalo hide. I can't send her to collect dried buffalo dung for the cookfire because she will run off. If I make her raise the tipi, the lodge poles fall, and so does the tipi. And she is always wiping water from the streams on herself. And once, once, she caught a fish in her hands and wanted to roast it on my cookfire! *A fish!* The Nermernuh don't eat fish! They are nasty, unclean creatures, and she wanted to curse my cook fire by throwing it in the embers!"

Green Willow's voice rose with each sentence until her last words were uttered in a high-pitched screech that pierced Spotted Tongue's ears. Other warriors ignored arguments between wives or pretended they did. Of course, it helped if each wife had her own lodge, then, the warrior could choose which wife to favor without having them all fight like badgers in the same burrow. Green Willow had her own lodge, but Spotted Tongue had to keep Little Flower by his side so she could not run away. He supposed Green Willow felt her place as chief wife was threatened, but he could not think of another way short of binding Little Flower hand and foot, and that was not a good way to gentle a wife, certainly not a wife like Little Flower.

"Little Flower doesn't understand our ways," he said, dropping to his knees and pulling his knife from his belt.

"And she will not try to learn!" finished Green Willow, still in that high screech.

Little Flower flinched away from Spotted Tongue, her eyes fixed on the knife in his hands.

"No, no, pretty one, I won't hurt you," he crooned as he reached behind her and cut the rawhide binding. "See, that's better. Let me rub your shoulders to take away the pain and stiffness."

He heard Green Willow utter what sounded like the snort of a bull buffalo as he massaged Little Flower's narrow shoulders and slender arms. He wondered how such a delicate woman, almost frail compared to the thicker bodies of Comanche women, could have so much strength and fight. If she were a man, she would make a magnificent warrior.

He smiled down at her face, so different from his own. Wide, round eyes the color of the sky, a thin nose, a face thin instead of round like a Comanche, sharp cheekbones rather than broad ones, full lips and a chin that was more pointed than not. And hair, chopped now below her ears, curled like the fur of a buffalo. He wondered why he thought her beautiful when she was so alien to his eyes. It must be her spirit that entrapped him. Her spirit was so much like a warrior's. She never gave in, and he suspected she never would. If she ever accepted the ways of the Nermernuh, it would be because she chose to.

He would never give her up.

Little Flower looked over Spotted Tongue's shoulder at Green Willow. *"Filthy squaw! Tie me up like an animal! I will be free! Do you understand? I will be free of you cruel savages!"*

"What is she saying?" asked Spotted Tongue.

"How should I know?" said Green Willow. "I don't speak her ugly tongue. And that is another thing, she refuses to speak Comanche."

"She has not had time to learn. She's only been with us a few moons."

"Fat Belly's wife, Slow Like a Turtle, could speak many words in fewer moons than Little Flower has been in our lodge. She either doesn't want to learn, or she is slow in her wits."

Spotted Tongue circled Little Flower's shoulders with one arm and pulled her against his chest. He hoped she would not scratch. "She isn't slow in her wits, Green Willow. If all my warriors had her wits and spirit, we would soon drive the Tejanos and other white men from the Comancheria."

Little Flower laid her hands on either side of his face and gazed into his eyes as though she would read his thoughts. *"You've been kind to me, as much as a Comanche can be, I suppose, but no matter how kind you are and how much I like you sometimes, I can't stay with you. You're a Comanche! You raid settlers that haven't done you any harm. You carry off women and children and slaughter their husbands and fathers. Sometimes, you torture the women. You don't wash, so you stink, and you put buffalo shit on your hair! How can you expect me to willingly be your wife? I won't have children only to watch my sons paint their faces and ride off to scalp my kind and watch my daughters forced to share their husbands and perhaps be beaten. I won't be a Comanche! Perhaps, if you were different, or I was, but we're not. Nothing will change my mind. I have to be free. I have to be with my own kin. You should understand that."*

The feel of Little Flower's hands against his face lingered. He cleared his throat of the hoarseness touching and being touched by her always brought to his voice. "What do you think she's saying now, Green Willow? Do you think she is thanking me for freeing her?"

"I told you, I don't know what she's saying, and I don't care. We need to ransom her back, Spotted Tongue. She is trouble. Think what the white man would give for her: his flour and coffee; sugar and beads, cook pots and blankets. . ."

"You have a cooking pot already. What do you want with another? And what is wrong with buffalo robes? One robe will keep you warmer during the cold moons than four of the white man's blankets," said Spotted Tongue, but Green Willow ignored his words. She was good at that.

". . . another mirror for you and maybe one for me. It would be easier to put on my paint if I had a mirror, too. And guns, Spotted Tongue, maybe one of those long guns that fires many bullets without re-loading. You have been wanting one of those."

"I can trade with the Comancheros for one."

"You said the Comancheros want too many ponies for a single gun, then more ponies for the bullets. I remember when you said it. I was scraping a buffalo hide for a new winter robe for you, and you were filing a piece of the white man's iron for a new point for your lance. It was before you captured Little Flower."

"I remember, woman! Now, please shut up! I will never send Little Flower away, no matter what the white man may offer in ransom. And he isn't offering any. Phillip McCusker told me. The white war chief will send the soldiers to kill us all if we don't give back our white captives. Phillip McCusker told me that, too."

"No ransom! Who will pay for the buffalo meat they eat? And sharing our lodges?" Green Willow's voice rose in such a screech of outrage that Spotted Tongue wanted to slap his hands over his ears.

"It doesn't matter! I'm not giving her to the white war chief anyway. But we must not let anybody see her or anyone in our band talk about her. No gossiping to women in the Kiowa or Kiowa-Apache camps. Dressed as she is, other tribes will think she is a Nerm if they see her. Just don't let anybody get too close."

"But look at her hair, Green Willow," he said, running his hands through her soft curls. "This doesn't look like the hair of a woman of the Nermernuh. You didn't put buffalo dung on it to make it straight. Why not? It was the last order I gave you before I rode to join my warriors."

"I tried, but she pushed my hand against my face. I had buffalo dung all over. I had to paint my face over again. That's when I tied her hands, and it took two other women holding her to do that. Then, I threw a blanket over her head. I couldn't even ride my pony into camp. I had to walk with her, dragging her along like I was pulling a travois. If she had not been afraid, I would have pulled her through the brush, and she would not have walked on her feet at all. You want buffalo dung on her hair, you do it!"

Spotted Tongue heard the hurt and anger in his first wife's voice and wished he was on a raid somewhere many days away---like Mexico. All powerful warriors rich in ponies had more than one wife, and he was powerful and had many ponies. Why did Green Willow have to act like a bear with one cub? It was not the way of the Nermernuh. When they returned to their winter camp, he would tell Green Willow so.

"Will the white war chief really come to kill us if he finds out about Little Flower?" Now, Green Willow sounded worried.

"That is what Phillip McCusker says."

Green Willow frowned, her face becoming all lines under her face paint as she glared at Little Flower. "I told you she was trouble, but no, you wouldn't listen. Now, we are the ones in trouble."

Spotted Tongue knew where Green Willow was going with her words. She would remind him of every time he had been wrong, and she had been right, and his shoulders were already slumping like an old man's under the weight of the fears he carried: his medicine leaving, what the white Commissioners were planning, the discovery of Little Flower. He didn't need Green Willow pointing out his past failings, and she never forgot a single one.

He put Little Flower away from him and rose to his feet. "I will seek out Wild Horse, Shaking Hand, and Fat Belly. We will hold counsel with Phillip McCusker to learn what will happen tomorrow. You watch Little Flower."

He ducked out of his lodge and darted away. He heard Green Willow shouting behind him and ran faster. There was warrior's business to see to. Maybe his women would be sleeping when he came back to his lodge, and he could find peace.

CHAPTER FOUR

"The brother and sister, thus separated, gradually forgot the language, manners, and customs of their own people, and became thorough Comanche as the long years stole slowly away."

-Remarks on the fate of the Parker Children in
Indian Depredations in Texas by J. W. Wilbarger;
A Reproduction of the Original,
Eakin Press—Statehouse Press, 1985, Page 315

A warrior at least a head taller than Spotted Tongue loomed out of the darkness. Silhouetted against the flickering light of the camp's many fires, the warrior stood with long legs spread a little apart, his hands on his hips, silent and motionless, but with such an air of intentness about him, that Spotted Tongue reached for his knife. Whoever stood before him was no one he knew and, therefore, was an enemy.

"Hold, Spotted Tongue," said the warrior in a voice as deep as he was tall, a voice that rumbled from his throat like thunder rumbled from the sky. He turned slightly so the light from the campfires dimly illuminated his features. Light blue-gray eyes glimmered beneath heavy lids, and a wide mouth with full lips opened in a smile. "Don't you know me, my friend?"

Spotted Tongue felt his own mouth fall open in astonishment. "Quanah?" Is it you? You have grown since I watched you practice with your bow and arrow as a boy when we both lived with the Nokoni band. How many winters are you now?"

"I will soon be twenty winters when the leaves return to the trees, but I am a warrior now, not the boy you knew."

That much was true, thought Spotted Tongue. Quanah was a man grown and nearly as tall as his father, who had been taller than any Comanche in the Comancheria. There was much talk among the bands about Quanah, that he had already ridden the war trail into Mexico and that he would be a great war chief one day. Spotted Tongue suspected he already was.

"But the Kwahadi have spurned the peace council, and you're a Kwahadi, or that is what is said."

Quanah, son of Peta Nocona, a Nokoni chief, and a Tejano white captive whose Comanche's name was Naudah, frowned and shook his head. "Don't talk of the Kwahadi. I don't want to be known to the white men."

Spotted Tongue bent his head in a sign of agreement and respect. For a lone warrior to ride across the Comancheria without his band or a single friend was a feat of courage. To be alone on the prairie is to welcome death. "Then why are you here if not to touch the pen? And does Phillip McCusker know you are here?"

"I will not touch the pen to any paper. I will not go to any reservation to be penned like the white man's horses. I will not go until the white man comes to make me. I came to Medicine Creek only to listen to what the white man says and to learn which chiefs of which bands will touch the pen."

"Better to learn which chiefs mean it," said Spotted Tongue. "Old Horse's Back of the Nakoni may touch the pen but says it means nothing because his young braves will choose for themselves. Or maybe he will touch the pen only to be sure his band receives their share of the presents. He may touch the pen because he believes it is the only way to save the Nakoni. They grow small in number, and he is afraid. I don't know his heart."

"I will know which chief means it when I see who tries to lead his band to the reservation. Not that his young warriors will stay on the reservation if I call them to ride with me on a war party. They will join me. What does the reservation have to offer a young warrior that he wants? Does it offer ponies or women or guns? Does it offer the buffalo hunt? I will listen to what the white commissioners offer, and then I will ride back to the Kwahadi and tell them what the white man plans to steal. I think many young warriors and their wives and children will be joining the Kwahadi. Kiowas will raise their lodges next to ours, too. What of you, Spotted Tongue? Your name is known to us as that of a great war chief with strong medicine. Will you and your warriors join the Kwahadi?"

"My band rides with the Kosoteka now. I and my warriors have left the Nakoni," said Spotted Tongue, his belly shriveling at Quanah's mention of medicine. He had no medicine and would bring only bad luck to the Kwahadi.

"I was one of the Nokoni," said Quanah, his voice suddenly rough with anger dark as the night that surrounded them.

"I know you were. Have you forgotten we were of the same band?"

"I have forgotten nothing of those days!" Quanah's voice was as bitter as a green persimmon, and he spit out each word as though they were sour in his mouth. He turned abruptly away toward a lodge set apart from the others. "Tell no one why I am here, and tell no one I am here who does not already know."

Spotted Tongue watched Quanah's tall figure fade into the darkness and let out a breath he didn't know he was holding. He had heard many things about Quanah since that warrior son of a white woman had left the Nokoni band after his father had been killed by the Tejanos and his younger brother died of some mysterious fever. As an orphan, Quanah had no standing in the tribe and no wealth. He was an outcast.

Quanah had been elected a war chief after a battle with the white soldiers when the band's war chief had been killed. Quanah killed a soldier and led the band across the Red River without losing any of the large herd of stolen horses. Another time, while on a raiding party, Quanah and his warriors came across some white soldiers with a herd of sixty mules. When the soldiers went to sleep, Quanah and his band stole the mules.

Spotted knew that Quanah's influence was growing among the Kwahadi even though he was not twenty years old yet. Spotted Tongue admitted to himself that he had no such influence when he was Quanah's age.

Quanah was different, and not just because he was half-white. He was a wise old man in a young man's body. He never lacked warriors to follow him on a raid or to war. But he carried sorrow and anger with him like Spotted Tongue carried his knife: he was never without it, and Spotted Tongue believed his time and treatment as an orphan still lay in his belly like spoiled meat.

Spotted Tongue shivered, unsure if it was the cold temperature or Quanah's warning that chilled his skin. The air *was* cold and carried that peculiar scent of falling leaves and the coming winter that only animals and those men who lived close to the earth could smell. But he knew it was Quanah, whose medicine came from the bear and the eagle, and like the eagle, could see further than any man Spotted Tongue knew---even into a warrior's heart.

Shivering again, Spotted Tongue stumbled away from the darkness that had swallowed Quanah and toward the nearest campfire. By the time he realized whose fire it was, it was too late to avoid the squat figure who lurched up to face him.

"Coyote Dung!"

Coyote Dung was a short man whose bulky shoulders, bandy legs, and a massive head with heavy features made him look like he was molded by a young child playing with mud. He was man-shaped, but that was the most complimentary thing Spotted Tongue could say. He had a temper that exploded like a bullet from a white man's gun. As a ferocious warrior and superior horseman, Coyote Dung earned the other warriors' respect to temper the revulsion his appearance caused. Fat Belly always said that Coyote Dung's looks would make a vulture throw up, but even a vulture would go behind a bush where Coyote Dung could not see him do it.

"Did you see Stinky?" demanded Coyote Dung, his lip curling as though he smelled a rotting buffalo carcass.

Coyote Dung was quarrelsome, cruel to his wives, and not above stealing from his own band, although Spotted Tongue could not prove it yet. "Have your eyes gone white like an old man's? Quanah is the tallest man I have ever seen among the Nermernuh, and ice on the Canadian River in winter looks warmer than his eyes. And he will remember you, Coyote Dung, because you're the one who gave him that name after his father was killed. No one dared to while Chief Peta Nacona lived."

"His mother was a Tejano, and Stinky and his brother had no relatives after the Tejanos killed his father and took his mother back to her own people. The Nokoni have no charity for a half-breed white with no kin. It was good he ran away before we threw him out." Coyote Dung folded his arms as though he had just spoken in council.

"Not all the Nokoni refused him food and a place by their fire," said Spotted Tongue. Given how big Quanah was and how fierce his expression was, Coyote Dung would be a wise man to forget he had ever called the warrior Stinky.

Coyote Dung laughed, a sound Spotted Tongue always found unpleasant because he knew the squat, ugly warrior was only copying what other men did. He doubted Coyote Dung even knew what humor was. "Some of the Nokoni are as weak as white men with their gifts like they are beggars pleading for their lives," said Coyote Dung.

Spotted Tongue debated pulling his knife but decided not to let the other warrior bait him. Coyote Dung was a fool. Drawing his blood would teach him nothing, even if Spotted Tongue did resent the insult of being compared to a white man. Better to let Quanah take his revenge. A good beating by a man he had tormented as a child might send Coyote Dung to his lodge to cower in his blankets until the council was over. The white man wouldn't care if one Comanche beat another, and Spotted Tongue had no doubt who would win that fight.

"If you were close enough to recognize Quanah, then you were close enough to hear what he said since your ears are always ready to hear what doesn't concern you."

"I don't fear Stinky," boasted Coyote Dung.

"Then you are a fool," said Spotted Tongue, stepping around him to walk toward the next tipi, where he saw Wild Horse, Shaking Hand, and Fat Belly, who had been crouching in a circle gambling with the little square objects the Comancheros called dice. The warriors abandoned their game and rose to their feet, Fat Belly awkward as always, and watched Coyote Dung with alert eyes. They were not alone. Many Comanche left their campfires and lodges to stand in the shadows and watch the two warriors quarrel. Sometimes, the Nermernuh were like children: always curious. A man had no secrets from the band except those held inside his own head and never spoken aloud. At times, Spotted Tongue wondered if even those were safe. Certainly, Green Willow acted as if she could see inside his head. Not all the time, but enough to make him uncomfortable.

"What did you call me?" said Coyote Dung in a voice that promised violence as he grabbed Spotted Tongue's arm with crushing strength.

Spotted Tongue pulled his knife and whirled around, pulling his arm from Coyote Dung's grip at the same time. He was glad the other warrior had not grabbed his knife hand. If he had, then his right hand would be as numb as his left. If Coyote Dung had no other virtue, he at least had a strong grip.

"You heard what I said. Take it as a warning not to cross Quanah. Because you are a Nerm won't shield you from his anger, and you have no kin or friends who will stand with you against him."

Wild Horse, with Fat Belly and Shaking Hand on either side, soundlessly encircled the two warriors like a wolf pack, each with a hand on his knife. "Did I see you put your hands on our war chief?" asked Wild Horse in a soft voice that carried a snake's venom in its tone. Wild Horse seldom raised his voice, but only a brave who could not hear would miss the undertone of a promised threat.

Startled, Coyote Dung's eyes darted from Spotted Tongue to Fat Belly to Wild Horse while he hunched his thick shoulders against Shaking Hand's presence at his back. His tongue flicked out to lick his lips, the only sign of nervousness, and his broad, heavy features took on a sullen expression. "We are not on a raid or in a war party now, so he is no chief, just a brave who speaks to an outcast and whose women order him about like a young boy."

"You get of an Apache squaw!" said Spotted Tongue, holding his knife at waist level to counter any thrust by Coyote Dung. Between his wives and Quanah's warning, his evening had been plagued by poor luck, and he would take no more insults.

"What did you call me?" demanded Coyote Dung, outrage and disbelief combined in his voice.

"Are your ears suddenly stopped with mud? You heard Quanah easily enough. I called you the son of an Apache squaw. I could have called you a Tejano or a Mexican, but I'm not sure even you deserve that. But I could be wrong."

Fat Belly snickered.

Unfortunately, so did most in the watching crowd.

Snarling like the animal he was named for, Coyote Dung lunged for Spotted Tongue, his hands reaching for his throat. Spotted Tongue leaped aside and sliced the other warrior's arm with his knife as Coyote Dung blundered off-balance past him and into Wild Horse and Fat Belly. Wild Horse hooked one leg behind Coyote Dung's knees and upended him. Coyote Dung fell heavily on his back and immediately rolled over in an attempt to get his feet beneath him, but he reckoned without Fat Belly, who sat on Coyote Dung's back and not only flatted him face down on the ground but pinned the sullen brave's arms with his knees.

Wild Horse knelt in front of the writhing brave, jerked back his head by his braids, and held his knife at Coyote Dung's throat. "Threaten Spotted Tongue again, and I will spill your blood on the ground." Again, his soft voice held venom.

Spotted Tongue locked his knees to keep his trembling legs from folding under him. "No, Wild Horse, Fat Belly, the Nermernuh do not kill one another! Let him up."

There were a few muttered agreements from the watching crowd, but fewer than Spotted Tongue expected. It could be a sign of Coyote Dung's unpopularity among the band, or it could be one more sign that what Spotted Tongue believed about his own people was not true, that the Nermernuh would not fight and kill one another. Given the right circumstances, one Comanche would turn against another.

Wild Horse waited a few heartbeats before bounding to his feet and returning his knife to his belt. Fat Belly took longer to get to his feet, managing to step on Coyote Dung in the process. What little breath remained of Coyote Dung left his body in an explosive hiss.

Wild Horse leaned over the prone warrior. "Remember what I said."

Spotted Tongue walked to Fat Belly's lodge, where the white dice lay scattered around the fire, and sank cross-legged to the ground. "I should have kept my temper. It isn't good to fight among ourselves. We need to save our anger for the white man, not waste it on each other."

Shaking Hand sat down beside him. "Coyote Dung doesn't think as you do. Don't show your back to him, Spotted Tongue, or he will put a knife or arrow in it."

"Then he'll be dead before he can brag he killed Spotted Tongue," said Fat Belly, none of his usual humor in his voice.

"Is it true Quanah is here?" asked Wild Horse in his usual soft voice.

"You heard our talk? Coyote Dung and I?" asked Spotted Tongue, grateful that Wild Horse had changed the subject. Any more talk of Coyote Dung would only raise the fever in his friends' blood. One day, Coyote Dung's vicious talk would end in death, but this was not the day, not in the middle of a treaty council.

"Half the camp did, and the other half will know before the sun rises," said Wild Horse. "But no one will tell the white man, and it would mean nothing to them anyway. Phillip McCusker says the Commissioners worry only about the Dog Soldiers of the Cheyenne."

"That is an insult!" exclaimed Fat Belly. "The Dog Soldiers can't fight like the Comanche. The Commissioners should worry about us."

Spotted Tongue shook his head. "No, it's good that the Cheyenne distracts them. If your enemy always looks in another direction, then he won't see what is behind his back."

"Then we sneak up behind and kill them!" said Fat Belly, a broad grin splitting his face.

Spotted Tongue let his shoulders droop with despair. His friends, the sons of his father's and mother's brothers, his brothers in the way of the Nermernuh, didn't understand. It was not about ambushes. They couldn't see that the white man's distraction allowed the Comanche to ride free on the prairies, to hunt the buffalo, to raid, to avoid the plow and the reservation, for a little while longer, maybe until the Nermernuh met death. At least, they would die as free men, as their fathers and grandfathers did, and be buried beneath the prairies. His friends didn't see what he did. Fat Belly, Wild Horse, and Shaking Hand believed the Nermernuh would live as they always had and that nothing would change.

Spotted Tongue wished he could believe the same, but he couldn't. When he lost his ability to make medicine, something shifted inside his head. He saw what he had never seen before, thought as he had never thought before, and was more frightened than he ever was before. He stood naked on the earth, had no defenses to protect him, and saw the earth was different.

CHAPTER FIVE

"I never knew the Indians to jest. In their boasts, there is always a meaning."

- General Harney, Medicine Lodge, Kansas, October 18, 1867

"Spotted Tongue! Spotted Tongue!"

"Your first wife calls," said Fat Belly, grinning at Spotted Tongue. "What have you done now to displease her?"

"She's not displeased; she's worried," he replied, his heart suddenly pounding as he pushed himself to his feet. "Green Willow, here, at Fat Belly's lodge."

She rushed toward him, her short, sturdy legs churning across the sparse brown grass between the trees along Medicine Lodge Creek. "I told you she was trouble! And you untied her, and now she's gone. Sneaked out of the lodge when my back was turned."

Spotted Tongue grabbed her arms and shook her, his belly suddenly hollow with fear. "I told you to watch her, woman!"

"I did, but I had to relieve myself. I squatted behind the lodge, but I could see to either side of it. I didn't see her run to the right or left of it, but she's gone."

"Little Flower is one smart woman," said Shaking Hand. "She must have ducked out of the lodge and run straight ahead until she lost herself in the darkness before she changed directions. Too bad she's a woman. She would make a clever warrior."

"She's running to the white men's tents, the commissioners. I must stop her before she reaches them. I must get my lance and shield." Spotted Tongue began running toward his lodge.

"We need our ponies!" shouted Shaking Hand, seizing his own lance and war shield. "We may have to catch her and flee. The white men will be angry if they see her. They will keep her, and Spotted Tongue's blanket will be cold this winter."

"Don't let Green Willow hear you say that," whispered Fat Belly to Shaking Hand.

"Little Badger's son is bringing the ponies to our lodge," panted Green Willow, running after the men. "I sent him as soon as I saw Little Flower had run away."

Spotted Tongue knew he should thank Green Willow for her forethought, but he was too angry. He grabbed his war shield from the tripod of poles where it hung when not in use. A warrior never took his shield inside his lodge where someone, particularly a woman, might touch it and destroy its magic. Only its owner could touch a war shield without bringing bad luck. He had not worked out whether his lack of medicine might render his shield worthless. He would worry about that later.

A young boy came running up to the lodge, leading four ponies, one of them Spotted Tongue's white stallion. None had saddles since the boy knew how quickly the warriors needed their ponies, but it didn't matter. A Comanche could ride bareback as well as he could with a saddle. When speed was urgent, when there was no time to tie a rawhide strip around the animal's lower jaw, a Comanche could also guide his pony with just the pressure of his legs.

Spotted Tongue grabbed a fistful of his pony's mane and vaulted onto its back, kicking it into a gallop. He heard the hoof beats of his friends' ponies behind him, heard the rising sound of voices as the Nermernuh, the Kiowa and their allies, the Kiowa-Apaches, poured from their lodges like the Canadian River in flood. His pony's hooves scattered cook fires and knocked over cook pots, women screamed as they pulled children out of the warriors' path, and a crowd of Arapahos and white men dressed in their strange long trousers, sweaty and clumsy from drinking crazy water, stumbled from a large Arapaho lodge. Spotted Tongue ignored it all, the shouts, the milling figures, the questions yelled out in heavily accented Comanche. The tongue of the Nermernuh was the language used by nearly all with whom the Comanche traded, so Spotted Tongue was not surprised to hear it used now.

Followed by his friends, Spotted Tongue turned his pony toward the bluff where the Commissioners slept in their lodges of canvas. With luck, he would reach the white man's encampment before Little Flower did and cut her off. Then he remembered he had no medicine, and for the first time, he felt anger instead of despair at his lack. He must have offended the Cannibal Owl to be cursed with such bad luck.

Suddenly, he jerked his pony's mane to bring it to a rearing stop as he neared the lodges of those who drove the wagons hauled by mules. They were called *teamsters* in the white man's tongue, a word he remembered the Comanchero using.

In the cleared circle around their campfire, he saw Little Flower struggling with a teamster whose long, gray beard was streaked with the yellow stains of tobacco. He held both her arms behind her back and was pressing his hairy face against hers, muffling her screams. In her buckskin poncho and skirt, her black hair cropped, her face painted, and in the flickering light of the campfire, Spotted Tongue realized the teamster thought she was an Indian. She must have stumbled into the teamsters' camp, thinking it was that of the Peace Commissioners, and was attacked before she could speak.

Teamsters gathered at the edge of the cleared area, some yelling in their incomprehensible tongue, others watching in tense silence while a younger man with hair the color of a sunset pulled on the gray-bearded man's arm. The sons of Tonkowa squaws were fighting over who got to rape her first!

"Yiii!" With the high-pitched war cry that was the last sound ever heard by many Tejano and Mexican enemies, Spotted Tongue kicked his pony's flanks and lifted his lance.

At that instance, distracted by the red-headed teamster's attack, the gray beard loosened his grasp on Little Flower. She screamed as she lifted her knee toward his crotch, while at the same time, she pulled one arm from his grip and raked her nails down the side of his face.

"You whoreson's bitch!" screamed the gray beard, twisting his body to avoid Little Flower's knee. But he didn't avoid her nails, and Spotted Tongue felt a moment's satisfaction at the sight of the bleeding furrows across the teamster's cheek. His satisfaction turned to blood lust in the space of a heartbeat when he saw the teamster's fist slam into Little Flower's chin. Like a buffalo calf pierced by a hunter's arrow, her legs folded under, and she toppled heavily to the ground. Immediately, the graybeard fell to his knees, jerked her legs apart, and shoved up her skirt with one hand while fumbling with the buttons on his trousers with the other.

Spotted Tongue leaped from his pony's back, landing on his feet, as any worthy Comanche warrior could do from childhood, and ran toward his unconscious wife and her would-be rapist.

"You filthy son-of-a-bitch!" screamed the redheaded teamster as he kicked the graybeard in his ribs with his square-toed boot. The rapist rolled off Little Flower, clutching his side and trying to scramble to his feet. The younger teamster kicked him in the crotch, and the greybeard collapsed with a high-pitched shriek. Turning his back on his writhing victim, the redheaded man leaned over and tugged at Little Flower's skirt.

Pushing the teamster away, Spotted Tongue switched his lance to his left hand, knelt and lifted Little Flower's limp body over his right shoulder.

"Get her out of here!" Wild Horse yelled at Spotted Tongue as he pointed his lance at the young teamster who was crouching on the ground with his hands up. Fat Belly and Shaking Hand whirled their ponies between the silent crowd of watching teamsters standing motionless around one side of the cleared circle and Spotted Tongue. Other than the groans of the graybeard curled up and holding his crotch, the shuffling of mules' hooves from where the animals stood tied to a picket line, the howling of the many dogs in the Indian camps, and the distant enquiring calls of army sentries, there was no sound.

"Don't kill him! He's mine! And don't kill any of the others! They have guns and many more numbers than us!" shouted Spotted Tongue as he laid the unconscious Little Flower face down across his pony's back.

The rising sound of confused and excited white voices made him spare time to glance around. A crowd of peace Commissioners and soldier chiefs, accompanied by tribal chiefs and warriors, ran toward the teamsters' camp. The Commissioners had been meeting late to talk about an argument between General Hancock and a band of Cheyenne under Chief Gray Head, according to what Phillip McCusker told him. Spotted Tongue knew little of the argument, only that it had nothing to do with the Comanche.

Grabbing a fistful of its mane, he vaulted on the pony's back behind his unconscious wife. He jerked the animal's head around, kicking its flanks at the same instant, and galloped toward his lodge.

Behind him, Spotted Tongue heard the two teamsters shouting at one another over the guttural threats of his three friends as they backed their ponies away from the camp. He spared the time of a heartbeat to give thanks that Comanche warriors were taught from childhood to obey the war chief instantly and without question. Otherwise, his friends would have pierced the teamsters' bellies, and the white soldiers would have turned their guns with many barrels on the three warriors, and their bodies would jerk from the bullets, punching holes.

Fat Belly and his other two friends galloped up to him before he reached his lodge. "The two white men drew knives on each other. They feared the Nermernuh too much to argue with us, so they argue with each other," he boasted.

"May they open up each other's bellies and save me the trouble," said Spotted Tongue.

"And the other white men stood like rocks on a canyon wall, even the Peace Commissioners, who yelled and waved their arms," said Wild Horse. "The teamsters never moved, although they outnumbered us. It's as Fat Belly says, the white men all fear the Comanche."

With that part of his mind that was a wholly Comanche warrior, Spotted Tongue thought the teamsters' behavior strange. It wasn't his experience to see so many white men, all with guns, cowering in fear against so few warriors. He doubted they were all cowards; in fact, he doubted any of them were. Years of raids on these men who drove their wagons full of trading goods across the prairies with no protection except themselves had taught him that the teamsters would fight until all were dead or the raiding party overran them, which amounted to the same thing. They were worthy enemies who fought well. It was curious they did not fight this time when they held the advantage of weapons and numbers and even white soldiers close by. But the teamsters' lack of fight was something to ponder later, as were the redheaded man's intentions after he and Green Willow tended to Little Flower.

Spotted Tongue slid off his horse and lifted Little Flower into his arms.

"Where did you catch her?" demanded Green Willow.

"At the teamsters' camp. Two white men were fighting over her."

Spotted Tongue heard Little Flower moan, then her body stiffened, and with a scream, she raked her nails down his bare chest, leaving bloody, stinging furrows in his skin. He jerked his head back so her flailing hands with their bloody nails missed his face. He dropped her on the ground and followed her down, grabbing her hands and pinning her body under his. Her eyes were blank of expression, and he knew she was lost inside her head where images of her abuse by the teamsters were all she could see. He had seen that same blankness in the eyes of other captives, but it had never touched his sympathy before. Captives should be afraid; it made them more agreeable to obedience. As long as they were not too frightened, then they lost their minds and were worthless. But Little Flower had never been afraid; at least, not so afraid that she failed to be defiant. She had even defied her rapist until he knocked her unconscious. So now that she was safe, why had her mind fled?

"It's all right, Little Flower," he crooned. "I have you. You are safe with me."

Little Flower writhed under him, her mouth wide open as she screamed, "*Get off me, you savage! Will you rape me, too?*"

"Little Flower, it's me, Spotted Tongue!" He looked up at Green Willow. "Her mind is lost inside her head. She doesn't know who I am. Why is she so afraid now when she is safe?"

Green Willow seized his arm and jerked him, catching him by surprise and tumbling him off Little Flower. "Get off her, you fool! A man just lay on top of her to hold her still, and now you do the same thing! Don't you understand that she sees all men as animals who will hurt her? That is why her mind is hiding. Let me take her inside the lodge and wrap her in a buffalo robe so she will feel safe and warm. It will help her get her mind back."

"What if her mind stays hidden?" asked Spotted Tongue, his stomach twisting with his fear that his defiant second wife might never be more than a mad woman.

Green Willow gave him a disbelieving look. "Little Flower will recover to make more trouble for me, but she must first feel safe. Did the man rape her?"

"No, I found her before the old teamster, or the young one either, could force his body on her. If that was what the young one intended."

"What else did he intend?" Green Willow draped a buffalo robe around Little Flower's fragile shoulders and led her toward the lodge. "Her greatest shock was that men of her own kind would rape her. She expected them to save her from you, and instead, you saved her from them. That is backward to what she planned. She must think about that and accept that she is different now. She is no longer the white woman that you captured. She is now a Comanche wife. Nowhere that she runs, and nothing she does can change that."

"Will she accept that?" asked Spotted Tongue. "Will she finally accept me?"

Green Willow frowned. "Who knows what she will do? She is strange, even for a white woman. Now, you go away while I tend to her. She will not want men around her, even a man who saved her."

Showing none of the dislike and impatience she usually felt toward her husband's second wife, Green Willow held open the tipi's flap and gently pushed Little Flower inside, leaving Spotted Tongue standing outside pondering her words.

CHAPTER SIX

*"...the next morning, when the argument was
resumed with Colt revolvers, one teamster was seriously wounded."*

*The Treaty of Medicine Lodge: The Story of the Great Treaty Council As
Told by Eyewitnesses by Douglas C. Jones, University of Oklahoma Press,
1966, page 96.*

"So, Spotted Tongue, you will kill the white teamsters?" asked Fat Belly, his broad face as somber as any had ever seen it.

"The old one, certainly. He attacked my wife," said Spotted Tongue, sitting with crossed legs in front of his lodge and peering into a small mirror as he painted alternating white and black strips across his face, then outlined his lips in red and yellow. Satisfied with his appearance, he put his paint away and lifted his headdress from his tubular-shaped war bonnet bag. Spotted Tongue followed the traditional Comanche way. His headdress was a buffalo scalp with the horns still attached. Some Comanche had started wearing a feather in their scalp locks, but he felt that was copying the Kiowa way or the Cheyenne way. Not only that, no number of feathers would ever frighten an enemy like a horned buffalo scalp.

He tugged the headdress securely over his head and stood up. He slung his quiver of arrows over his shoulder so that it lay snugly against his back just above his left hip, so he could pluck arrows one after another in rapid succession, as fast as a white man could fire his revolver. He slung his bow over his right shoulder, lifted his shield from the tripod of sticks, and slid its band over his left arm.

"What about the young one?" asked Wild Horse. "Will you kill him?"

"I will think about that. I must be sure he meant to harm Little Flower, not save her. If he meant to save her, then I owe him thanks."

"Ha! Once a snake, always a snake," said Fat Belly.

Spotted Tongue straightened to his full height and faced his companions and relatives of his blood. "I will ride to the Kiowa lodge, where they meet before the ritual of the sun dance. It is a sacred place, even if just to the Kiowa, and there I will sing my death song. Then, I will ride to the teamsters' camp and kill the one with the long grey hair that grows from his chin. I must do this, for no man may attack the wife of a Comanche warrior. It is an insult that no warrior can accept. I will not escape the soldiers' guns, so you must demand my body back and bury me with honor."

"Would that we could ride with you," said Wild Horse, his face as solemn as Fat Belly's. "It is a thing that friends do. It is our duty."

Spotted Tongue shook his head. "No, I go alone. I was dishonored, and I must avenge myself, but I don't want my friends to die with me when there is no reason."

"What are you talking about?" asked Shaking Hand. "Comanche friends and family always ride with a warrior who looks to claim vengeance for a wrong done to him. It is the way of the People."

Spotted Tongue felt the now familiar isolation from the People. He understood the consequences of his actions, but his friends and family did not. "There is no need for you to die with me, and I will die. I am one warrior against all the teamsters and the white soldiers."

"But you have strong medicine," said Fat Belly. "It will protect us when we ride in, kill the teamsters, and ride out before any of the white men can fire their guns."

"My medicine will not protect us!" shouted Spotted Tongue. "No warrior's medicine will. Don't you understand? The Comanche are small in number, while the white men are many. His numbers will bury us like a rock slide. I will not waste the lives of warriors on the quest of a single man. As your war chief, I must save your lives for the time we will fight the white soldiers to save the People. That is your duty; not following me on the trail of vengeance!"

"But the Comanche always support their brothers when they seek vengeance for an insult done to them. It is justice for a wrong," protested Shaking Hand, repeating his argument... Fat Belly and Wild Horse nodded their heads in stubborn agreement.

Spotted Tongue's shoulders slumped in frustration and anger, anger that his loss of medicine has forever separated him from his brothers. What he saw clearly was lost to them in a perpetual mist. He drew a breath, knowing his next words would further separate him from the People. "You have chosen me as your war chief for many winters, whether we go raiding or to war against the Apaches. As your war chief, I order you to stay here. I don't want your help."

He braced himself for his brothers' reactions, whether anger or hurt, but neither hit him. Instead, a soft body pressed against his chest, and two hands seized his horned buffalo scalp, pulling it off his head.

"Spotted Tongue! *You won't fight that teamster! I won't let you give up your life for a man's pride. It's stupid and not your right, anyway! I didn't ask you to commit suicide for me. Do you understand?"* Little Flower jerked on the ends of his braids hard enough to bring water to his eyes. Suddenly, she released him and spun away. *"Of course, you don't understand me! All you speak is that heathen tongue. But I won't let you go."* She dropped to the ground and wound her arms around his legs.

Spotted Tongue gazed down at the stubborn expression on his second wife's face. He heard the laughter of his friends at the sight of a Comanche warrior held in place by a captive woman and a rather fragile one at that. Most of all, he heard the sound of his name---in his tongue---screamed out by his white wife. She knew his name! She spoke it!

"I don't think she wants you to go," said Wild Horse.

"She's being disrespectful," said Fat Belly. "No woman should hold back a warrior."

"You spoke my name," said Spotted Tongue.

"Did she touch his shield?" asked Shaking Hand. "If she did, it would lose all its magic and bring bad luck to Spotted Tongue."

Panting for breath, Green Willow rushed up from the creek, carrying a water bag made from a buffalo's stomach. "I only went to the creek for water, but I can't take my eyes off her for a heartbeat, or else she causes trouble. Let go of Spotted Tongue, you skinny, pale-skinned witch! I tell you, Spotted Tongue, you should have let her go last night. She's nothing but trouble, and now she will get you killed, going after a white man in the middle of his camp with all his friends willing to make your body leak blood from their bullets."

Green Willow dropped the water bag, grabbed Little Flower's arms, and dragged her away from Spotted Tongue and toward the lodge. "Get in there! It's not bad enough that you are the reason that my husband will die, but you have to shame him and possibly bring him bad luck by hanging on to him like a snake wrapping itself around his legs. Except I never saw a white snake." She gave Little Flower a shove that sent the white woman sprawling to the ground.

"Don't hurt her!" shouted Spotted Tongue.

Green Willow gave him a disgusted look despite the tears that ran down her face. "She's going to hurt you. She's going to kill you!" She dragged Little Flower into the lodge.

Spotted Tongue cleared his throat but could think of nothing to say. He darted a quick glance around the Comanche camp to see most of the People watching him. Several of the women were already packing cook pots and robes to load them on a travois. The Comanche were preparing to leave Medicine Lodge Creek and the Peace Council. They knew he would die at the hands of the teamsters and soldiers, and then all the People would become targets of the white men. Those of the People present must save themselves so that they might fight another time when they are not so badly outnumbered. His friends must also save themselves for leading war parties of which he would not be a part. Such is the life of a Comanche warrior: short and brutal.

Spotted Tongue mounted his waiting pony. As he turned it downstream toward the Kiowa medicine lodge, he paused to lift his hand to his brothers. "Save our People from what will come."

As he kicked his pony's flanks, he saw a tall Comanche standing apart. He recognized Quanah and raised his hand in a farewell salute. Quanah returned the gesture, then walked toward his own lodge, still separate from the rest of the People, as he had been separated from the day his father was killed. Spotted Tongue identified for the first time with Quanah's loneliness among his own people. He now shared it, if for a different reason.

As he rode downstream, he cleared his mind of all but his coming journey beyond the rising sun. There, he would ride free forever, hunting for the plentiful buffalo and other game, never sick, never hungry, never cold, always a warm lodge and full cook pot. He might not be able to make medicine anymore, but he could still believe there was existence beyond his own death. Faith and medicine were two different things, after all. He pushed away doubts that this was so, and when the large, round lodge loosely built of poles and tree branches came into view, Spotted Tongue was ready to sing his death song.

This was a sacred place, at least to the Kiowa, for it was where they held their Sun Dance each year. The People had no Sun Dance, not seeing the sense of self-mutilation and self-torture as their enemies would inflict enough wounds without giving them help. Still, a lodge that was the focus of a sacred ritual, even if it was not a Comanche ritual, must hold spiritual strength. Certainly, many thought so, for hanging on the outside walls were brightly colored talismans.

Slipping off his pony, Spotted Tongue entered the Kiowa Sun Dance lodge, where he found more talismans: feathers, arrows, beads, brightly painted gourds, and hanging high on the center pole, a decorated buffalo skull. The early morning sun sent slivers of light between the poles of the walls, and the still air was filled with dust motes and the aura of an unseen spirit.

Spotted Tongue knelt on the earthen floor, beaten hard by many feet, leaned back his head to look upward, stretched his arms out, and began his chant.

> Father Sun, I have been a worthy Comanche,
>
> A warrior who has counted many coup, killed
>
> Many enemies, taken many scalps and captives,
>
> Given as gifts all I have taken in raids except
>
> Ponies and captives. I have been a mighty hunter,
>
> Killing many buffalo to feed my kin and my band,
>
> And to provide hides for robes and lodges. I
>
> Have cared for my wives and have not beaten them,
>
> But my protection of them failed. Now, I must kill
>
> The man who dishonored me that I might restore
>
> Balance. I will ride beyond the sunrise this day. May I
>
> Find peace in my mind and body. I now go forth to
>
> Die. . .

"Spotted Tongue! Come out now! I must talk to you!"

The high-pitched voice speared his ears like an enemy's war lance, and Spotted Tongue gritted his teeth. One day, he would lose all patience and beat Green Willow. He rose to his feet and stalked through the lodge's door. "What in the name of the Cannibal Owl do you want? You have interrupted my death song. You know a woman must not do that. All you are allowed to do is mourn. Now I must start my song again and hope the bad luck you brought will not keep me from killing the teamster."

Green Willow had the decency to look worried. And something else, some other expression that came and went so fast, he did not recognize it. Maybe shame. She ought to be ashamed. "Forgive me, husband, but I knew you would want to know that Little Flower has escaped again. She cut a flap out of the back of the tipi, so she's probably crossed Medicine Lodge Creek. I think she'll steal a pony and ride toward the sun. After last night, she won't trust her own kind to help her. She doesn't know how to survive by herself on the prairie, so I suspect she'll die. I thought you might like to know before you go to let the white men kill you."

Spotted Tongue was so angry that, at first, he was unable to speak. He just breathed fast and hard until he felt himself grow lightheaded. That made him angrier still. He gritted his teeth and slowed his breathing. "Why didn't you tie her up, and if you didn't tie her, then why did you leave her alone? Oh, never mind trying to answer! I'll deal with you later."

He leaped on his pony and pulled on the rawhide strip tied to the animal's lower jaw, kicking the pony's flanks at the same time. He splashed across Medicine Lodge Creek and rode east toward the Comanche herds. He needed to know which pony Little Flower stole to judge its speed and training, as well as to study its track so he would recognize its hoof prints. The one thing he never doubted was that it would be a long and difficult chase if Little Flower chose a good pony--and she would. Spotted Tongue had captured her in the first place only after a long chase on horseback. Little Flower was a good rider, almost as good as a Comanche warrior. If her horse had not stumbled into an animal burrow, she might have escaped capture. No, catching her would not be easy, but catch her he must. Even a Comanche could die alone on the prairie despite his skill; Little Flower had almost no chance of surviving. He had to see her safe before he went to die.

Women! Sometimes, they were more trouble than the pleasure they brought. But only sometimes.

By the time Spotted Tongue returned to his lodge, the sun was several hands' width above the earth's end. He saw the chiefs of the various tribes and the white Peace Commissioners seated under a large lodge made of tree branches woven together to make an arbor while warriors and women, old men, and children stood or sat on their ponies where they could watch. There was barely room in the open, circular area in the grove of elm trees for all who wanted to watch, although few would know their fate was the real subject before the Council, and judgment would be rendered by the Commissioners whatever the Indians might want. It was late in the morning and later still in the lives of his People, the Kiowa, and others waiting in front of the giant lodge.

He had already decided his own fate, but that of the People rested in white men's hands. For once, his luck had returned. Better to choose the time and manner of your own death than have others decide it for you.

He slid off his pony in front of the buffalo hide lodge, his heart as sick as it had ever been, and rested his head against the side of the animal's neck. He had not found a trace of Little Flower. The young boys watching the large pony herd swore they had not seen her and that no pony was missing. Spotted Tongue believed them. No Comanche boy trusted to watch the pony herds would fail to notice an animal missing. The boys knew all the ponies.

"Spotted Tongue!"

He raised his head at the sound of Green Willow's voice. "What do you want now, woman? I have found no sign of Little Flower, neither pony prints nor her footprints."

"I found her, Spotted Tongue. She was hiding among the Kiowa lodges. And a Kiowa woman told me that the two teamsters who touched Little Flower fought with guns this morning. The gray-haired man is dead, so there is no reason for you to seek him out. You do not have to die, and I do not have to cut myself in mourning." Green Willow looked extraordinarily pleased.

CHAPTER SEVEN

"...we are greatly rejoiced to see our
red brothers so well disposed toward peace."

*Senator Henderson of Missouri, Peace Commissioner, at Medicine Lodge Creek,
October 21st, 1867, as Reported in Various Newspapers*

Still wearing his war paint and buffalo headdress, Spotted Tongue rode toward the teamsters' camp accompanied by his three friends. He must see the grey-bearded teamster's body; he must make sure the man is dead. Spotted Tongue was not sure how he should feel about the teamster's killer. Should he owe the man gratitude for killing Little Flower's would-be rapist and consequently saving him from the guns of the soldiers and the other teamsters? Or should he be angry that another man interfered? A Comanche did not forfeit his own vengeance to another man's hand, particularly when the other man is most likely to be white.

Spotted Tongue's head ached with questions that each pointed to different answers. He did not know himself anymore, did not feel the ground beneath his moccasins was solid, but shifted like the sand along the Canadian riverbanks since he lost his medicine many moons ago when he called upon the wolf, and the wolf did not appear. Despite his fasting and vigils alone on the prairie, Spotted Tongue knew in his heart that the spirit animal would never visit him in a vision again. There was a chasm between himself then and himself now, between himself and the Comanche, wide as the Palo Duro Canyon. It was a chasm he could not cross. He could not walk backward in his moccasins, only forward.

He was a Comanche, yet at the same time, a man separate from the People, a man lost in the darkness who must find his way in an unfamiliar country.

"Spotted Tongue, what do you want us to do when we reach the camp of the men who drive mules?" asked Fat Belly, raising his voice to be heard over the squealing of children, the barking of dogs, and the distant drone of voices from the Medicine Lodge Council meeting in the grove of elms.

"Learn what happened. I would know who killed the teamster?"

"What does it matter? He's dead, may the worms feast on his body, and you can go back to your second wife who has caused so much trouble." Fat Belly looked puzzled or maybe confused; sometimes, it was hard to tell the difference.

"The man was mine to kill!" said Spotted Tongue.

His companions nodded their heads. "That's true," said Wild Horse, "but maybe the man who killed him thought the same. How do you know which of you lost the most honor? Maybe the spirit of the wolf will guide you."

And maybe the wolf spirit doesn't exist, thought Spotted Tongue. At least he no longer exists for me. "I spoke in hot blood. I will not risk our lives to kill the killer. The People will need all its warriors strong and unwounded when the white man comes for us."

"Then you agree with what old Horse's Back said? That the white man will make war with us?" said Shaking Hand in disbelief; "that the soldiers will force us onto reservations? It's just a vision of an old man who has lost his wits, Spotted Tongue."

Spotted Tongue hesitated to answer. Yes, he did believe Horse's Back, but a warrior going into battle against such great odds must never doubt a victory nor have cause to fear a defeat.

"We are the Comanche! The white man's army has never fought such warriors as we bring to war!"

It was the answer his brothers wanted, the one they believed, and who was he, a war chief who had lost his medicine, to tell them that the Comancheria soon would be littered with the dead bodies of the People, that the wails of wives and children would echo within the walls in the Palo Duro Canyon, where the last tipis of a free people would stand among the groves of cottonwood trees.

Spotted Tongue shivered, although the morning chill that greeted the rising of the sun was gone. The chill was inside him, freezing his blood like water in tiny Palo Duro Creek when the snow fell, and the wind set the ice-covered limbs of the cottonwood to rattling. Seeing what is, the many soldiers with their guns, and seeing what must come because of those soldiers and guns are visions he does not want. Still, he will fight, and his warriors will fight because they are Comanche, and it is what the Comanche do.

He listened to his pony's hoof beats, muffled on the hard ground, as the white stallion carried him toward his death.

But not this day. He would not travel to meet his ancestors beyond the rising sun.

This day, he would learn who stole his vengeance against the gray-haired teamster and why.

Spotted Tongue guided his pony into the teamsters' camp, where a huge crowd of mule drivers and a few hard-faced women, pushing and shoving to get closer, surrounded a redheaded man, the same one who attacked the greybeard the night before. Two soldiers held the man by his arms while gesturing at the crowd to move back. The teamsters were yelling at the soldiers and their captives; the soldiers were yelling at the teamsters; dogs were barking, nipping at every available leg, whether a teamster's or a soldier's and the large gray mules were braying. A cloud of dust hung over the pushing, yelling men, the dogs, and the mules, kicked up by the boots of restless men.

The noise was enough to hurt Spotted Tongue's ears. Even a war dance before a raid, with drums and chants, was quieter. War dances were certainly more dignified.

Suddenly, a white soldier rode up, fired a shot in the air, and looked as if he might fire another shot, only with a man as a target. *"Sergeant, push those teamsters back before they step all over the body or lynch the killer or both! I'll have no mob running amuck here!"*

From the soldier's uniform with its shiny buttons, the man's rigid back, his angry face, but especially his sword, Spotted Tongue guessed the man must be a war chief. From his few times watching soldiers, mostly when they were unaware they were being watched, he noticed only war chiefs wore swords hanging from a leather belt around their waists. Certainly, the other soldiers were quick to obey him, pushing the teamsters away with the butts of their guns until the redheaded man stood alone except for the two soldiers holding onto his arms.

Lying inside the empty circle created by the ring of soldiers around the captive and his two captors was the body of the graybeard. A pool of blood spread outward from a wound in the man's side, soaking into the bare earth and already attracting a swarm of flies. Blood from a wound in the greybeard's shoulder had soaked one side of the man's shirt, from the entry hole to the waist.

Spotted Tongue looked from the teamster's shoulder to the bloody hole in the man's side and frowned at what he saw. The wounds in the man's body, one bringing death, the other not, though Spotted Tongue hoped both were very painful, were not right, not right at all.

He guided his pony through the crowd and slid off its back to kneel by the body, ignoring the startled looks of the two soldiers.

"Hey, you, Indian, get away from here," yelled one soldier, hanging on one of the teamsters' arms while grabbing Spotted Tongue's shoulder with the other.

Spotted Tongue pushed the soldier's hand away and sat back on his heels, perplexed by what he saw. The bullet wound to the greybeard's shoulder came from a shooter directly facing him, but the wound in the teamster's side that allowed blood to pool beneath him and surely was the killing shot could only have come from a bullet fired from beside and slightly behind the old man.

The redheaded man did not kill the old teamster. Someone else did.

"Now, what in the devil is this fight about? Damnation, we can't have white men fighting and killing each other. We got enough Indians to do that. Don't you fools know we've got four generals among the Peace Commissioners, and any one of them will horse whip the first man who causes trouble, and this looks like trouble to me." The officer gestured at the greybeard's body, then seemed to notice Spotted Tongue for the first time. *"Hey, you, Indian! What are you doing by that body?"*

"Hell, let him scalp old Pap, Major. The bastard don't deserve any better," shouted a man from the midst of the crowd of teamsters.

"That way, the old reprobate would be good for something, even if it's nothing but decorating a Comanche's lance," yelled another, spitting tobacco juice on the ground close to the body to emphasize the victim's utter worthlessness.

"You men shut up," ordered the soldier chief. *"I intend to get to the bottom of this mess without stepping in shit, and I don't need any advice from any of you or interference from an Indian. Hell and damnation, is he wearing war paint?"*

"That's the one, sir, the Indian I've been trying to tell the sergeant about. He's the one who rode off with the squaw old Pap was fixin' to rape. Maybe she was his

sister or wife or something. He didn't try to kill Pap, I guess, 'cause he saw there was more of us than there was of him, and his friends just watched his back for him." The redheaded captive gestured toward Spotted Tongue while never looking away from the soldier chief. Sweat dripped down his forehead, although it was a cool morning.

Spotted Tongue knew that sweat would be colder than the ice on Palo Duro Creek during winter. The sweat of fear always was, and this redheaded man was afraid his war chief did not believe whatever he was hearing. Spotted Tongue assumed he was the subject of the conversation and wondered what he should do. Wiser to do nothing.

"That's right, Major," said a tall, thin, white-haired man older than those in the crowd around him and whose bent shoulders Spotted Tongue knew came from a lifetime of driving mule teams. *"That's the same Indian, all right. He probably came back all painted up to kill old Pap. Bet he's pissed that Evan done it for him. Got all dressed up and got nowhere to go. Can't let him scalp him, though. Pap's a white man even if he's been such a piss poor one that he gives the whole race a bad name."*

"All right, Old Bill, I hear you and the rest of you men, too. The man deserved killing, and this Indian had cause to do it, but he didn't. What the hell was the old man thinking? Five thousand Indians in this encampment, we're outnumbered ten to one, if not more, and that damn fool was going to rape the squaw?"

"Not just any squaw, Major, a Comanche squaw. Might as well throw gunpowder on a campfire to make a Comanche mad. You and General Harney and the rest of the Peace Commissioners can fret all you want over the Cheyenne Dog Soldiers, but I'd take my chances against them before I'd go up against the Comanche. The red savages don't show mercy to any man. The prairie's empty one minute, and the next minute, there's a hundred of them screaming savages, sending arrows through the air faster than a man can shoot. The next minute, they disappear and leave everybody around you dead and missing their scalps. If there's any women or children, then they're gone, too, and their folks won't see them again until the Comanche ransom them back—if they do. They generally raise the kids as their own and take the women as wives after they break their spirits. The women they ransom

back are in such poor shape, mutilated and tortured in most cases that they mostly die within a year. Old Pap was damn sure a fool to mess with a Comanche squaw."

"No need to preach at me, Old Bill," said Major Elliott, nodding impatiently. *"I've known my share of Indians, fought them, too. I'm with the Seventh Calvary under Colonel Custer, and he knows a thing or two about Indians."*

Old Bill spit on the ground and wiped his mouth on his sleeve. *"Beggin' your pardon, Major, but Custer's got no respect for Indians, and that makes him a fool, all yellow hair and hot air. A man doesn't have to like the red savages, but if you live in this neck of the woods, you better respect them. They are damn fine fighters."*

"No disrespect for Colonel Custer if you please, Old Bill. He was a highly deco-rated officer during the Civil War."

Old Bill shook his head. *"Custer and them Rebel generals, Lee and that crowd, they all learned to fight out of the same book. The Indians never read that book, so you can't count on them to fight like the Army does. They're here, there, and gone, and you're picking arrows out of your carcass—if you're still alive—and wondering what the blue belly hell just happened. If Custer doesn't learn that, then his scalp will likely be decorating some Indian lodge. Mark my words, Major, that man is going to get you killed one day."*

"You give the Indian warrior too much credit, Old Bill, and underestimate Colonel Custer's fighting skills."

"Don't never say I didn't warn you," said the old teamster, turning and walking away.

The officer watched the old man disappear into the crowd, He frowned, then shook his head as if dismissing an unpleasant thought. He dismounted and walked toward Spotted Tongue, careful to avoid stepping in the pool of Old Pap's blood. *"Now, you, Mr. Comanche, get away from the body."*

Spotted Tongue, not understanding the speech between the old teamster and the soldier chief, had used the time to further examine the body, studying the size of the wounds and finding them the same or nearly so. There were faint black specks around the shoulder wound but not around the hole in Greybeard's side. He wiped a finger over one of the black specks, then smelled the resulting smear. Gun powder! He had fired enough guns that he recognized what those specks of gunpowder meant. Whoever shot Greybeard in the shoulder stood closer to the old teamster than whoever shot him in the side.

Spotted Tongue didn't realize the soldier chief, who he later learned was named Major Elliott, was talking to him until the man grabbed his arm and tried to pull him away from the greybeard's body. Spotted Tongue jerked his arm out of the major's grip and pulled his knife. At the same time, Fat Belly, Shaking Hand, and Wild Horse reined their ponies in a circle around the warrior and the soldier. The other two soldiers abandoned the prisoner and ran toward Spotted Tongue and the major, their guns pointed toward the warrior. The tableau of warriors and soldiers froze as each side stared with suspicion at the other. The tension between the two groups of men pulled tighter as if it were a piece of rawhide stretched between them.

CHAPTER EIGHT

*"The Great Father has sent us here to hear from your
own lips what were those wrongs that prompted you
to commit those deeds if you had committed those acts of violence."*

-Senator John B. Henderson on the First Day of the Peace Council,
Oct. 19, 1867, as Reported in Various Newspapers

"Spotted Tongue, what's happening here?" asked Phillip McCuster, panting as he stepped between the Comanche and the soldiers. "Some old teamster came to the Council meeting and told me I'd better get over here before an Indian war started. I just left the Council high and dry, and I'm the principal interpreter for the Comanche chiefs. Let's get this settled so I can get back to my job."

Phillip McCusker's voice broke the frozen tableau as Comanche and soldiers turned to stare at the newcomer. All but Spotted Tongue. He had stayed alive on raids and war parties by never relaxing his watchfulness in the presence of an enemy. Those warriors didn't leave their wives as widows and their children orphans.

McCusker touched Spotted Tongue's shoulder. "What are you doing here? What's going on? Why are you in warpaint?"

"I came to kill the greybeard for trying to rape my second wife last night, but someone else killed him first."

Phillip McCusker pointed toward the redheaded man. "That teamster did, and it's a good thing, too. Otherwise, you would've started a war and busted up the Peace Commission. The soldiers, not to mention the teamsters, would've filled your carcass so full of holes that you would leak blood like a sieve, and your hair would be hanging from some teamster's wagon."

"Two men shot at the old teamster, Phillip McCusker, the man with hair of fire, and someone else. The other man killed him. Look at the wounds!"

"It doesn't matter who killed him, Spotted Tongue. He started the fight, according to the teamsters who witnessed it, and now he's dead, and it's not a good idea for you to be here. You and your brothers stand over there while I explain the situation to General Harney. He's a Peace Commissioner and the soldiers' principal chief who came with me to make sure no one starts a fight."

Spotted Tongue finally turned toward the interpreter. Standing by Phillip McCusker's shoulder was the General Harney he spoke of, a tall, aging soldier with thinning white hair and whiskers on his face and under his nose. His eyes were narrow under jutting brows and narrowed even more as he looked at Spotted Tongue. He was an imposing figure even though he wore a dark coat and trousers instead of a dark blue uniform. The coat had two large brass buttons, so perhaps it was a special soldier's coat. At any rate, Spotted Tongue recognized a warrior comfortable with leading other men on a war party.

Spotted Tongue watched Harney's face while Phillip McCusker told the old soldier about the greybeard's attack on Little Flower. He didn't understand anything that was said, but he recognized the growing disgust on Harney's face as McCusker talked.

"Hellfire and damnation!" said the soldiers' war chief in a voice loud enough to be heard over men, dogs, and mules, loud enough to echo off the bluffs of Medicine Lodge Creek. *"I won't have this Peace Council ruined because the teamsters can't keep their trousers buttoned, and the Indians can't keep their womenfolk in their own camps."*

The general marched up to the captive and addressed one of the soldiers holding him. *"Sergeant, I sent you and your men to arrest a man for killing one of his fellow teamsters. Instead, I find you barely able to secure the prisoner and nearly overrun by men too long unacquainted with bathwater and razors and a bunch of Indians in war paint!"*

"There's just one, Sir," said the soldier.

"Eh? What did you say, Sergeant?"

"I said there's just one Indian in war paint, Sir," replied the sergeant. Spotted Tongue noticed that the soldier was sweating, but he doubted it was from the heat.

"I don't recollect asking you for the number, Sergeant. Is my memory failing me?"

"No, Sir, Sorry, Sir," replied the sergeant. A drop of sweat rolled off his forehead and into his left eye, making him blink rapidly.

The General shook his head slowly like an old man receiving sad but expected news. He tilted his head back to look at the sky. *"I tell you, this man's army is trying my patience. First, it's Major Elliott and some of his friends from the 7th Cavalry riding off on a buffalo hunt before the Council started, but **leaving the dead buffalo to rot!"***

The old general suddenly lowered his head and turned to glare at Major Elliott. *"Chief Santana of the Kiowa complained about it being a waste of food, among other things. I think he would have taken scalps if given half a chance. As it was, I had to arrest several officers. And now I have this business with a dead teamster. Was there ever a man so put upon as me!"*

The soldier called Major Elliot, now red-faced and stiff, saluted. *"No, Sir, General, Sir."*

"I'm glad you agree, Major Elliott, because you're responsible for part of my aggravation."

The General turned to face the teamsters. *"As for you teamsters, I don't want to have to visit your camp again. If I do, well, you better make sure that doesn't happen. Now, I'm not General Sherman, but right now, my temper is on just as short a fuse as his usually is. You just better be glad he got recalled to Washington and won't be at the Council. I shudder to think what he might have done if faced with this situation."*

General Harney gave the teamsters a disapproving glare. *"I have responsibilities greater than a dead teamster; this Council is getting off to a rocky start. The Cheyenne aren't here; the Arapahoe are out chasing a band of Pawnees they claim stole two hundred heads of their horses, and the other chiefs are late. The tent is set up under the trees; the Commissioners are all seated at the table—except for me— but the Indians are late. The chiefs who are there are arguing over protocol—who gets to sit where. Some tribe, I think the Kiowa, or maybe the Arapahoe, had an all-night pow-wow, so nobody got much sleep last night, including me, which means I'm in a piss poor mood!"*

Harney let his words sink into the hungover brains of the teamsters, nodding with satisfaction as he watched the bedraggled men shuffle backward. Spotted Tongue watched him turn toward the redheaded man. *"You, prisoner, what's your name?*

"Evan Flynn, Sir."

"And the dead man's name?"

"Pap—Pap Dickerson, Sir"

"So, Mr. Flynn, why did you kill Mr. Dickerson? Fighting over a woman, were you? And an Indian woman, at that, is what I heard. Bad business. The Peace Commissioners, the Army, and you teamsters all moved our camps a mile away from the Indian lodges specifically at the request of one of the chiefs, just so there wouldn't be this kind of business."

Flynn looked so relieved that his knees buckled, and the two soldiers had to pull him back upright. Spotted Tongue thought he heard a sympathetic note in the General's voice. Or maybe not. He couldn't speak the general's tongue, but something he said seemed to take away the teamster's fear.

"He was messin' with her, Sir, and it didn't look like she was willin', so I pulled him off. He didn't much like me interfering and came lookin' for me when he sobered up. He pulled his pig sticker on me, and I pulled out my revolver. A revolver is better than a knife in a fight, provided you get off the first shot before the other man gets too close with his knife, but then he pulled a revolver, and I knew I had to shoot before he did ."

"What did he say, Phillip McCusker?" asked Spotted Tongue, frustrated by the white man's tongue he couldn't understand.

"General Harney asked that man, Evan Flynn, why he killed the victim, Pap Dickerson. He said Dickerson came looking for him, mad as a hatter 'cause Flynn pulled him off your wife. Flynn killed him. Sounds like self-defense to me, but who knows what the Army will do?"

The soldier, General Harney, Spotted Tongue remembered, began to speak. *"We got Indians in front of us; we got Indians on both our flanks; and for all I know, Indians creeping up behind us. There are over 5,000 Indians here! One damn thing I don't need right now is some damn warrior getting his nose out of joint over some teamster interfering with his squaw. Hell, Mr. Flynn, if I had known what Mr. Dickerson was doing, I would have shot him myself for being a damn fool, not to mention endangering this Treaty Council and the life of every white man here. And I know for sure General Sherman wouldn't hesitate to do the same. Hells' belles, some men are too stupid to live, and Mr. Dickerson fell into that category."*

General Harney took a deep breath, put his revolver back in his holster, and glared at Flynn. *"However, Mr. Flynn, much as it pains me, I'll have to arrest you for murder. Can't have your teamsters killing each other. Who would drive the wagons of supplies?"*

"But it was self-defense, Sir! What was I supposed to do? Let him kill me?

"What are they saying, Phillip McCusker? Tell me!" said Spotted Tongue.

McCusker sighed. "It's none of our business, Spotted Tongue, but I'll interpret."

General Harney held up his hand to silence the teamster. *"Don't get snippy, boy. I don't have time for snippy this morning—too much responsibility for this Peace Council to have any patience with men trying to kill one another. But I'll be fair, Mr. Flynn, because I'm a fair man, everyone says so, even General Sherman would say so if he wasn't in Washington, and he thought about it long enough. Major Elliott will investigate the circumstances of the fight, but I look with severe displeasure at men killing each other—except in war, of course, or to protect the innocent, such as the fair sex or children."*

"But I was protectin' the fair sex, Sir!"

Evan Flynn was screaming at General Harney, his face nearly as red as his hair, whether from anger or blood lust. Spotted Tongue couldn't tell. He had noticed at those few times he had met white men that their faces would change color, or red spots would appear on their cheeks, depending on what they were thinking. Spotted Tongue thought that it was not a good thing to reveal which way you were thinking, particularly if you were a man and a warrior.

It occurred to him that he might be wise to learn to interpret what the change of color in Little Flower's face might mean. Not that he was afraid of his second wife, but since he lost his medicine and had only himself to depend on, he had learned to be cautious. Like a man walking across the prairie learned to look for snakes before taking a step, Spotted Tongue had learned to watch a man's face for signs of what he might do before he did it.

General Harney rubbed his chin, looking almost kindly at the young team-ster. *"Mr. Flynn, that red hair tells me you're probably Irish, so you pop off at the drop of a hat, but I won't have it. Now I can see you're still almost a boy, your beard is just beginning to sprout, and boys don't always think before they act until they find themselves knee-deep in a pile of shit and sinking fast. Did it ever occur to you that maybe that Indian girl wasn't so innocent after all? Why in Christ's good name did she run into a teamsters' camp? And she had to run a mile from her lodge to get here! You would have been in a lot less trouble if you had poured a bucket of water over Mr. Dickerson's head and reminded him that I'd make fritters out of his balls if he caused any trouble with the Indians. We need them sweet, boy, so they'll sign the treaty."*

"I don't think I had time to get a bucket of water, Sir."

General Harney rubbed his chin before sighing loud enough to be heard all over the camp. *"Never mind, Mr. Flynn, what is done is done. Major Elliot, lock up Mr. Flynn until he gets his temper under control. Do I make myself clear, Major?"*

"We don't have a stockade, General."

"I know we don't have a stockade, Major! Chain him to a wagon wheel if you must, but keep the peace between the teamsters and the Indians!"

Phillip McCusker barely finished interpreting before Spotted Tongue ap-proached General Harney. "Mr. Flynn—he stumbled over the word—Mr. Flynn did not kill the graybeard. If Mr. Flynn was in front of him, face to face, then someone else shot the teamster here," Spotted Tongue placed his hand on his own side to indicate the location of the graybeard's wound. "There were *two* men!"

General Harney put his hand on his revolver, and the other soldiers turned their rifles on Spotted Tongue. *"What's this Indian doing here? Comanche, isn't he, Major Elliott? Got his war paint on. If he owns that squaw that caused all the trouble last night, then he's got his dander up about what happened. Somebody tell him Dickerson's dead. McCusker, parley with this man, tell him he's got no cause to take anybody's scalp this morning. Tell him and his warriors to go back to their lodges; they have no business here. Tell this one to keep better watch over his squaw and stay away from the teamsters and their camp. Nothing but trouble will come of his coming around here."* The General directed a last glare at the teamsters, then stalked off like a stiff-legged dog toward the elm grove where the Council was meeting.

"Did you tell him what I said? What did he say?" Spotted Tongue asked Phillip McCusker.

Phillip McCusker was sweating, and Spotted Tongue wondered why when it was a day chill with the coming winter. "I didn't have a chance to tell him anything; I was too busy listening to what he was telling me. He told you the business with your second wife was over and for you and your friends to go back to your lodges and stay away from the teamsters. He also said to keep a better watch on your wives—and that sounds like good advice to me." He nudged Spotted Tongue toward his waiting pony, then abruptly stopped in mid-stride. "How do you know two men killed Pap Dickerson? How can you be certain? You weren't there."

Spotted Tongue waved his hand at the teamster's body, still lying in the middle of the circle cleared by the soldiers. "Look at the graybeard. He has a wound on his shoulder where he was shot by someone standing in front of him, but he also has a wound—the killing wound—in his side. If Mr. Flynn was standing in front of him, how did he also shoot him in the side at the same time?"

Phillip McCusker rubbed his chin as General Harney did. Spotted Tongue wondered if it was something white men did when they were puzzled. "Maybe Flynn approached him from the side, shot him, then stepped around to face him and shot him again. Or maybe he shot him in the shoulder first, then stepped to Dickerson's side, and boom, shot him." McCusker rubbed his chin again. "No, that won't work. The shot in the side probably hit his vitals, like his liver, and dropped him to the ground. No point in shooting him again in the front. Just a waste of a bullet; the wound in his side was going to send him to Hell on a fast train."

Spotted Tongue wasn't sure where this Hell was or why a dead man would ride an iron horse there, but there was much about the white man, even Phillip McCusker, that he didn't understand.

"But did you tell General Harney," Spotted Tongue stumbled over the soldier war chief's name, "did you tell him that there were two men?"

Phillip McCusker shook his head. "No, I didn't, but I think maybe you're right about there being two different shooters. I was too anxious to get you and your friends out of the General's sight. Besides, if I had told him, he wouldn't believe you. To him, he has one dead body, one man with a gun in his hand, and that makes it simple, and he's in no mood for anything that's not simple."

"What about that teamster, the one called Evan Flynn?" asked Spotted Tongue, not moving. And he didn't intend to until he learned what the soldiers had in mind to do with the man.

"I guess Major Elliott will tie him up for a few days, then let him go. I don't know exactly, and what difference does it make to you?"

"But he was trying to save Little Flower from the man the others called Pap Dickerson! I owe him my gratitude even if he stole my right to avenge Little Flower."

"Let it go, Spotted Tongue, and stay away from the camp," said Phillip McCusker, showing impatience as he nudged Spotted Tongue again, less gently this time.

"McCusker's right, Spotted Tongue," said Fat Belly, taking his arm and pulling his friend toward the ponies. "It's just one white man killing another. That's one less white man to cheat us."

"But it's not right. The white man did not kill the graybeard teamster," insisted Spotted Tongue, walking toward his pony on reluctant feet.

Fat Belly shrugged his shoulders. "What difference does it make if he is punished this time when he did nothing? Maybe he did many bad things before, and no one knew."

Spotted Tongue felt so frustrated that his face would be turning red if he were a white man. He understood Fat Belly's words. He even agreed with them as far as they went. Justice must come to every man eventually, but it was not right that it came to this man for a wrong he did not do. "Someone else killed the graybeard teamster, then did a greater evil by hiding like a coward behind Evan Flynn. Besides, Evan Flynn may have tried to save Little Flower. I can't be certain. If he did, then I owe him gratitude. If he did not, then I owe him death. I must know which it is."

Phillip McCusker shook his head. "What is wrong with you, Spotted Tongue? Leave the white man to the white man."

Wild Horse shook his head at Spotted Tongue. "Phillip McCusker is right. Your worry is foolish, and your thoughts are dangerous. Who cares how the white man thinks or why, whether he is a coward or not? The graybeard teamster is dead, and you didn't have to kill him. You lose no honor. Let the white men settle who is honorable among themselves—if they have any honor. Better we look to our own needs, which are how to keep the white man from the Comancheria. It is our land even if we do allow the Kiowa and their allies, the Kiowa-Apache, to share it."

Wild Horse's words were like the whine of the mosquito in Spotted Tongue's ears: familiar and very irritating. He had heard them all before from Fat Belly and even Phillip McCusker: it's none of your business. Why do you care what happens to the white man? Leave it alone.

But he couldn't, and he didn't know why—except he felt he would lose his honor if he didn't help the white man. He had already lost his medicine; he couldn't lose his honor, too. His honor is the last, best Comanche thing about him.

But he could tell Fat Belly, Wild Horse, or Phillip McCusker nothing of his thoughts. They would not understand, and he knew of no way to make them understand.

Spotted Tongue suddenly stopped and put away his lonely thoughts as his eyes focused on a white man some twenty paces away. Neither a soldier nor a teamster, but dressed more like one of the white chiefs from Washington, the man was staring at him as a wolf would: as if the teamster camp had disappeared, and Spotted Tongue was the only man remaining.

"Who is that white man, Phillip McCusker?" Spotted Tongue whispered, then wondered why he didn't speak his words out loud. He didn't know—except that you never disturbed a wolf.

CHAPTER NINE

"The commission was primarily concerned with affairs north of the Arkansas and the supposed general war in Kansas, they took relatively little notice of Comanche and Kiowa relations with Texas and New Mexico. But their solution to all three was a policy of collecting the Indians on reservations."

The Comanches: A History 1706-1875 by Thomas W. Kavanagh, University of Nebraska Press, 1996, page 411

Phillip McCusker looked at the white man staring at Spotted Tongue. "Oh, that's William Fayel. He's a newspaperman here for the Council. He writes words down on paper so other white men can read them and know what is happening at Medicine Lodge."

"I know what is happening," said Wild Horse under his breath. "The white man wants us to touch paper with a pen, wants us to promise not to raid, not to make war on our enemies, not to hunt the buffalo, and go to the reservation and live like children being told what to do."

"Maybe you can tell him that, and he will write it down for white men to read," said McCusker as he waved the man over. *"Mr. Fayel, meet my Comanche friend, Spotted Tongue, and his brothers Fat Belly, Wild Horse, and Shaking Hand. Spotted Tongue is a war chief of his band."*

Fayel glanced at Fat Belly and Wild Horse and noticed Shaking Hand's deformity before again looking intently at Spotted Tongue. He held out his hand. *"A war chief, eh? Of the Comanche."*

When Spotted Tongue ignored his outstretched hand, Fayel pulled it back and arched his eyebrow at McCusker. *"I take it shaking hands is not a Comanche custom?"*

McCusker shook his head. *"Not for Spotted Tongue, it isn't, no matter what the other Indians do, but don't worry, he won't hug you either. I heard how Senator Henderson accepted a hug from a chief and came away with a yellow nose, red streaks on one cheek, and green patches on the other."*

"The war paint didn't bother the Honorable Senator from Missouri as much as the lice the chief also shared. Being a politician, you would think he wouldn't notice," said Fayel.

"I don't recommend getting close enough to our Comanche chief to pick up any such critters. He might take it wrong and take my word for it, you don't want that. Spotted Tongue might be some shorter than you, but he's a lot stronger with no give to him."

"Give?" asked Fayel.

"A Comanche warrior, especially Spotted Tongue, keeps coming at you no matter how wounded he might be. He keeps coming until one or the other of you is dead. It's hard to win against a man like that."

Fayel nodded his head slowly. *"Well, since I prefer my hair on my head and not hanging from a Comanche lance, I guess I better start my conversation over again."*

He turned his gaze toward Spotted Tongue again. *"Have you come to sign the treaty? I had heard the Comanche were more distrustful of the* government *than even the Sioux and just as determined to defy the Great White Father in Washington, keep settlers off their land, and live as they always had. Am I wrong, McCusker?"*

"No, you aren't wrong. Spotted Tongue and his band are here to see who will surrender to the government and go to the reservation; at least, I think that's Spotted Tongue's main reason. He wants to see how many young warriors will follow the old chiefs and how many will join another band. The rest of the Comanche are here primarily for the presents the Commissioners will hand out. No point in turning down presents. As for the treaty, it doesn't matter what chiefs like Ten Bear and Horse's Back do, the Comanche will follow their lead or not as each warrior pleases."

"I never saw much honor in dying to the last man unless it is to buy time until an offensive can be launched or reinforcements arrive. But Indians, the Comanche included, don't hold back warriors as reinforcements, do they? They don't fight like organized armies, but individually, each man fighting as hard as he can, but not as any cohesive unit. Those fighting ways are fodder for poets with bloodless faces and soft hands but damn ineffective against a modern army of several hundred or several thousand men led by the likes of General Sherman. The Comanche are doomed, McCusker. Haven't they ever heard of running away to fight again another day?"

"But there won't be another day, will there, Mr. Fayel?"

"No, McCusker, I don't suppose there will be. Like the late Confederacy, I'm afraid the Comanche are fighting for a lost cause."

"Do you think your newspaper would be interested in telling the Comanche side of the story? Maybe something sentimental that will tug at the ladies' heartstrings?"

Fayel's mouth puckered as if he had tasted something sour. Spotted Tongue wished he knew what words tasted so bitter to the white man. For the first time, he wished he could speak the white man's tongue.

"There are some ladies in the East, society ladies in the main, with too much time and too much of their husbands' money on their hands, even a few men along with them, who are fond of talking about 'The Noble Red Man,' as I've heard them called. I tell you, McCusker, in all my life, I've never met a noble man, red or white. We're mostly rapscallions to a more or lesser degree. I never expect more than fifty percent goodness from my fellow man, and I'm frequently not surprised when they fail to reach even my modest expectations. Besides, those society ladies don't read my newspaper."

Fayel shook his head, looking beyond Spotted Tongue at vistas only he could see. The Comanche warrior shuddered, thinking the journalist had witnessed firsthand whatever he was seeing.

"I'm afraid I can't accommodate you and Spotted Tongue, McCusker. I write for a St. Louis newspaper, and Missouri is like the rest of the country: divided between Northern loyalists and Southern sympathizers, and not many signs of reconciliation. The Civil War is barely over; the blood hardly soaked into the soil of battlefields where the two armies clashed in a futile attempt to annihilate one another. When the armies withdrew, they left behind thousands, sometimes tens of thousands, of the dead, some hastily buried, many not. Those who lived near the battlefield and had the stomach for it did most of the burying. The civilians at Gettysburg told me that the air stank of death for days afterward, and they could hear the buzzing of the blow flies like bees in a hive from hundreds of yards away. Every time it rains hard, bones and rotting body parts are washed out of shallow graves. Then there are the poor souls still stumbling over the bodies of soldiers from both sides, skeletons still wearing what is left of their uniforms, the dead lost in the woods and swamps of the South, and never found by their comrades."

Fayel stopped to take a deep breath before continuing in a less passionate voice while switching his attention back to Spotted Tongue. *"Those loyal to the Union don't want to hear about any Lost Cause, and the only Lost Cause the Confederates care about is their own. But both sides want the Indian problem solved and the West safe for white settlers. Most of my readers would see the Comanche as standing in the way of progress, not to mention all the stories of raiding parties capturing white women and children and scalping their husbands and fathers would remind people of Quantrill and all that bloody business at Lawrence, Kansas."*

Fayel's mouth twisted into that sour pucker again, and his words sounded even more bitter. *"There is a school of writing I call 'Bugles and Drums' that write sentimental pig slop about the Civil War if you can imagine, all about the brave soldiers dying for the South or the North, sacrificing themselves for others, thinking about their wives, children, or sweethearts. Never any mention of arms or legs severed by an artillery shell or bodies blown apart in those stories. I never read so many euphemisms for blood and guts in my life. For damn sure, none of those writers ever saw a battlefield, not close enough anyway to be splattered by blood. Maybe you could interest one of those writers in the story of the brave but doomed Comanche. Be interesting to see what euphemism some of them could come up with for scalping."*

"What is he saying, Phillip McCusker? Interpret his words," said Spotted Tongue, stepping closer to McCusker. His curiosity was an itch inside his head he could not scratch.

Reluctantly, McCusker translated, but Spotted Tongue felt the words whirl around in his head. He had heard of the white man's war—who hadn't?—but the Comanche's only interest was in how many bluecoats would die and how long their war would last. If the white men were fighting in the east, there were fewer soldiers to bother the Comanche. That just left the Texas Rangers to contend with. The Rangers were fewer than the soldiers but much more troublesome.

And all this talk of dead soldiers left behind by retreating armies. It was dishonorable! The Comanche never did that! Spotted Tongue wasn't sure how many soldiers made up thousands, but he thought the dead must have equaled the numbers of buffalo on the Comancheria in the days before the buffalo hunters came with their loud guns. There weren't many such white hunters yet, but he sensed in his heart that the few would become the many.

It wasn't the talk of dead soldiers that made the skin on the back of Spotted Tongue's neck feel tight; it was the talk of Lost Causes. If this man, who made marks on paper for other men to read, thought the Comanche were fighting a Lost Cause, what did the white soldiers think? What did the war chief, General Harney, think? Did he think the Comanche were a people on the edge of defeat, and that is why he sent them to their lodges like children for whom he had little regard?

"Why does he keep looking at me, Phillip McCusker? Has he never seen a Comanche in war paint before?"

McCusker turned to Fayel. *"Spotted Tongue wishes to know why you are staring at him. I'd like to know, too. It's not really considered polite to stare at a man so long."*

"Why is he so interested in the teamster's killing? He seemed downright agitated when he was haranguing General Harney. He seemed desperate that Harney understood him, which, of course, the General didn't."

"Spotted Tongue believes that Evan Flynn is innocent, that there were two shooters."

"And you told General Harney that?" asked Fayel.

"I didn't get a chance. The General was more interested in sending Spotted Tongue and his brothers back to their lodges. I doubt he would have paid much attention to anything Spotted Tongue had to say anyway. He's just interested in keeping everything peaceable."

"Why would Spotted Tongue care about two teamsters trying to kill one another? That's what I really want to know. It hasn't been my experience that Indians, no matter what tribe, care much about white men fighting among themselves."

"What is Fayel saying, Phillip McCusker? His tongue flaps more than yours. What is his answer?" asked Spotted Tongue, impatient at having to wait for McCusker to interpret.

"He wants to know why you care about the teamster's death. I told him about you thinking there might be two shooters and that Flynn's being innocent. He still wants to know why you care. Let me talk to him some more."

Phillip McCusker turned back to the reporter. *"It's like this, Fayel. Spotted Tongue has a second wife named Little Flower..."*

Spotted Tongue listened to the strange tongue the two white men shared and watched Fayel's face change from a curious expression to one of interest. What was Phillip McCusker telling the white man that made him study Spotted Tongue like a Comanche would study the footprints of a stranger lurking near the lodges? Spotted Tongue felt his belly turn hollow.

He reached for McCusker's arm and squeezed it. "What are you telling him?"

"I told him about the dead teamster trying to rape Little Flower and how the young killer stopped him. He's really interested, Spotted Tongue. He says his paper might be interested in a story about the rescue of an innocent Indian maiden. A fight over a woman that ends in a killing, especially during a Peace Commission, is the kind of thing that sells newspapers. He wants to talk to Little Flower, hear her side of the story."

Spotted Tongue felt the hollow place in his belly spread to his chest until he had trouble breathing. Phillip McCusker might be married to a Comanche woman, but he talked too much like the white man he was. And Fayel was wrong on two different points: Little Flower wasn't an innocent Indian maiden—she would have knifed the teamster in his belly if he hadn't knocked her witless--- and Fayel was not going to talk to Little Flower. He wasn't even going to see her. One look at Little Flower's white skin and blue eyes, and Fayel would know she was a captive. Then the soldiers would come and take Little Flower and maybe him, too. Maybe they would put a rope around his neck and let him dangle from a tree limb.

That was no way for a Comanche to die, not the Comanche way at all, and Spotted Tongue did not intend for any of it to happen. If he couldn't outwit this white man, with or without his medicine, then he was no Comanche worthy of the name.

Spotted Tongue touched his fist to his chest. "I will find the real killer. I will hunt him like I would the buffalo." He folded his arms and waited for Phillip McCusker to interpret his words.

There followed more talk between McCusker and Fayel while Spotted Tongue waited, feeling hollow now from his belly to the top of his head. He would not have talked of finding who else besides Evan Flynn shot the teamster; he would have stayed silent if he hadn't needed to interest Fayel in something besides talking to Little Flower. Much as he hated to admit it, Green Willow was right: Little Flower made more trouble than one man could handle. Right now, he would trade her for a good cook pot.

Curses on Phillip McCusker and his flapping tongue.

Phillip McCusker turned back to Spotted Tongue. "Fayel called you a detective, like a Pinkerton agent, except you're an Indian. A detective is a man who hunts down other men who do bad things like murder. Anyway, Fayel thinks your hunt for the killer will make a good story for his newspaper, and he wants to help you. I don't think you ought to go along with it, Spotted Tongue. General Harney and the army don't want you going near the teamsters' camp again. Poking your nose into this business will just get you into trouble."

"I'm not an Indian; I'm a Comanche," said Spotted Tongue, closely watching Fayel's face for some expression that would reveal his thoughts. He didn't trust the reporter; his words twisted first one way, then another, like a feather in the wind. First, he wouldn't write about the Comanche because they were a Lost Cause, and no one cared but a few society women, whatever they were, and the Noble Red Man. All of a sudden, Fayel changes his mind and wants to write about the Comanche, whom he calls a detective, and furthermore, wants to help. Spotted Tongue never knew of a white man who helped an Indian without an ulterior motive. He wondered what Fayel's was.

Spotted Tongue felt as if he stood at the juncture of two trails, and he must choose one or the other. "How can he help me? He doesn't speak Comanche, and I don't speak his tongue. How can I tell him what questions to ask the teamsters? Besides, I don't trust him. No white man helps an Indian except for his own benefit. Why should this Fayel be any different?"

McCusker walked around in a small circle, then stopped to look around the camp as if he was searching for an escape. He pulled off his hat and slapped it against his thigh, something Spotted Tongue had seen him do before when he was confused or felt trapped. "Damn it all, Spotted Tongue, between you and this reporter, I'm between a rock and a hard place. If I don't go along to interpret, you're just going to get into trouble, and that reporter is liable to get himself killed. Don't you know how dangerous it is to stick your hand in a rattlesnake nest? And that's what you two would be doing. A man who kills another man ain't anxious to get caught, and he ain't gonna have no compunction about killing a reporter and an Indian!"

Spotted Tongue grasped McCusker's shoulders. "Thank you for helping. You, I will trust. And don't worry about rattlesnake biting me; it is the rattlesnake who should worry."

And may the teamsters never guess that a Comanche is hunting for an evil man who kills his own kind.

CHAPTER TEN

"We are especially glad because we as individuals would give them all the comforts of civilization, religion, and wealth, and now we are authorized by the Great Father to provide for them comfortable homes upon our richest agricultural lands. We are authorized to build for the Indian schoolhouses and churches and provide teachers to educate his children."

- Opening Remarks by Senator Henderson of Missouri at the Opening Council Meeting with the Comanche, Kiowa, and Kiowa-Apache, October 19, 1867, at Medicine Lodge Creek, Kansas, as recorded by Henry M. Stanley in *My Early Travels and Adventures in America and Asia, Second edition Published by Gerald Duckworth & Co. Ltd., 200l, page 263.*

As eager as Spotted Tongue was to begin the hunt, Fayel and Phillip Mc-Cusker had to attend the Council. Fayel had to make marks on paper to send back to his newspaper, and Phillip McCusker had to interpret. At least, the Comanche and other Indians would know exactly what the white men from Washington were saying instead of the best guess or, even worse, words an interpreter twisted, so the Indians might hear one thing, but the white men had said something different. At least, Philip McCusker was trustworthy, he was kin even if he was a white man.

Spotted Tongue wasn't as sure of the other interpreters, the principal of which was a half-Arapahoe woman Philip McCusker called 'Mrs. Adams.' Spotted Tongue admired her bright red dress and wished he could give Little Flower one like it. Of course, he would have to give Green Willow one, too, or there would be a screaming, rolling-in-the-dirt, hair-pulling, face-scratching fight between the two women, and his friends would laugh at him for not being able to keep peace in his lodge.

Spotted Tongue sighed. A warrior, a respected war chief, should not have to suffer the jealousy of the two women. A warrior had more important things to worry about. He wondered if his loss of medicine brought discord into his lodge.

"Spotted Tongue," said Philip McCusker. "I must leave you to walk beside Ten Bears. I should have been here earlier; he isn't pleased. In fact, none of the chiefs of the Comanche, Kiowa, or Kiowa-Apache are happy. The Cheyenne demanded six more suns before they would come to Council to talk. The Council agreed, and now the other tribes are mad. The other chiefs want to begin now so their tribes can leave. The Commissioners don't know what to do."

"The Cheyenne always want their own way," said Spotted Tongue. "Give them one pony, they want ten. It is always so. But six more suns will be good for me; I will find the killer in six more suns if you and Fayel help. I must see the gun the Army says killed the teamster, and I must talk to the other teamsters. I do not believe that Little Flower is the only one the graybeard wronged."

"I will help you, but I still think it sounds like a good way to get on the wrong side of the Commissioners—and General Harney. They won't put up with you sticking your nose where it doesn't belong. General Harney is liable to chop it off with his sword."

Spotted Tongue rubbed his chin as he had seen General Harney do. Perhaps it would help stir his wits into making a plan. "Fayel said he wanted to help, but he doesn't speak the Comanche tongue, so I need you to interpret. I don't think General Harney and the Commissioners would be angry with Fayel, do you? They don't want him to make bad marks about them for other men to read. And the Comanche—maybe not the chiefs whose spirits are weak—but all the warriors would make big trouble if I am hurt. I think the Commissioners want the Indians to be happy, to listen to their words, don't you, Phillip McCusker?"

McCusker rubbed his jaw until Spotted Tongue wondered if the man's flesh would peel off his face. "Damn it, Spotted Tongue! If I couldn't see you and know you're an Indian, I'd think you were one of those politicians from Washington."

Spotted Tongue didn't know if the word 'politician' that Philip McCusker used was good or bad, but he waited for the interpreter to surrender.

McCusker sighed. "All right, Spotted Tongue, I'll help you and Fayel, but no good will come of it. First, I have to see if I can help settle the chiefs down. Damn the Cheyenne; they're doing this on purpose!"

Spotted Tongue gazed at the great clearing amid a large grove of tall elm trees. Logs were arranged in front for all the principal chiefs who would speak for their bands to sit upon. Along one side were folding tables and stools for William Fayel and other men who made marks on paper for other men to read. In a semi-circle in front of the principal chiefs sat the Commissioners. A few branches were arranged over the Commissioners and the men who made marks on paper. These white men were not friends of the sun like the Comanche.

Behind the principal chiefs were the lesser chiefs, those who came to watch and listen but not to speak. Spotted Tongue supposed he was a lesser chief, but he stood close by Philip McCusker so he would not miss what the white man might say, but also to watch Phillip McCusker in case the interpreter might try to slip away after the Council without helping to find the second shooter.

Spotted Tongue gazed again at the Commissioners. He recognized General Harney but none of the others. Though he knew their names, he could not match names with faces. The war chiefs were Terry, Sanborn, and Augur, besides Harney. Of the other Commissioners who were not war chiefs, he knew neither names nor faces. Phillip McCusker had taken him to meet them all, but they looked too much alike with hair on their faces and their mostly light eyes and strange names. White men did not name themselves after animals such as Ten Bears and White Eagle, Horse's Back, and Dog Fat, were called, nor did their names say something about them like Gap in the Woods, Standing Feather, or Painted Lips. These names were strong and told something of the men who carried them.

To Spotted Tongue, the white men's names meant nothing.

One of the Commissioners who was not a war chief was a man with no patience, like Green Willow, when things did not go her way. His shoulders were stiff, and so was his face, and he tapped his fingers together like a warrior with a drum. Spotted Tongue doubted the Commissioner would hear the words of the chiefs, as he was a man in too much of a hurry to leave one place to reach another. To understand, a man must stay still and listen.

The principal chiefs shifted restlessly on their logs, waiting for the Commissioner to speak. Except for Santana, Kiowa chief, who sat in what he had heard Phillip McCusker call "a camp chair." Spotted Tongue noticed that the Kiowa chief wore a white man's Army coat and clutched his bugle. If luck was with the other chiefs and all the warriors, Santana would not blow on it, for he made an awful noise.

Behind the principal chiefs were lesser chiefs, and behind them, warriors in all their paint and headdresses. Then there were the women and the old members of the bands and the ponies of the chiefs and warriors. The sight made Spotted Tongue proud and sad at the same time. How many more times would the peoples of the Comanche, Kiowa, Kiowa-Apache, Cheyenne, and Arapaho be free to gather in one group to confront the white man?

Not too many more times, he thought.

Phillip McCusker squatted in front of the Comanche chiefs, ready to interpret. Comanche was the trade language for the plains. Other tribes knew enough Comanche to trade with them, and of course, there was always sign language, although most Comanche didn't use sign language very well. Why should they when the other tribes know Comanche?

"Six sleeps! No!" said Santana.

Spotted Tongue cringed, waiting for the Kiowa chief to blow his bugle, but Santana was too busy arguing to use his breath for such an action.

"Six sleeps is too many. The Comanche, the Kiowa, and the Kiowa-Apache need to return to our lodges in the Comancheria. We have much to do before snow covers our hunting ground. We want all the talking done and our presents given in four nights of sleep. We will not wait for the Cheyenne to come to the Council. They may come in six sleeps, or they may not. To depend on a Cheyenne is to depend on a broken stick."

The Kiowa chief sat back in his camp chair and folded his arms over his chest. Spotted Tongue wanted to grab Santana's bugle and bend it over the other chief's head. Instead, he grabbed Phillip McCusker's arm. "I need more sleeps. What if I can't learn who the other shooter was in only four sleeps? "

McCusker pulled his arm from Spotted Tongue's grip. "You're one Indian, and all the other Indians outnumber you. If we only have four days, then you will have to make do. Now be quiet so I can hear what the Council will do."

Spotted Tongue shuffled his feet in the dirt as he watched the white men sitting at the table. He couldn't quite hear them, but it didn't make any difference; he didn't understand their tongue anyway.

Finally, the impatient one stood up. *"If we can't all meet together, then we will parlay with each tribe separately, beginning with the Comanche and Kiowa. We have selected a great peace man—a member of the Peace Council at Washington—to tell you what we have to say. Listen to him."*

Spotted Tongue straightened, squaring his shoulders, his hands on his hips close to his knife. He did not need to know this impatient one's tongue to hear the threat in the man's tone.

When Phillip McCusker turned the white man's words into Comanche, Spotted Tongue felt his belly sink and tighten all at the same time---as if he saw an arrow coming that he must dodge. The white man's words didn't sound like the Commissioners came to make a treaty that both white men and Indians could honor. The man's words ordered the Comanche to listen to what the white man's chiefs wanted the Indians to do.

A very tall, thin white man rose to his feet, and Spotted Tongue wondered if all white men were tall as trees or only the ones he had seen. Senator John B. Henderson sounded like an important name for an important chief. At least he didn't twitch like a dying buffalo, so maybe he would speak true. If he did, Spotted Tongue could overlook the hair on the man's face.

Spotted Tongue listened to the white chief's voice, a very pleasant one, as Senator Henderson greeted the different tribes, as was the right thing to do. Then he mentioned the treaty signed two winters ago that many claimed the Indians broke. Spotted Tongue's band had not signed that treaty, so how could they break it? Besides, the white man had broken the treaty first.

Then the white chief said words that caught Spotted Tongue's attention when Phillip McCusker turned them into Comanche, words that made his belly hurt as if he had been eating green plums.

"We are authorized to build the Indian schoolhouses and churches and provide teachers to educate his children. We can furnish him with agricultural implements to work and domestic cattle, sheep, and hogs to stock his farm. We now cease and shall wait to hear what you have to say, and after we have heard it, we will tell you the road to go. We are now anxious to hear from you. If the Commissioners will tell the Indians the road to go, then they will not listen to the Indians. The white men have already made up their minds.

CHAPTER ELEVEN

"...All the land south of the Arkansas belongs to the Kiowa and Comanche, and I don't want to give away any of it. I love the land and the buffalo and will not part with any. ...I hear a good deal of fine talk from these gentlemen, but they never do what they say. I don't want any of these medicine homes built in the country; I want the papooses brought up just exactly as I was...I have heard that you intend to settle us on a reservation near the mountains. I don't want to settle there. I love to roam over the wide prairie, and when I do it, I feel free and happy, but when we settle down, we grow pale and die."

Speech by Kiowa Chief Santana in Response to Senator Henderson's Opening Remarks at Medicine Lodge Creek, October 19, 1867, as Recorded by Henry M. Stanley in My Early Travels and Adventures in America and Asia, Second Edition Published by Gerald Duckworth & Co. Ltd., 2001, pages 264-265

Spotted Tongue's head was heavy, like he was wearing many buffalo headdresses, all of them too tight, as he walked away from the great circle under the elms where the Peace Commissioners met with the Kiowa and the Comanche. He was not a close brother of Santana, but he admired the Kiowa chief for his words. Well, most of his words. Santana and his tribe hadn't always walked the path of peace the past two winters, but if he wanted to tell the white men the Kiowa had, then Spotted Tongue would not say otherwise. If Santana spoke with a forked tongue, it was less than the white man did.

Spotted Tongue wished the Comanche could walk backward through many winters to the time before the white man built their lodges along the People's creeks, or white soldiers in their blue clothes cut Comanche timber to build their log forts, and all the strangers who didn't belong on the land killing the buffalo for their hides, but left the meat on the plains to rot under the sun.

But no warrior can walk backward on the path he has already walked, so Spotted Tongue straightened his shoulders as if the words he heard from the Commissioners and from Santana and Ten Bears didn't blind him like a night without the moon or stars to give light.

Spotted Tongue couldn't make medicine to save the People from what he saw coming; all he could do was lead his warriors against the soldiers as a war chief should until a white man's bullet found him and sent him to ride the trail beyond the rising sun.

Until the Comanche faced the white soldiers in their last fight, Spotted Tongue had nothing to do---except find the second shooter so the redheaded man called Flynn would be free. If he did try to help Little Flower, and more and more Spotted Tongue believed he had, as visions of last night's actions repeated themselves inside his head. Yes, he was convinced that he must help the white man with the fiery hair. A Comanche's gratitude for a white man's freedom. It would be a good trade, a fair trade---better than the white government was giving the Comanche.

"Why did you leave early, Spotted Tongue?" asked Philip McCusker, catching up to the Comanche. "You missed old Silver Brooch of the Panateka Comanche. He flat-out told the Commissioners that he would wait until next spring to see if the white man would keep his word about everything they promised to give the Comanche and the Kiowa. If they don't, Silver Brooch said he and his young warriors will leave the reservation to live with their wild brothers. He meant the Kwahadi, I guess."

Spotted Tongue felt a cold spot in his belly growing bigger. "Did the Commissioners listen to him?"

McCusker looked as worried as Spotted Tongue. "Hell no, Spotted Tongue. Their faces were as empty as the plains on a hot day. They heard, but they didn't understand. The only man who looked like he knew Silver Brooch was talking straight was that newspaper editor from Kansas, Lawrence, Kansas, I think he said. Reynolds is his name. If the government doesn't live up to its word, Silver Brooch's band won't be the only one that heads for the Staked Plains of Texas, and Reynolds knows it. That would be bad for the Comanche. It would mean war for sure, and that would bring in the Texas Rangers and the Army. The Comanche can't replace every warrior killed with another warrior. The Army can bring in fresh soldiers for every man killed and keep bringing them in until the Red River dries up. I don't want to see that happen."

Neither did Spotted Tongue, but he knew in his heart that the white man wouldn't keep his word, and each warrior must decide whether to take the warpath until the Comanche were gone with no one left behind but women and children and old men, or whether they would take the trail to the reservation. The choice was between living free or mere survival. The chiefs didn't understand that the treaty would make them beggars at the mercy of the white man and his agents. The Commissioners didn't understand that a Comanche may accept or reject the decisions of a council chief as each man chooses.

Spotted Tongue tried to draw a deep breath, but his chest was tight. Never had he missed the power of his medicine more. With the strength, cunning, and intelligence of the wolf, he might yet save the Comanche.

In the space of a heartbeat, his vision of the power of his medicine faded. He had no medicine, and he knew he never would again. He had no spirit animal he could call on for help. There was no one but himself. He didn't know why it had happened, why he had changed, but he had.

"Here comes Fayel," said McCusker, waving at the newspaperman walking toward them. "Let's get your search over with, Spotted Tongue, before General Harney finds out what you're doing. I still don't understand why you're so set on interfering. It's not like the army will hang that teamster."

"Flynn, he is called Flynn," said Spotted Tongue.

Phillip McCusker rubbed his chin, and Spotted Tongue wondered again about the gesture. "I'm surprised you'd remember his name since you don't speak the language."

"I remember a man I owe."

"What did he say?" asked Fayel.

Phillip McCusker translated, and Fayel raised one eyebrow. Spotted Tongue watched in fascination and wondered what the man's gesture meant. He decided he should learn what white men's strange motions meant. He might need to know one day. You could never know too much about your enemy.

"If I weren't such a cynical bastard, I would believe Spotted Tongue was a man of honor; however, I can say he is a man who pays his debts, and maybe that's the next best thing to honor. Now, what does our Comanche detective want to do first? Talk to the innocent teamster?"

"Fayel wants to know what you will do first, Spotted Tongue?"

"I want to see the two guns," said Spotted Tongue, walking at a fast pace toward the military camp, followed by Fayel, with McCusker lagging behind.

Spotted Tongue stood stiff as a tree along Medicine Lodge Creek, feeling the sweat run down his face, smearing his war paint. He watched the soldiers, who also watched him. He was surrounded by the men in blue coats, some holding their long guns, and none of them looking friendly. He wasn't afraid, but he wasn't easy either. He didn't believe the soldiers would touch him or shoot at him, but no one liked to be surrounded by an enemy.

"Sergeant, please tell Major Elliot that Mr. William Fayel of the Missouri Republican newspaper of St. Louis wishes to speak with him." Fayel leaned toward McCusker and lowered his voice to a whisper. *"That will bring the man out of his tent in a hurry. I've never met a soldier who rode with George Armstrong Custer who didn't have a taste for seeing his name in the newspaper as much as our flamboyant general does."*

Phillip McCusker looked worried. *"How are we going to explain why Spotted Tongue wants to look at Flynn's and Dickerson's guns?"*

"Don't worry, McCusker. I know how to make a silk purse out of a sow's ear, meaning like every other newspaperman, I can lie when it's called for."

"What's he saying?" asked Spotted Tongue, tired of the white man's language filling his ears.

Phillip McCusker interpreted Fayel's words, and Spotted Tongue nodded. He didn't know who this Custer man was and what he had to do with the lesser chief called Elliot, but he didn't care as long as Fayel told a good enough lie to persuade the soldier to show them the gun.

Major Elliot did produce Flynn's gun, but when Spotted Tongue reached for it, Elliot jerked it away.

"What are you playing at, Mr. Fayel?" demanded Elliot. *"You think I'm giving a gun to an Indian?"*

"My readers will be interested in a story about the offended brave examining the gun that killed the man who assaulted his wife. In the interests of peace between the government and the Indians at the Treaty Council, Major Elliot explains to Chief Spotted Tongue how justice was done by the teamsters. Our brave learns how

white teamsters saved the virtue of a beautiful squaw. It's a wonderful story that the ladies will love," said Fayel with an earnest expression on his face.

"Ladies don't read the newspaper," said the major, frowning at Fayel.

"I don't know what part of the country you come from, Major, but in St. Louis, ladies read the paper. Our womenfolk are very well informed. The next thing we know, they will be wanting to vote."

"What are they saying, Phillip McCusker?" demanded Spotted Tongue. After McCusker translated, Spotted Tongue thought the women William Fayel talked about sounded a lot like Comanche women: always more interested in men's business than they should be. Perhaps white men and Comanche warriors had more in common than he thought. They both had nosey wives.

"I'm not just a chief," said Spotted Tongue. "I'm a war chief. That's different from a council chief, headman, or any lesser chief. I want Fayel to tell the soldier."

"No, you don't," said Phillip McCusker. "If Major Elliot learns you are a war chief, he might think you are planning to lead your warriors on the warpath and lift a few scalps. All the soldiers, from the officers down to the privates, are jumpy as frogs after a bug. Major Elliot is really fond of his hair, so he's twice as jumpy as the other soldiers. Another thing, he doesn't like Indians much at all, especially after General Harney reamed him out about shooting the buffalo just to see how many he and his men could kill in an afternoon. Santana and the rest of the Kiowa demanded Elliot be punished, and he was."

"But that was the Kiowa, not the Comanche. The Comanche haven't done anything to him yet," said Spotted Tongue, offended at being confused with the Kiowa.

"Elliot can't tell the difference; not many soldiers can. That's why General Hancock rode out to punish the Sioux and ended up burning a Cheyenne village instead and killing any Cheyenne that couldn't get away, including women and children. Hancock ended up in hot water, but it didn't help the dead Cheyenne. So you just keep quiet about being a war chief 'cause I don't want to listen to Green Willow wailing over your dead body if some soldier gets the urge to shoot himself a Comanche for no good reason, except everybody is twitchy and jumping at their own shadows. The air is still smoky from the prairie fires to the west of here, and the weather feels unsettled, like the earth is holding its breath before bursting out with a terrible storm. Can't you feel it, Spotted Tongue, like the air is squeezing your body?"

Spotted had felt unsettled since he lost his medicine, but maybe it was the coming of the frost on the next moon with his band far from its winter camp, the Grand Council and the soldiers, and the other tribes, some enemies not so long ago, created a feeling greater than merely being unsettled. He felt uneasy with an itch down his back that he couldn't scratch. He felt surrounded by men and changes he could not control.

But he could control whether or not Pap Dickerson's killer would be identified. Not that he intended to make the killer's name known to Major Elliot. Pap Dickerson earned death, and Spotted Tongue intended his killer to stay free and unknown—except to himself, who owed the man a debt.

"Spotted Tongue?" said Phillip McCusker, a worried expression on his face at the warrior's continued silence.

Spotted Tongue blinked and replied to Phillip McCusker's warning but not to his feelings. If Phillip McCusker had an itch of his own, it was up to him to figure out how to scratch it himself. "I will stay silent as you say. I just want to see the gun," he said, continuing to hold out his hand toward Major Elliot. "And I want to see Dickerson's gun," he added.

"Dickerson's wife kept his gun according to the major," said Phillip McCusker.

"Then we will talk to her," said Spotted Tongue. The Major handed him the revolver, but with a scowl on his face that remained Spotted Tongue of Coyote Dung, except Elliot wasn't as ugly.

Spotted Tongue had a gun exactly like Flynn's, Phillip McCusker said it was made by two men named Smith and Wesson, and he had traded for it with the Comanchera several moons ago. The men, Smith and Wesson, had done a bad job. The gun was worthless further than about twenty paces because it might or might not hit what the warrior aimed at, and it might or might not kill anyone if it did. Flynn was standing closer to Dickerson than twenty paces, maybe ten paces or less, and the young teamster still didn't manage to kill Dickerson.

Spotted Tongue counted the bullets left in the revolver. There was only one bullet missing, meaning Flynn only fired once. The bullet went through the teamster's shoulder, and the impact should have slowed it down.

"The bullet should be somewhere in the teamster's camp," said Spotted Tongue, explaining his reasoning to Phillip McCusker and Fayel.

"Makes sense," said Phillip McCusker. "Let me tell Major Elliot and Fayel, then we'll walk over to the teamster's camp and find that bullet."

"Tell Fayel, but not the officer who likes his hair. Look around," said Spotted Tongue, waving his arm at the camp. "See all the braves? Kiowas, Comanche, Arapahos, Kiowa-Apaches, and Cheyenne wandering among the white men like curious children? The army will blame one of them for the old man's death if they can't blame Evan Flynn. It is the way of men to accuse those who are not their own. I will not see this Evan Flynn go free only to have an Indian take his place."

"Then what will you do, Spotted Tongue? You can't free Flynn if you don't convince Major Elliot that one bullet fired from one gun couldn't cause those two wounds," said Phillip McCusker. "I think you ought to leave well enough alone."

Spotted Tongue wished people would stop arguing with him. He saw the trail before him so clearly; at least, he saw part of it. First, find the bullet, then talk to Evan Flynn to learn who hated the old teamster enough to kill him, and let someone else take the blame. Then---what?

CHAPTER TWELVE

"A long time ago the band of Penekdaty Comanches were the strongest band in the nation. The Great Father sent a big chief down to us, and promised medicines, houses, and many other things. A great, great many years have gone by, but those things have never come. My band is dwindling away fast. My young men are a scoff and a byword among the other nations. I shall wait till next spring to see if these things shall be given us; if they are not, I and my young men will return to our wild brothers to live on the prairie... Do what you promised us, and all will be well. I have said it."

Speech by Penateka Comanche Chief Silver Brooch in Response to Opening Statement by Senator Henderson at Medicine Lodge Creek, October 19, 1867, as Recorded by Henry M. Stanley in My Early Travels and Adventures in America and Asia, Second Edition Published by Gerald Duckworth & Co. Ltd., 2001, pages 266-267.

The teamsters' camp smelled even stronger of burned coffee, mule dung, dust, and a crowd of unwashed men than it had the night before. The odor of unwashed bodies was familiar to Spotted Tongue. Living in a land with little water, the People didn't waste it on their bodies. Water was to quench the thirst of warriors and ponies, to use in the cook pots, wash blood off after a raid, and clean wounds. The teamsters smelled like they followed the Comanche habits.

The mule dung, however, stank; it smelled worse than pony dung, a lot worse. The Comanche stole mules whenever they found a herd because mules could be traded to the Comancheros, who sold them to the white man's army. You could also eat a mule---if it was winter, and the snow was deep, and the band was starving, and you didn't mind the taste. No band Spotted Tongue had camped with had eaten a mule, but he had heard of other bands who did.

"Let's look for that bullet, Spotted Tongue," said McCusker, "so we can get out of here. None of these teamsters look friendly. You Comanche have lifted too many teamsters' scalps over the years."

Spotted Tongue looked around at the crowd of white men, most with hairy faces and cloth shirts tucked into dark pants. He agreed with Phillip McCusker that the teamsters didn't look friendly, but they didn't look like men planning to kill themselves a Comanche either. They were watchful, mostly quiet, as men were waiting for something or someone. For what or who, Spotted Tongue didn't know.

He walked into the center of the camp, noticing the teamsters moving back as if giving him room. He heard the rattle of Elliot's sword and the officer's loud voice and wished Phillip McCusker and Fayel had managed to keep the army's lesser chief at the military camp. He wished all the Indians in the teamsters' camp would go back to their lodges.

Spotted Tongue stopped at the scuffed dirt where the old teamster he remembered was called Pap Dickerson died in a pool of his own blood. Someone had kicked up the dirt to cover the blood, but there was still a dark spot. Spotted Tongue looked beyond where Dickerson had stood, then walked toward a wagon where he saw a fresh gash in the wood just above the big iron wheel. He pulled his knife from his belt.

"What's that Indian doing pulling his knife?" demanded Major Elliot, putting his hand on his sword as he took a step back.

Spotted Tongue ignored the major other than thinking the man lacked war sense. By the time Elliot could pull his sword out, any Comanche warrior would have already gutted the man. He heard Phillip McCusker trying to calm the white man, or he assumed that was what the interpreter was trying to do. Kneeling down, Spotted Tongue pried a bullet from the wagon with his knife. The bullet had not flattened badly enough when hitting the wagon that Spotted Tongue was unable to identify it as being fired from Evan Flynn's revolver or a revolver just like it.

Spotted Tongue held up the bullet between his thumb and forefinger. "See, Phillip McCusker, if this is not magic, then the bullet could not have hit Pap Dickerson's arm, changed direction into the old teamster's side deep enough to kill him, and followed its path out of the body, and embedded itself in the wagon." Since he did not believe in magic anymore, Spotted Tongue knew his words were true. "Tell the lesser chief Elliot what I said so Evan Flynn goes free."

"What about the other Indians, Spotted Tongue? Aren't you still afraid that Major Elliot will arrest one of the Indians that are standing around watching?" asked Phillip McCusker.

"I have thought about that, but which Indian would he choose? One of the Cheyenne? They are still angry about Sand Creek, and now the village the white War Chief burned. They might leave. The same with the Arapaho. The Kiowa and the Comanche don't trust the Peace Commissioners already and would leave if Elliot picked an Indian out of the crowd. The Kiowa-Apache will follow with the rest. There would be no peace treaty, and all the tribes would follow the warpath again. I don't think the Great White Father and the Peace Commissioners would like that. I think lesser Chief Elliot would be punished if the Treaty Council fails. Tell him so, Phillip McCusker, and maybe William Fayel would tell him, too."

Spotted Tongue folded his arms as he had seen Silver Brooch do. "I have said all. I am done talking—until I talk to Evan Flynn."

Phillip McCusker frowned at Spotted Tongue as he rubbed his chin. "I hope you know what you are doing, Spotted Tongue, because I can already tell that you are pissing off Elliot."

Fayel studied Spotted Tongue, the hint of a smile on his lips. *"You know, Mc-Cusker, I believe the Comanche would be better off if Spotted Tongue negotiated on the tribe's behalf. Seems to me that he sees both sides of the argument, picks the best side, turns it on its head, and persuades everyone that he's right. Really unusual for an Indian."*

"Yeah, well, Spotted Tongue is just a little different. Don't know how he comes by it, but he can see things his warriors can't. Be a hell of a politician if he was white." McCusker turned to Spotted Tongue. "Don't worry about Elliot. Fayel and I will talk to him. Maybe we can cool him down before this whole situation blows up like an overheated cannon."

Spotted Tongue watched Phillip McCusker and William Fayel as they each talked to the Lesser Chief Elliot. He watched the white officer turn to look at the wagon with its fresh gouge surrounded by splinters where he had dug out the bullet with his knife. He watched Elliot frown but finally nodded his head. Spotted Tongue knew the officer had accepted what he had been told. Elliot wasn't happy, but Spotted Tongue didn't care. He wasn't here to make the white officer happy; he was here to prove him wrong.

"Come on, Spotted Tongue," said Phillip McCusker, walking toward a wagon at the end of the line. "Evan Flynn is chained to a wagon back here. "

In the flickering light of the campfires, Evan Flynn's face was all shadows and hollows, with bloodshot blue eyes and his red hair lending color to his visage. One end of a greasy chain encircled his right wrist, while the other end was looped through a wagon spoke with a padlock holding it closed. A ragged blanket was draped over his shoulders to keep out the chill that arrived with the setting of the sun. A dirty tin plate with the residue of dried beans and biscuit crumbs sat on the ground next to his left hand. There was a spoon laying in the middle of the plate. There was no knife in sight, which Spotted Tongue supposed was a good idea. Never give a prisoner a knife.

Spotted Tongue listened to Phillip McCusker while watching Evan Flynn. A man's facial expressions and the movements of his body reveal more than what his tongue says. What they reveal is that Evan Flynn is afraid, confused, and unaware that his bullet didn't kill Pap Dickerson.

"I kicked him last night because he hit that Indian squaw. It ain't right to hit a woman even if she is dirty Injun squaw. Nobody liked Dickerson. He was a liar, a braggart, and too quick to beat his wife and his mules. He cheated at gambling games, bullied younger teamsters, and taunted others into knife fights and killed them. It wasn't nothing more than murder 'cause he never picked on anybody who could beat him, and if he did, it was in some underhanded way that never led back to his doorstep. If I hadn't been so mad, I never would have got into it with guns against him. I ain't no killer, and he knew it. He thought I'd pull off my aim, and I thought I did. I never meant to kill him, but I did. But he had it coming. I never figured out why his wife, Lizzie, didn't take after him with a cast iron skillet to his head some night when he was sleeping off a drunk. Nobody would have thought less of her if she had."

McCusker leaned over and patted Flynn on his shoulder. *"Don't worry about it, son. Spotted Tongue proved you didn't kill Dickerson, although it sounds like it would have been a public service if you had. Your bullet went through his shoulder, but somebody else shot him through the side."*

"What does that Injun have to do with it?" asked Flynn, staring at Spotted Tongue with a puzzled look.

"That squaw was his second wife," said McCusker. *"He figured he owed you a debt of honor even if he doesn't like white men."*

"I ain't fond of Injuns, but I appreciate what he did. Maybe there's hope we can get along with each other, do you suppose?"

"Don't know, son; I just don't know. Lots of differences need to be ironed out." McCusker turned to Spotted Tongue and translated his conversation with Evan Flynn.

Spotted Tongue didn't like Flynn's calling Little Flower "a dirty Injun squaw." Little Flower wasn't an Injun squaw; she was a Comanche warrior's wife. He would think about Flynn's appreciation. He guessed it hurt the white man to have to thank a Comanche, but he did it. Maybe the white man and the Comanche could get along—if the white man stopped killing the buffalo and stayed out of the Comancheria.

"Let's go talk to Dickerson's wife. It sounds like she won't be wailing and cutting herself because he is dead. Where is she?" asked Spotted Tongue.

McCusker and Fayel exchanged a few words with Flynn before Fayel waved toward a woman whose face looked worn down to the bone and decorated with fading bruises, sitting in front of a dirty canvas tent. Several women who looked equally hard used but without the bruises were gathered around Lizzie Dickerson, the new widow of the late, unlamented Pap Dickerson.

"The ladies comforting Lizzie Dickerson are camp followers," said Fayel, waiting while McCusker interpreted his words for Spotted Tongue. *"I don't imagine their lives are much better than Mrs. Dickerson's."*

"They are a little more free to pick and choose," said McCusker to Fayel before explaining to Spotted Tongue what a camp follower was.

Spotted Tongue thought it was one more thing he didn't understand about white men. How did a father increase his pony herd or collect extra buffalo hides if a warrior could take a woman to his lodge without paying her father to take her as a wife? If the same woman visited many different lodges, there might be fights among the warriors. No, the whole thing seemed like a bad idea to Spotted

Tongue, but he was here to question Lizzie Dickerson, not to learn about these camp followers.

"May I offer my condolences for your loss, Mrs. Dickerson," said William Fayel.

"Weren't much of a loss to me," said Lizzie Dickerson, eyeing Fayel with suspicion before glancing at Spotted Tongue, then dismissing him as inconsequential. *"I don't know what it is to you, but he was a hard man, and I waited most of my married life for somebody to kill him. Well, somebody finally did, and now he's dead and ain't ever gonna hit me again. I picked up his gun when he fell. I figure I will sell it when I get back to Fort Larned. It ought to be worth something, and I ain't got no use for a revolver that can't kill a man until you're close enough to see the whites of his eyes. That never bothered Pap any 'cause he got close to a fellow like he was going to slap him on the back-friendly like, then he'd shoot him in the gut. No, I don't want anything to do with that gun. Got too much blood on it to suit me. I want a revolver, I'll buy a nice Colt."*

She held up Dickerson's revolver, its cylinder still full of bullets. "I got this and his Spencer rifle, the wagon and mules. I'm good with mules, better than he was. I'll make out. "

Spotted Tongue tugged on Fayel's coat. "Did she reload the revolver, and who saw her pick it up after Dickerson fell?

Fayel looked at McCusker, one eyebrow raised. McCusker translated, and Fayel nodded before turning back to Lizzie Dickerson. *"Madam, did you happen to re-load the revolver after Mr. Dickerson fired it?"*

"Fired it? Pap didn't fire it at all. Evan Flynn shot first, hit Pap in the shoulder, and he dropped the gun. Molly here saw it all. Tell him, Molly!"

Molly was an attractive woman with nice skin and curly blond hair, although she was missing a few teeth, so her voice whistled when she spoke. *"It's like Lizzie said. Evan fired, a real loud shot it was, too, and Pap grabbed his shoulder. The bullet must have done something to his arm, numbed it or something, so anyway, he dropped the gun. He kind of staggered a bit, then fell. Lizzie waited a minute to make sure he was dead before she picked up the gun. That's when we saw he was shot in the side, too."*

"How many shots did you hear, Molly?" asked Fayel.

"Well, that first shot was loud, had kind of like an echo, so maybe it was two shots we heard. Do you think so, Lizzie?"

"There were two shots, but I don't think Evan Flynn shot twice. He dropped his own gun when he saw Pap grab his arm. Evan is so kindhearted, I'm surprised he fired once. He ain't one to see blood spilled."

"Did she see anyone else fire a gun?" asked Spotted Tongue.

After a whispered translation from McCusker, Fayel turned back to Molly. *"Did you see anyone else fire a gun? Did anyone else have a gun?"*

Molly rolled her eyes in disgust at the question. Spotted Tongue saw Green Willow do the same thing when she was disgusted with him. He was beginning to wonder if white women and Comanche women were more the same than different. What if they met each other and no one was a captive? What if they formed a band? He shivered. It was too horrible to think about.

"Everyone has a gun. They are all teamsters! You think they drive a wagon full of goods across the prairie without a gun?"

Spotted Tongue didn't need Phillip McCusker to translate Fayel's words. The Cannibal Owl must have stolen his brains to ask such a question. Of course, the teamsters had guns. Only men missing their wits would cross the Comancheria without guns. The teamsters were white, but they didn't lack wits---except when they tried to cross Comanche land in the first place. Most lost their goods and their scalps even when several teamsters traveled together. He had several teamsters' scalps on his own lance.

"What do you want to do now, Spotted Tongue?" asked Phillip McCusker. "It doesn't sound like old Pap's wife killed him. It's too bad since it sounds like she earned the right to send him to meet the Devil, but some women are just too soft-hearted to kill a man even when he needs it."

Spotted Tongue wondered if Green Willow would kill him if he beat her like Pap Dickerson did to his wife. He wasn't sure about his first wife, but he felt that Little Flower would absolutely kill him. Little Flower didn't have a soft heart; she had a determined heart. Best to keep knives out of her hands.

"Spotted Tongue, what do we do now? Major Elliot is glaring at you. You spoiled his case against Evan Flynn. He thought he had the murder all wrapped up with a bow on it until you came along and pissed on his parade. Now he's got to start over finding the killer. The Army doesn't like loose ends---unless it finds a way to cover up its mistakes."

Spotted Tongue thought he would never really understand white men's talk, even when the white man was Phillip McCusker. "I never pissed on the officer, and what is he wrapping up?" demanded Spotted Tongue.

Phillip McCusker sighed. "It just means you proved him wrong, and he's mad about it. So, let's leave and let him stew in his own juices."

Spotted Tongue looked at the teamsters standing silently in front of the wagons. He closed his eyes to bring up an image from that morning: Pap Dickerson's body lying in the dirt, white like bleached buffalo bones from loss of blood, and teamsters crowding around the stiffening body, muttering words he could not understand.

Spotted Tongue opened his eyes, the image from the morning superimposed over the crowd of teamsters. He pointed at an older man. "You! I want to talk to you!"

CHAPTER THIRTEEN

"If the Texans had kept out of my country there might have been peace. But that which you now say we must live on is too small. The Texans have taken away the places where the grass grew the thickest and the timber was the best. Had we kept that we might have done the things you ask. But it is too late. The white man has the country which we loved, and we only wish to wander on the prairie until we die…I want no blood upon my land to stain the grass."

Remarks by Yamparika Comanche Council Chief Ten Bears in Response to Senator J. B. Henderson's Opening Remarks at the Indian Peace Commission At Medicine Lodge Creek, October 19, 1867.

A young teamster whose good looks were marred by a healing knife wound on one cheek, and wearing a faded blue shirt made of some course material and worn-looking black pants stuffed into tall boots filthy with mud and old splotches of blood, probably from a newly slain buffalo, looked startled. He looked at the other men around him before pointing to himself and clearing his throat.

"What does that Indian want?" he asked, looking first at Spotted Tongue, then at Phillip McCusker and William Fayel.

"He wants to know what you saw when Pap Dickerson was killed," said Phillip McCusker. "Just tell me, and I'll tell Spotted Tongue. The woman Dickerson grabbed was his wife."

The young man looked at Spotted Tongue and nodded. *"We're all sorry about his wife. Pap Dickerson wasn't worth the powder it would take to blow him to Hell. He was a bad man. However you looked at him."*

There was a foot-shuffling, throat-clearing mumble of agreement from the crowd of men. Many wore an uncomfortable expression on their faces as they found themselves defending an Indian woman against a white man. It was a situation most weren't used to dealing with since their stance meant they saw the Indian woman as the same as their own women: someone to protect rather than to ignore.

Spotted Tongue heard Phillip McCusker's translation of the young teamster's words, but he already sensed that the crowd of men around him were ashamed of Pap Dickerson's actions. He nodded his head to acknowledge the embarrassed apology of the teamsters while wondering at the same time when his life had changed so much that he believed a bunch of men, white men, were actually sorry about how one of their own treated an Indian girl. Maybe his inability to make medicine left him open to strange ideas. He wished he could call on his spirit wolf once more. He would ask why his wits were twisted around and up and down until he wasn't sure what the Comanche trail was and what the new trail he walked was. He didn't feel he fit in his own skin anymore.

The young teamster cleared his throat again, then spoke to William Fayel, who had asked a question from Spotted Tongue. *"My name is George Carter, and I'm a teamster. Well, I guess you knew that already. Anyhow, you asked if I was sorry Pap Dickerson was killed? Hell, no, I'm not sorry. He marked my face in a knife fight before we left Fort Larned for no better reason than he thought I was trailing him too close, making his mules skittery. He woulda killed me if Old Bill over there hadn't knocked him in the head. Left him with a big knot on the back of his head that woulda killed an ordinary man. But not Pap Dickerson. He had a skull thicker than the leather sole on a boot."*

A runt of a man in the crowd handed Carter a tin cup full of whiskey if the smell of the fumes was anything to go by, and Spotted Tongue thought it was. He could almost feel his own throat burn as he watched the teamster empty the cup in a few swallows. He had drunk the white man's firewater the last time he and his band had traded with the Comencheros, but Spotted Tongue didn't like the taste of it, didn't like losing his wits when drinking it, and certainly didn't like the sickness in his belly and head the next morning. He forbade the members of his war band from drinking the white man's firewater, and his band mostly obeyed.

He listened as William Fayel translated Carter's words and thought the young teamster had a good reason to kill Pap Dickerson. But he didn't think Carter did it. Maybe the young white man would kill someone in the heat of battle or to defend himself, but Spotted Tongue doubted George Carter had the cold spot in his belly needed to plan a killing and carry it out.

George Carter gave the tin cup back to the scrawny teamster and wiped his mouth on his shirt sleeve. *"Old Bill paid for saving me, though. Somebody fed his mule team locoweed, and two of his animals died. I reckon it was Dickerson getting his own back, and Old Bill thinks so, too. It didn't pay to be a good Samaritan, as far as Dickerson was concerned. He was a mean son of a bitch, and I reckon the Devil's got his biggest furnace saved for Pap."*

Spotted Tongue listened to McCusker's translation and wondered who these Samaritans were. Another kind of white man? He had heard Phillip McCusker refer to this devil many times, and he sounded worse than the Cannibal Owl.

Old Bill, a white-haired teamster whose bent shoulders still exhibited the strength of a life spent driving mule teams, spat out a stream of tobacco juice, leaving a streak down the middle of his long white beard, *"I was biding my time to get my own back from Dickerson with interest, but somebody beat me to it. Lizzy offered to give me two of Pap's mules, so I came out all right. It's just the principle of the thing. I wanted to put paid to Pap Dickerson's account, and somebody canceled it before I could… I figured if the law ever caught me for it, well, I've had a good long run of life, past my three scores and ten, so if they hanged me from a limb, I haven't got much time left this side of the grave anyway."*

"No jury would send you to the hangman, Old Bill, not if any of them knew Pap Dickerson," called a voice from the crowd of men. There was loud agreement from several different voices among the teamsters. *"And we'll all claim you were in the bawdy house with us,"* continued the first voice.

"Well, I didn't do it much as I planned on it, so I don't have to worry about no jury. And don't be talking about me being in a bawdy house. My daughter might hear it and disown me," said Old Bill.

He looked at Spotted Tongue but spoke to William Fayel. *"Tell this Injun that I didn't kill Pap Dickerson, and he's right about Evan Flynn. That youngster didn't kill him either. If I saw who did, I'd take it to my grave. Pap Dickerson deserved killin', and you ain't gonna find no one here who says different."*

Spotted Tongue studied the old man as Phillip McCusker translated. He believed this man didn't kill Pap Dickerson, but he had wanted to, and the old teamster had that cold spot in his belly needed to plan a killing. Anybody as old as this man had learned that some men needed killing, asked for it almost, and he was one to do it. But the old man knew something, but what, Spotted Tongue didn't know. Did he see who fired that second shot? And what else was the old man trying to tell him other than he knew who killed Pap Dickerson? But why didn't he tell the army man, Major Elliot, especially since he knew Evan Flynn was innocent, and he seemed to like the boy? Or was he like most white men: saying one thing but meaning another?

"Lots of us had a reason to kill Pap Dickerson. You can point your finger at about anybody and find a man with a grievance, maybe nobody as much as Maintain Mike Flynn, Evan's brother. He caught Dickerson abusin' his own daughter and laid the old bastard up for a month with ruptured privates. The first time Dickerson was up and around, we heard screaming from Mike's camp. It seems two rattlesnakes crawled into his bedroll and bit him all to hell. He swelled up like a toad and died the next morning. We all knew Dickerson had done it, including Evan, but he swore he was in camp with Lizzy. We couldn't prove no better, and she was too scared of him to say differently. We were all laying for him, but Pap finally picked on the wrong person, and he died of his bad judgment before the rest of us could do for him. Good thing we all saw the fight, though. We can tell the major when he asks if Dickerson started it. Evan Flynn was just defending himself. Good thing someone else stepped in to save Evan 'cause a bullet in the shoulder wouldn't stop a man as mean as Pap. He'd have gotten up and killed Evan." Old Bill nodded his head for emphasis, switched his wad of tobacco from one cheek to the other, and spat.

Phillip McCusker translated Old Bill's speech, and Spotted Tongue felt a chill run up his spine as he met the old teamster's eyes. The old man's eyes reflected curiosity as if he was wondering what kind of a man Spotted Tongue was, weighing him as one would weigh a lance for balance but withholding judgment. Age and hard life had formed the teamster into a man like few Spotted Tongue had met, and he realized with a shock that he hoped Old Bill saw the worth of a Comanche warrior. He was even more shocked to realize he wanted approval from this white man when he usually only wanted fear.

CHAPTER FOURTEEN

The harmonious business of examining witnesses was interrupted by a rush and hurry of Indians, who stated that a couple of white men had been having a fight down in the timber, and that one had shot the other. It was ascertained that a couple of these gentlemen of six-mule power had gotten into a scrimmage on some subject, and that one had shot the other through the arm, the ball lodging in his side, where it now remains.

Excerpt from the Dispatch of Correspondent S.F. Hall to the Chicago Tribune, Chicago, Illinois, Thursday, 24 October, 1867, Page 2.

"*I had a run-in with that SOB, too,*" said another teamster, a stocky man with massive, bull-like shoulders. "*The name's Pinkie Jones and I got Pap Dickerson to thank for this.*" He held up his left hand, which was notable for two missing fingers.

"*I'm left-handed, and Pap knew it, so it ain't no coincidence he left me half crippled. You drive mules, it's best that you have all your fingers on both hands, not just one. Pap was cheating at cards; he was really clever at it, but I caught him. I reached for the pot, thinking the two of us would have some fisticuffs, and I'd put him on the ground, missing a few teeth, but that ain't what happened. He pinned my fingers to the ground with his Bowie knife. They started turning black, and I had Old Bill cut them off. Like to have lost my whole hand from the poison.*"

Pinkie gestured at the audience of grizzled men and a few hard-used women, all with dirt and grease embedded in callused hands and under ragged fingernails. "*There ain't anybody here that wouldn't give a metal to the party that finally put an end to Dickerson. But it ain't Evan Flynn, and we shoulda said so to start with and not let that major haul him off.*"

McCusker translated Pinkie Jones and several other teamsters' accounts of Pap Dickerson's abuse but as witnesses rather than victims, which Spotted Tongue concluded meant they avoided Pap Dickerson like they would a rattlesnake. Only Evan Flynn, George Carter, Old Bill, Pinkie Jones, and Lizzy Dickerson had been injured enough to demand vengeance, and Evan Flynn only fired one shot.

Spotted Tongue wondered why someone hadn't killed the man before now. No Comanche would have let him live. The People knew many ways to kill a man slowly, so he had time to regret his evil acts. Lots of time, maybe two sleeps, maybe three.

Spotted Tongue studied the men and women in front of him. "Ask each man where he was standing when the bad man was shot," he told Phillip McCusker.

The men looked at one another, seeming puzzled at Spotted Tongue's question, but he didn't believe the teamsters were really surprised. Unless they thought he was just another dumb Indian, they should have expected the question, and unless they were all still missing their wits from drinking firewater the night before the fight, then they knew where they were standing. When you see a man die, you remember who stood next to you.

After many exchanges of looks, chin rubbing, and head scratching, Old Bill finally answered for the other teamsters. *"Best I remember, Lizzie was standing on the far end next to her tent, and George was next to her. Pinky was on my left, near the end of the line of us that stood closest. Evan was in front of Pap, of course, but none of us was directly behind Pap 'cause no one knew where the bullets might go. None of us figured Evan would shoot to kill, but you can't always tell where a man might aim when he's nervous, and Evan was really nervous. I could see his hands shaking some from where I stood. I was surprised he hit Pap at all, especially with that Smith and Wesson revolver of his. That gun ain't worth a cup of warm spit."*

Old Bill turned first one way, then another to look at the crowd. *"Ain't that right, boys? None of us seen a man shoot Pap?"*

A murmur of agreement came from the crowd, along with the sound of shuffling feet that raised small puffs of dust as the teamsters backed away before turning to find their way to bedrolls stashed under wagons.

Spotted Tongue listened to Phillip McCusker's translation but still found the teamsters' behavior strange. Fayel only spoke after McCusker interpreted the Comanche tongue, yet the white men acted as if he was not present. In his experience, no white man ignored a Comanche warrior, not if he wanted to keep his hair. The teamsters had to know that all the questions were coming from him, even if they never looked at him. And they answered so quickly as if they had already decided what they were going to say. For that matter, why did the teamsters answer at all? Why did they answer an Indian's questions while pretending he didn't ask them at all. Why did Old Bill say that Dickerson had picked on the wrong person when the teamsters knew that Evan would not kill Dickerson, or else he would have already avenged his Flynn brother's murder?

Phillip McCusker nudged Spotted Tongue. "I don't think you'll get any more out of them, and the Grand Council meets again tomorrow when the Peace Commissions will tell us what the government wants out of the Indians and what the government plans to give to them. I am not expecting much, but I need to be there anyway so I can tell the Comanche what's what. The government figures that it has the Indians between a rock and a hard place, and maybe that's true. Fayel has to be there to hear it all so he can write a dispatch to his newspaper. Right now, he wants to wander around the Indian camps to learn how the Indians live and what he thinks of all this."

"Indians all different," replied Spotted Tongue, a cold spot suddenly forming inside his chest. He didn't want the white man looking around the Comanche lodges. He might see Little Flower, or she might see him, he wasn't sure which would be worse, but either way, he was liable to find himself on the wrong end of a white soldier's gun. Or maybe several guns. If the white soldiers didn't kill him, Green Willow would for bringing trouble into their lodge.

"Indians all different," Spotted Tongue repeated. "Kiowa visit our lodges. They think they are wilder than us, but they are wrong. The Arapaho were different from the Cheyenne, and the Cheyenne were different from the Comanche. Why do white men think all Indians are alike when not even our skin is all the same color, close but not the same. White men are foolish."

He heard Phillip McCusker talking to Fayel in his own tongue but ignored them and turned toward the Comanche camp and his lodge. "I'll go to the Grand Council when Father Sun rises, see what this treaty will say," he said to the two white men as he walked away.

Spotted Tongue felt Fayel staring at him. He glanced over his shoulder at the white man in time to see a strange expression on the man's face or at least one he hadn't seen before. For a moment, Spotted Tongue thought Fayel was studying him like a Comanche would to decide if he was a danger or a man who saw visions of truth. If Fayel thought that, he was wrong. Spotted Tongue was a man without visions, a man who was never sure what was true and what was not. He could only see how one action could lead to another. What wisdom was there in that? Better to have your spirit animal guide you on the right trail to truth. To decide for yourself made a warrior's head hurt.

But he must decide for himself what was the truth about Pap Dickerson's murder.

He reached his lodge to find Green Willow leaning over the cooking pot, stirring a rich broth made of chunks of buffalo meat and wild onions she had picked and dried last summer. He heard his stomach rumble as he realized how long since he had eaten. Not since Father Sun had risen, and now he had long since sank and left the sky to a bright moon shedding pale light on the world of lodges and pony herds, and white men's tents and ambulances and bedraggled teamsters and mules, and soldiers restlessly walking about their camp, stopping to stare at the Indian camps. It was getting colder, and a light wind caught the smell of the broth, enticing Spotted Tongue to squat by the cooking pot and spear a large chunk of buffalo meat with his knife.

"It took you long enough to come back to the lodge. Where were you? The Council ended before Father Sun left the sky, and I had the food ready, but you had disappeared with Phillip McCusker and that other white man. Who is he, Spotted Tongue, and what were you doing with him?"

"He is called a correspondent," replied Spotted Tongue, stumbling over the unfamiliar word. "He makes marks on paper and sends it to a newspaper so other white men can read about what happens at Medicine Lodge."

"So why are you with him? You can't speak his tongue, so you can't tell him anything about the Council. Besides, he was there; I saw him sitting at one of those wooden things..."

"Folding tables, they are called folding tables," said Spotted Tongue, interrupting Green Willow.

"Whatever," said Green Willow, waving her hand like she was swatting a fly or something else that irritated her---like anything Spotted Tongue had to say. "But I'm not talking about those folding tables; I want to know what you were doing with a white man after the Council. You need to stay away from white men, Spotted Tongue, especially since you have a white captive in your lodge. That Cannibal Owl army man with the hair the color of a campfire will burn our village and kill us all if that white man makes any marks on paper about Little Flower."

Little Flower, the object of Green Willow's shrill rant, pushed aside the tipi's flap and crawled out. She seemed to know that Green Willow was talking about her, and Spotted Tongue thought that meant she recognized her name. Soon, she would be able to speak Comanche; he just knew it.

For now, she stared at Green Willow, then switched her attention to Spotted Tongue, studying them both as if they knew the answer to a question she was unable to ask.

"Be at peace, Little Flower. The white man who tried to force himself on you is dead. You don't have to be afraid anymore. I don't know who killed him, but I will find out and give him a fine pony to thank him."

"First, you won't random her, so we get no goods from the white man, then you want to give away a fine pony just because one white man shot another, and you think he did it because the dead man bothered Little Flower. Spotted Tongue, I think your wits are leaking out your nose. Listen to me! You must stay away from the white men and their troubles. We have troubles of our own, like these reservations and building medicine houses that the white men talked about in the council."

Sometimes, Green Willow surprised him. He didn't think his first wife would understand what reservations meant. She must have listened very closely to what the Peace Commissioners said. Spotted Tongue didn't see the reservations as trouble. He would not lead his band to a reservation to be penned up like the white man's hogs. It was not the Comanche way.

A sudden thought struck him like a lightning bolt. "Were you at the Council?"

"I said I was, didn't I. That's where I heard of these reservations and where I saw you walk off with Phillip McCusker and that white man following you. I worry about you, Spotted Tongue. You lose your way trying to follow what another person says." Green Willow shook her head as a mother might at a disobedient child.

"If you were at the Council, then where was Little Flower? You didn't leave her tied up in the lodge, did you?" demanded Spotted Tongue.

"Of course not! She might try to bite through the buffalo hide rope and run off again. She is very clever sometimes, and I don't trust her. I left her at Fat Belly's lodge with Slow Like a Turtle to watch her. Little Flower speaks some of Slow Like a Turtle's Mexican tongue, so she is different around her, quieter, and doesn't cause as much trouble as she does with us."

Green Willow stopped to take a breath. "And I wanted to hear what the Peace Commissioners said for myself. Sometimes, men hear the same words as women but don't understand them the same way. Then I see you walk off with that white man, and I know you are not thinking of what all this means to the Comanche but worrying over something that only matters to the white man. That's what you do now, Spotted Tongue, worry over what you see coming the next sun or even the next moon, something that no one else sees. Sometimes you scare me."

"Be quiet, woman! I have much to think about, and I can't listen to your complaints and think at the same time. I am a Comanche warrior and do as I believe best."

Spotted Tongue walked away and closed his ears to Green Willow's shrill voice. She saw too much, saw that he was different! She didn't understand, but she soon might. Between her observations and the sounds of dancing, a few drums, children's squeals, dogs barking, and drunken laughter coming from the lodges where Indians and white correspondences meet together in mutual misunderstanding, he couldn't hear himself think, His head pounded in time with the occasional drumbeats from the few who wanted to make noise to impress the white man.

Spotted Tongue walked down Medicine Lodge Creek toward the medicine lodge. There, he would find quiet to sort through his own actions. First, there was Pap Dickerson's murder; second, there was his obsession to find the killer. Dickerson is dead, Flynn will not be blamed for murder; Spotted Tongue will not accuse another teamster even if he knows who fired the shot. Why, then, does he have this unsettled feeling in his belly that it is important to know the truth? Did teamsters fear he would kill the man who stole his vengeance?

CHAPTER FIFTEEN

There was no lack of evidence that Comanches and Kiowas had been active south of Red River. It was a time of war parties west of the Brazos—stolen horses, shattered families, captured children, missing travelers, and deserted ranches. Yet, for some unexplained reason, the Peace Commission seemed unconcerned with what had happened in Texas. When Leavenworth and others spoke before the Commission, they made great to-do about the purity of the Comanche and Kiowa in Kansas while admitting that there were captive women, children, and grisly trophies—from Texas— in Comanche and Kiowa lodges.

Disregard of Comanche and Kiowa Depredations in the Commissioner's Report; The Reactions to Governor Crawford's Papers on Indian Depredations in Kansas by General Hancock and Agent Leavenworth as recorded in the Sherman Report, Short Summary by Douglas C. Jones in The Treaty of Medicine Lodge,: The Story of the Great Treaty Council as Told by Eyewitnesses, University of Oklahoma Press, 1966, page 58.

"Did you hear that Tall Bull and Gray Head of the Cheyenne rode in from their camp on the Cimarron?" asked Shaking Hand.

Spotted Tongue shook his head. "Then where are they? The only Cheyenne chief I know of being here is Black Kettle."

"Before we got here, they rode in late at night to talk to the tall army chief with the white hair."

"General Harney?" asked Spotted Tongue, proud of himself that he knew not only who Shaking Hand was talking about but how to speak his name.

Shaking Hand shrugged his shoulders. "If that is what he is called. They went into Harney's lodge and talked. They brought a war party with them that waited across Medicine Lodge Creek while they talked. They were all painted up, and the Arapaho, Kiowa, Kiowa-Apaches, and Black Kettle's band thought they were about to start a war. Every warrior was grabbing his lance, and the squaws were chasing children toward the timber to hide. That's why the camps and the soldiers were running around like they thought they were going to lose their hair when we rode over the ridge. Everyone thought we were the Cheyenne Dog Soldiers."

"And everybody knows the Cheyenne are close to going on the warpath after that white chief Hancock burned down a Cheyenne village," said Fat Belly.

Spotted Tongue wondered if his warriors ever did anything but collect gossip when they weren't busy raiding or hunting buffalo. Maybe he should order another raid when they got back to camp before the frost covered the ground and the creeks froze. Leave a warrior with nothing useful to do, and he would find something to do, and it often wasn't as harmless as listening to gossip.

"Tall Bull and Gray Head came to listen to what the white men say about Hancock and what he did, or so we heard, " said Wild Horse, not to be left out of the conversation. "Also, the Cheyenne will not come to the Grand Council for five days. They will stay in their camp on the Cimarron and make medicine. Some of the Commissioners are angry."

"More likely the Cheyenne are making trouble instead of medicine," said Spotted Tongue. He rubbed his belly, which had become sour from the conversation. The Cheyenne were always causing trouble, but on this occasion, maybe it was good. If the white man spent his time worrying about what the Cheyenne Dog Soldiers were going to do, then they wouldn't be worrying about what the Comanche and Kiowa were doing. Anything that would keep the white man out of Comanche's business.

"You missed a good fight with words between the white war chief, Harney, and that Peace Commissioner, Henderson. That was after Santana and Ten Bears had a word fight. Santana said the Comanche didn't think enough before they acted, and Ten Bears said the Kiowa talked too long before they acted," continued Wild Horse, snorting with laughter. "Santana stomped out of the Great Council, and the Peace Commissioners gathered together like a flock of prairie chickens with Peace Commissioner Henderson waving his arms. Phillip McCusker finally brought quiet to the Council. But before many heartbeats passed, Santana stomped back in and started a word attack on Indian Agent Leavenworth. Then Ten Bears jumped up and said the Comanche liked Leavenworth and wanted him left alone. You should have seen, Spotted Tongue! Santana's warriors and squaws were screaming for him, and Ten Bear's warriors and squaws were screaming for him, and Henderson was back to shouting for peace in the Great Council. It was a great commotion, but needed some drums."

"So what happened today," Spotted Tongue asked. His day of thinking at the medicine lodge had not shown him a straight path to follow to find Pap Dickerson's killer. But it had kept him away from the Grand Council.

"First, let me tell you about Little Raven, the Arapaho chief. He ran to the Commissioners, claiming the Pawnee ran off most of his pony herd, and he and his warriors were going to hunt them down. That happened before we got here, too, but the Arapahos came back yesterday with their horses and lots of fresh scalps taken from the Kaws," said Fat Belly, looking disappointed that the Arapahos didn't invite him on their hunt.

"I thought you said the Pawnees stole the ponies," said Spotted Tongue.

Fat Belly shrugged. "A white man said they were Kaws. All the same."

Spotted Tongue nodded. To most white men, all Indians were the same, but Fat Belly ought to know better. It wasn't worth fighting about, though.

"What else happened? "

"Little Raven told the Peace Commissioners that the Arapahos did not want to be with the Cheyenne but with the Apaches. He said the Cheyenne got them into trouble."

Spotted Tongue nodded. "He is right. The Cheyenne are trouble. What did the Peace Commissioners say?'

"That they had to stay with the Cheyenne. That answer got up Little Raven's nose. Then that white man, Henderson, said we had to come back tomorrow to sign the treaty, us, the Kiowa, and the Kiowa-Apache. That means today."

"Have we heard what the Peace Commissioners said with their marks on paper? Did they listen to Ten Bears, Silver Broach, and Santana? Has Phillip McCusker looked at the marks on the paper?"

Fat Belly, Shaking Hand, and Wild Horse shook their heads. They exchanged glances, looking suddenly worried. Wild Horse cleared his throat, glanced one more time at his friends, and spoke. "We do not know what the marks on the paper mean, Spotted Tongue, and Phillip McCusker does know what the marks mean either because no one has seen the treaty. The Peace Commissioner named Henderson said they had listened to our words and were certain we trusted the Commissioners, and the Commissioners trusted that we would follow the right path."

"The right path is their path," muttered Shaking Hand. "And do you know what else this Henderson said, Spotted Tongue? He said that we could still hunt the buffalo up to the Arkansas River like they promised us in the last treaty, but we needed to accept their medicine houses and learn to farm because the buffalo would soon be gone, and we must change our path, go to the reservation, or suffer and die. The buffalo would not be gone if the Peace Commissioners and the Great White Father would stop the other white men from killing the buffalo. And they don't even kill them to have food and hides to wear and to make lodges!"

"Is it true, Spotted Tongue? Are the buffalo going to be gone?" asked Fat Belly, looking hopefully at his war chief. "Can your medicine stop the white buffalo hunters?"

Spotted Tongue closed his eyes for a few heartbeats. When he opened them, he felt as if all the color had fled the earth, and nothing was left but grey and white. The sky was white, and his warriors, his friends, and his brothers were colorless shadows. Although it was the Moon when the Leaves Fall, there still should be color. The leaves themselves should still hold color as they made a blanket on the ground where the children would stomp upon them and laugh at the crackling sound they made. The pony herds, the women in their clothes made from the white man's cloth that was always included in the gifts given to the Indians, presents that stole a warrior's pride little by little, all should have color.

What could he tell Fat Belly, Shaking Hand, and Wild Horse, who looked to him for hope? He could not deny what Henderson said because he, too, had noticed the buffalo herds growing smaller season by season. When the buffalo were gone, the Comanche, Kiowa, and others who hunted the shaggy beasts to live would be forced onto the reservation. The Comanche would also be gone, reduced to shadows of who they once were. The Comanche and others would survive, but their spirits would be broken.

He also saw other signs of the coming end of the People: the iron horses that needed iron tracks that would run over Indian land; the flood of white settlers, more and more each season; the rise of the wooden building in groups the white man called towns. If the Comanche, the Kiowa, the Apache, and all the Indians in all the land came together to fight, they would lose the war. For every white man killed, many more would take his place. When a warrior died, the tribe must wait to replace him until a boy grew into a man.

Spotted Tongue's shoulders bowed with the weight of his thoughts. But he must tell his friends something without taking away their hope. He must tell them the truth, but not all the truth. "I think we live until we die. We hunt the buffalo and kill the buffalo hunter wherever we find them. We fight until we can fight no more because that is the Comanche way. I can say no more. Tomorrow, we go to the Great Council to see who touches the pen." And see who would bow to the white man, he thought to himself.

CHAPTER SIXTEEN

A treaty was signed to-day by the Indian Peace Commissioners on the part of the United States, and the Kiowa and Comanche tribes...The treaty is substantially the same as was made with the same tribes on the Little Arkansas river two years ago, and changes nothing but the establishment of an Agricultural Reservation...The policy is to give the Indians a permanent home, and induct them gradually into the pursuit of agriculture and the adoption of civilization.

Excerpt of Correspondence from William Fayel to The Missouri Republican---St. Louis, Published October 28, 1867.

Spotted Tongue watched and listened as Kiowa chief Santana walked up to the folding table where the treaty lay. His beloved bugle hung around his neck, and Spotted Tongue hoped he didn't blow it. The bugle made an awful noise and would change nothing, certainly not the minds of the Peace Commissioners.

"I do not want to settle down and live in houses. Silver Brooch's band tried to live like whites, and now nearly all his people are gone."

Santana's voice held much anger, and Spotted Tongue agreed with what the Kiowa said, but he should have argued more about the hunting ground instead. The Kiowa and Comanche lost much of their land, and what was left was too small to support the tribes. As Spotted Tongue understood it, all that was left was that part of the Comancheria in Texas. The treaty also said that the Comanche, Kiowa, and Kiowa-Apaches must not attack the iron horses, attack any white men traveling on roads, steal horses, capture any white women or children, scalp any white men, stay on the reservation unless hunting buffalo, not molest whites or their property, and stay on good terms with the GOVERNMENT. Nothing was said about the Government staying on good terms with the Comanche. And most of all, to take up the plow. In return, the Government will build houses the Comanche don't want, force Comanche and Kiowa children into schools, send a white Indian agent to watch the People, and once a year send presents, turning the People into beggars.

Spotted Tongue felt a sickness in his belly as he watched the chiefs step up to touch the pen to the treaty. First were the Kiowa: old Satank, Black Eagle, Kicking Eagle, Stinking Saddle, Woman's Heart, Stumbling Bear, One Bear, The Crow, and Bear Lying Down. Santana, the chief who argued the most, was the second to touch the pen to the treaty. Spotted Tongue felt both disappointment and doubt. Did Santana mean that he would follow the orders in the treaty? Or was he doing it to fool the white man?

For all that he watched the Kiowa chiefs, he did not care what they did. But he watched most closely the Comanche chiefs who stepped up to the table. These men were chiefs of Comanche bands; they were of the People, they were of his blood. He must remember them. Ten Bears was the first to touch the pen, but Spotted Tongue was not surprised. Ten Bears always pushed for peace with the white man.

Painted Lips was the next chief, followed by Silver Brooch, who threatened to join the wild Comanche on the plains if the Government did not keep its word to build on his reservation by next spring. Spotted Tongue wondered if the old chief would keep his word. Would he lead his young warriors to the Staked Plains to join Quanah Parker's band? Spotted Tongue did not know, but he would watch. Would the Comanche chiefs keep their word no matter whether the Government kept theirs or not?

Next to touch the pen were Standing Feather, Gap in the Woods, and Horse's Back. He already knew that Horse's Back would lead his band to the reservation; the chief had said as much when he met Spotted Tongue the day he rode in. Horse's Back saw as many white men as the blades of grass, and the only way the Comanche could survive was to take the reservation trail. Spotted Tongue knew the old chief was wise in his words, but Spotted Tongue could not follow Horse's Back. He could not.

Wolf's Name, Little Horn, Iron Mountain, and Dog Fat were the last Co-manche to touch the pen. Spotted Tongue did not know if those chiefs would ride the reservation trail or not. He had not spoken with them, and none of the chiefs spoke for their warriors. Every warrior spoke for himself; he could accept the treaty or not as he chose. It was the Comanche way.

After the chiefs touched the pen, Spotted Tongue watched as several white men made their marks on the treaty, but unlike the chiefs, they did not make the sign of the X. Phillip McCusker, and Fayel made their marks in what McCusker called a "signature." He offered to teach Spotted Tongue how to make the marks that would be his signature, but Spotted Tongue refused. There might be magic in his special marks, but it wouldn't be his magic, it would be the white man's. The marks that meant his name first came from the white man, so the marks would carry their magic,

Not that Spotted Tongue believed in magic anymore, but a warrior must be cautious of what power his enemy might have. Maybe they call their magic something else; maybe they call it "civilization."

Spotted Tongue pondered this as he turned to leave the Great Council. He was shoved aside as Comanche, Kiowa, and Kiowa-Apache warriors jostled one another in their hurry to reach the Peace Commissioners' Enclosure. Squaws and children followed the warriors, all leading ponies to be loaded with the white man's presents that, even now, the warriors were pushing and shoving to be the first to claim. Back at the band's lodges, each present would be examined to ensure that each warrior's present was equal to every other warrior's. To the tribes who fought to collect their presents, they feel no loss of pride. Food and clothes, not to mention treats like flour, coffee, and sugar, were hard to get and usually cost the Indians a lot in trade goods. If these presents were free, then why not take them?

Spotted Tongue felt sickened as he watched the Comanche warriors fight over the presents. Each warrior was less than he had been before.

"Hurry up, Spotted Tongue," said Fat Belly, trotting up to him in his usual clumsy manner. "We don't want to miss out on our presents that we don't even have to trade any ponies for. And I hear they are giving away pistols. Pistols, Spotted Tongue! We won't have to trade for them with the Comancheros. They demand too many ponies for pistols, then want more ponies for the bullets!"

"We know what the Comancheros want, Fat Belly. They want ponies. What does the white man want?" asked Spotted Tongue.

Fat Belly tripped on his moccasin's long fringe but caught himself before falling on his face in the dirt. He had a puzzled look on his face that had nothing to do with his near fall. That happened often enough that catching himself was something he did without thinking. It was thinking that put a puzzled look on his face. "But, Spotted Tongue, the presents cost nothing! They are free!"

"Nothing from the white man is free, Fat Belly. There is always something they want in exchange. We just don't know what it is this time," said Spotted Tongue.

Fat Belly still looked puzzled. "Until they ask me for something, I will take their presents. I think you worry too much, Spotted Tongue, and you had better get in line. If you miss getting your presents, Green Willow will scalp you in your sleep. Or burn the buffalo stew. She likes the white man's clothes; they have a lot of color in them. Slow Like a Turtle likes it, too. And she makes my blanket much warmer when she is happy."

Fat Belly is right, thought Spotted Tongue. Green Willow would scalp him or hit him over the head with her cook pot if he missed collecting the white man's presents. He would rather trade with the Comancheros, but Green Willow would see that as a waste of good ponies when you could get the same goods for free. She had a point, but not one he wanted to accept.

Spotted Tongue felt a cold spot on his back and looked around as he would at a war party. Standing near the wagon from which the Indian agent Leavenworth and another white man watched the presents being handed out was the tall figure of Old Bill. The old teamster was looking at him and didn't seem bothered that Spotted Tongue caught him at it.

Spotted Tongue started toward the old man when a loud noise rang out, followed by yips and shrieks and white man's curses. Putting his hand on his knife, he turned quickly, dropping into a crouch, ready to defend himself, only to see a young warrior, perhaps a Kiowa, with a bloody hand.

"The pistol blew up, everybody close got hit with pieces of metal, and that young warrior is liable to lose that hand. It's got a couple of fingers hanging loose," said Phillip McCusker, appearing at Spotted Tongue's side. "Better tell your warriors not to take one of those pistols until somebody checks the rest."

Before Spotted Tongue could yell out to Fat Belly, Shaking Hand, and Wild Horse, another pistol and then a third exploded as another warrior and a teamster were left with bloody hands and hot pieces of steel.

"Damn it to hell with the government for handing out defective pistols. Congress ought to investigate the company that made those—the Union Arms Company. They are either manufacturing shoddy guns, or they are as crooked as a dog's hind leg, or both. Somebody is making money out of this deal, and it's sure not the Indians," said Phillip McCusker. "We're going to have a bunch of Indians sharpening their knives to give these reporters a first-hand look at the proper way to scalp a man, or they will all get together and tell the Commissioners to stuff their treaty up their asses, that is if they can pull their heads out of the way first."

Phillip McCusker waved his hat and trotted toward the Indian Agent. *"Hey, Leavenworth, you better do something to straighten this mess out. Santana and the Kiowa already don't like you, and the other tribes will be lining up behind them if you don't make good on those pistols. My God, man, we already got three men with their hands all torn to hell from those guns exploding!"*

Leavenworth was the Indian Agent for the Comanche, not that Spotted Tongue ever talked to him or cared to, but he recognized him. Old Ten Bears could say what he wanted about Leavenworth, but Spotted Tongue didn't accept an Indian Agent, no matter who he was. The very idea of a white man watching the Comanche like they were a bunch of children and reporting to the Government on everything the People said, everywhere they went, and everything they did made rage burn like fire in his belly.

"What do the presents cost, Fat Belly?" asked Spotted Tongue. "So far, three wounded warriors. Who knows what more their presents will cost?"

Fat Belly looked indignant, or else his stomach was sour. Sometimes, it was hard to tell the difference by looking at his face. "What are we going to do for pistols, Spotted Tongue?"

Spotted Tongue felt his own stomach sour. Fat Belly sounded as if he was more unhappy at the loss of the pistols than the fact that three warriors might lose their hands. Sometimes he thought of refusing to accept being a war chief and hiding inside his lodge with Little Flower until it was all over—the war with the white man, the loss of Comanche land, the foolishness of his friends, and the Cannibal Owl damned reservation.

Spotted Tongue only saw one problem with hiding in his lodge. Green Willow would never give him any peace. She would be after him to bring home the buffalo; to help her put up and take down the lodge, even though that was a squaw's job; to do anything except lie around like a fat dog too old to chase rabbits.

Sometimes, there was no peace for a warrior.

"Mr. McCusker, it is not the government's fault that some of the pistols are defective. We generally have found the Union Arms Company to be trustworthy and always give the taxpayers value for their money," said Leavenworth, wiping his forehead with a handkerchief even though the weather was turning cold and dark clouds covered the setting sun.

Spotted Tongue didn't need McCusker to repeat Leavenworth's words in Comanche. He recognized a man trying to talk his way out of a mess of his own making. The sweat on the Indian agent's face when the air was cold, and a storm was coming is never a sign of a man comfortable with what he has done.

"What are you going to do about it?" demanded McCusker.

Leavenworth turned to the soldiers and teamsters handing out presents from a wagon. The men lifted out several different guns—Colt revolvers, the best and most dependable firearm on the market. The muttering of the Kiowa and Comanche ceased as members of each tribe jostled and shoved to be first to get one of the sought-after revolvers.

"That ought to calm things down, Leavenworth. You should have done that to start with," said McCusker, putting his hat back on. *"Damn government is always trying to cheat the Indian."*

"That's not a fair statement, McCusker. There are some bad apples among the Indian agents, but most of us try our best to care for our charges," said Leavenworth.

"Your best isn't good enough, Leavenworth," said Phillip McCusker. *"And your thinking is a big part of the problem. These Indians don't see themselves as your charges. They don't want you to care for them the way you're talking about doing. These are proud people, Leavenworth. All they ask is that you don't steal their land*

and keep the buffalo hunters out, and I reckon they will leave off scalping and stealing horses."

Leavenworth took a deep breath and let it out in a loud sigh. Spotted Tongue wished Phillip McCusker would stop talking in his own tongue and interpret what he was saying. It would tell him why Leavenworth looked so sad.

"You know that's not possible, McCusker. The settlers are coming, thousands of them, and they can't be stopped. And the government won't let the railroads be stopped either. We need the railroads to connect one coast with the other. I can't fight the inevitable; you can't fight the inevitable, and for damn sure, the Indians can't. It's progress; it's civilization."

"What's going to happen to my wife's people, the Comanche, to the other Plains Indians, Leavenworth?" asked McCusker.

"I don't know, McCusker. Would that I did," replied Leavenworth. He looked back to the wagon, then turned back to face the tribes. The wind was stronger, the air colder, but the tribes ignored the increasing rain as they loaded their presents on their ponies to make the trek back to their lodges along the banks of Medicine Lodge Creek.

"That's all for tonight. We will hand out the last of the annuities tomorrow. The weather is turning bad, and people need to seek shelter," said Leavenworth.

"What did he say, and what did you tell him, Phillip McCusker? There was much talk, and I would know your words and his words."

Phillip McCusker looked over Spotted Tongue's shoulder, always a sign that a man did not want to talk with a straight tongue. "That it wasn't the government's fault that the pistols exploded, that the government had been cheated. And that the weather was getting worse, and he would hand out the rest of the presents tomorrow."

"And what else, Phillip McCusker? What did you talk about that made Leavenworth look so sad?'

Phillip McCusker rubbed his chin again, looking toward the black clouds filled with forked lightning. The wind blew his hair back from his face, and he held his hat on with one hand. Finally, he looked at the war chief. "Spotted Tongue, that treaty the chiefs signed, I don't think you really understand some of it. When the buffalo are gone, and you know they are being killed off faster than they can breed, then your reservation will be like the white man's prison. You can't ever leave it without the agents or the government saying you can. You can't ride off across the Staked Plains just for the hell of it. You can't put up your lodge under the stars just anywhere you want. And your land? Once the buffalo are gone, and that won't be long, you can't leave the reservation, and your hunting rights won't mean anything. That land will be open for white settlement, and there's nothing you can do about it. I don't like to be telling you this, but you asked, and I think you are different enough to understand it. I don't know exactly when you became different, but you did, and I don't think you like it much."

"I understand what the treaty says, Phillip McCusker, and I don't know if I can save the People, but I will try," replied Spotted Tongue. Never would he have thought that of all who he knew, it would be a white man who recognized his change. Phillip McCusker might not understand how he changed, but he didn't fear it or was confused by it, as were Fat Belly, Wild Horse, Shaking Hand--and Green Willow.

"What will you do, Spotted Tongue, war chief of the Comanche?" asked Phillip McCusker.

"I will not ride the reservation trail with my band," said Spotted Tongue. "Now come with me, Phillip McCusker. I see Old Bill just across the Enclosure. He has been watching me, and I would know why."

CHAPTER SEVENTEEN

The first principal installed into the breast of an Indian is revenge. Time cannot efface the remembrance of an injury. It is kept alive like the hereditary feuds of the Scottish clans, and it goes down from one generation to another with the ardor of a burning coal. The blood of the offender can alone expiate the transgression....Even the women seem imbued with the restless spirit of revenge for injuries done them or their relatives, and nothing can satisfy them until the destructive passions glutted with blood of the offender.

William Fayel, Medicine Lodge Creek, October 16, 1867, Excerpt from the Dispatch to The Missouri Republican of St. Louis, Published October 24,1867

"Ifeel a great load will be removed from my heart if the Commissioners will wait and make a strong peace. I want to show my nation that I acted in good faith and that the Commissioners will be for our good, as I have told my people all along," said Black Kettle, Cheyenne chief, his voice hopeful.

Spotted Tongue pushed through the chiefs, warriors, and a few squaws still gathered around the folding table where the newly signed treaty with the Kiowa and Comanche lay. So Black Kettle was happy about the treaty because he believed it proved him right before his warriors. Spotted Tongue thought the old Cheyenne chief should not trust the white government so much. If the government did not keep its word, then Black Kettle would look like a fool in front of his people. But that was Black Kettle's gamble. Spotted Tongue would gamble on when the first snow would fall and believed he had a better chance of winning. The weather was more dependable than the government's word.

Spotted Tongue overheard many other voices, most of them about the hunting ground described in the treaty, as if that was the most important article and the others didn't matter. There were many fools at the Peace Council...

"I must stay to listen to the discussion about the Cheyenne Dog Soldiers," said William Fayel. *"There seems to be some disagreement about how long Senator Henderson and some of the Commissioners are willing to wait. Supposedly, the Cheyenne cannot interrupt their medicine rituals once they start. Senator Henderson*

doesn't understand why, and no one seems able to explain it to him. In fact, he and General Harney had a spirited discussion about it. If the Cheyenne interrupt their ritual, they have to start all over, and that would take longer than if the Commissioners just wait."

"Making medicine, especially renewing medicine arrows, is serious business to the Cheyenne or any other Indian tribe, Fayel, but the Cheyenne can deliberately be more irritating about it than stepping in a bed of red ants," said Phillip McCusker.

He touched Spotted Tongue's arm. "William Fayel and I have to stay a little longer. Black Kettle and some of the other chiefs want all the tribes to stay until after the Cheyenne and Arapaho sign the treaty. Black Kettle is strongly in favor of all the tribes supporting the treaty. He doesn't want any more massacres like what happened to his village on Sand Creek or that Cheyenne village in the Smoky Hills. Then, of course, there will be more presents."

Impatient with Phillip McCusker's delaying him, Spotted Tongue looked through the crowd of teamsters and Indians for Old Bill but could not see him. "Why should the Comanche and Kiowa stay? We need to prepare for the winter, and our winter camps are many sleeps away. I see no reason to stay because the Cheyenne want it, except it will give me more time to find Pap Dickerson's killer, so my band will stay until the Cheyenne and Arapaho touch the pen to their treaty and receive their presents." Spotted Tongue knew he sounded harsh, but he needed to get away.

"Fayel and I will catch up with you, although how you are going to talk to Old Bill without me, I don't know. Can't you cool your heels and wait for us?" asked Phillip McCusker. "It shouldn't take long."

"If Black Kettle and the other Cheyenne chiefs talk, it will take a long time. They take many words to say very little. I must find Old Bill. He knows more about Pap Dickerson's death than he has told us."

"You are one stubborn Comanche, Spotted Tongue, chasing after answers when nobody but you cares about the question," said Phillip McCusker. "We'll find you in the crowd. You will be the Indian surrounded by the teamsters wondering what you are doing chasing one of theirs. That is if they don't use you for target practice with their Big 50s. Those guns will blow a hole through you the size of my fist."

More impatient than ever, Spotted Tongue waved away Phillip McCusker's words. He knew about the big guns the white hunters used to kill his buffalo; no need to warn him. He began weaving his way through the crowds of Indians, soldiers, miscellaneous white men, and teamsters. Everyone was tall, taller than he was. No one was stronger, though, with his massive arms and thick chest. He needed both to hold his lance that was nearly three times his height, and no one was more fierce than a Comanche warrior on horseback.

Unfortunately, he was not on horseback; he was on foot, and the Commissioners, most of the soldiers and teamsters, the Cheyenne and Arapaho, and certainly the few Sioux who came to the Council for no reason known to Spotted Tongue, were taller. The Sioux certainly were. It didn't matter; the Comanche didn't fight standing on the ground. On horseback, they were invincible. Spotted Tongue didn't need his medicine to know that. He just wished he had his pony.

He ducked around a group of white men busy making marks on paper, correspondents, he supposed, rolling the strange word around on his tongue. He had learned many words in the white man's tongue at Medicine Lodge Creek, but none of them would help him talk to Old Bill.

Spotted Tongue finally saw the teamster on the edge of the crowd. He didn't seem to be trying to escape as much as leading Spotted Tongue away. If it was a trap, it wasn't a very good one. Father Sun still sent enough of his light that no one could hide in the dark waiting to attack him. And Old Bill was alone. The old man was losing his wits and would soon lose his hair if he thought to fight a Comanche warrior by himself.

Old Bill gestured toward Spotted Tongue to follow him as the teamster walked further away from the crowd. When he was several paces away, under a grove of trees close to the banks of Medicine Lodge Creek, he stopped to wait for Spotted Tongue.

Now more puzzled than suspicious, Spotted Tongue followed Old Bill while glancing around for signs of other men close by. No one seemed interested in one Comanche warrior and an old teamster. But whatever the old man wanted to say was a waste of breath as Spotted Tongue did not speak the white man's tongue, and Old Bill would not understand Comanche. Few white men did. Only the Comancheros who traded with his band and with the Kiowa and a few random white men like Phillip McCusker spoke enough of his tongue to talk together. Certainly, no one spoke Kiowa. Hardly anyone spoke Kiowa except the Kiowa. It was a tongue that was hard to speak and was unlike any other tongue spoken on the plains. Most other tribes who wanted to trade with the Comanche spoke the Comanche tongue at least enough to get by. It saved the Comanche from having to use the awkward sign language.

Spotted Tongue stopped ten paces from Old Bill to study the teamster. Old Bill held his hands out to show that he was not holding any weapons. He pulled up his shirt, exposing his loose, aged skin and turned all the way around until he faced Spotted Tongue again to prove he had no gun or knife hanging from his belt.

"Your name Spotted Tongue?" asked the old teamster.

Spotted Tongue lost his speech for a few heartbeats as he realized the old teamster had called him by name. "You speak Comanche?"

Old Bill held his forefinger and thumb a few inches apart. "Little bit. I rode with the Comancheros when I was young until I got sick of their ways. Picked up some of your tongue."

"Why did you not tell Phillip McCusker and Fayel? Why did you not tell me? Did you want to know about us without our knowing?"

Old Bill held out his hands. "You might say so, but don't you be getting after me with your knife. I wanted to know what kind of a man you were, and the best way to do it was to listen to you without your knowing I could understand what you were saying."

"I am a Comanche warrior. That's all you need to know."

"There are warriors and warriors. Some will lie to your face, then stab you in the back when you're not looking. Some white men would do the same. I just want to know what kind you are."

"Why do you need to know, Old Bill?"

"Oh, you know my name. I reckon there's a lot you know that you won't tell. I want to know if that squaw that Pap Dickerson bothered really is your wife and if she's all right. Pap didn't have no right to treat her the way he did and the way he was planning to."

Old Bill mangled the Comanche tongue, but Spotted Tongue could understand well enough. He couldn't be sure if Old Bill realized Little Flower was white, but he didn't act as if he did. It was dark that night, and Little Flower was painted like a real Comanche squaw. So maybe he really cared whether Little Flower was all right. All the teamsters he had seen seemed to care about Little Flower even though they thought she was Comanche. Or did they all know she was white, and they were trying to fool him. But why? If they knew she was white, wouldn't they take her to the Peace Commissioners, who would send the soldiers and their guns with many barrels to catch Spotted Tongue and his band? Green Willow would have much to say about his bringing such trouble into their lodge. Of course, Green Willow had much to say about everything.

"You have told me this already. Why do you tell me again?"

"I want to be sure you know the rest of us teamsters ain't gonna harm some young woman even if she was an Injun. We ain't all like Pap Dickerson. I wanted you to know that because we know you, Comanche, are big on revenge. We don't want you taking out your revenge on the rest of the men. And we do want to know how your wife is doing, if she really is your wife," old Bill added.

Spotted Tongue studied Old Bill's face, looking for signs of falsehood, but found none. The old man meant what he said, but what else could he say? Everyone who knew the Comanche, or thought they did, knew the warrior seeking revenge did not always stop at killing the one who wronged him, but all those around him as a warning.

A few seasons ago, before he lost his medicine, Spotted Tongue would have done the same. "Little Flower is my wife, and she is as well as she can be after Pap Dickerson mistreated her. She is safe in my lodge where I can protect her."

"Old Pap is dead. Why are you still sniffing around our camp? There is no one to take revenge on," said Old Bill.

Spotted Tongue wished everyone would quit asking him that. He wasn't after revenge now; he was paying a debt he owed Evan Flynn. And he wanted to know. Who killed Pap Dickerson was an itch as bad as the bite of a mosquito, and Spotted Tongue had to scratch it. He tried to explain his itch to Old Bill but doubted the old man understood. He didn't understand himself; he just knew it was something he had to do.

Old Bill rubbed his chin, a gesture Spotted Tongue had decided meant that a man was trying to make up his mind as to what to believe or which trail he should take. "You're not a common Injun, Spotted Tongue. What will you do when you find whoever killed Pap Dickerson? Will you kill them to take away your revenge? I know you, Comanche hug your revenge closer than you hug a squaw."

"I will do nothing. It was a revenge killing by someone whom Pap injured, maybe more than he injured me. Phillip McCusker tells me that nothing bad will happen to Evan Flynn, so I will not tell Lesser Chief Elliot who killed Pap Dickerson because he might tie that person to a wagon wheel in place of Evan Flynn. I believe revenge has been taken, and Pap Dickerson escaped being killed for too long. But his killer should not have let Evan Flynn be blamed; that is cowardly."

"If the killer had confessed, then the Army would be obligated to turn that person over to be punished, probably hanged, because that was deliberate murder. Pap Dickerson wasn't worth getting another man killed. Like you said, it was probably a revenge killing."

Spotted Tongue knew of white men hanging other men from a tree, and he felt a chill run up his back. There was honor in dying from another warrior's lance or arrow or a white soldier's bullet during a fight but hanging made a warrior less than an empty husk.

"Was it one of the teamsters that he had wronged?"

Old Bill hesitated a minute, then rubbed his chin again. Spotted Tongue knew whatever the teamster said would be only part of the truth.

"What if the killer didn't have a choice, Spotted Tongue? It was a revenge killing, but it also saved someone else from being killed. Likely, the killer didn't think about it being murder and didn't think about Evan Flynn being arrested. But you put paid to Evan's trouble, so the killer ain't going to confess. And I ain't telling nothing more. Just be happy with your wife. She seems like a fine woman; she sure didn't go down easy when Pap got hold of her. Just leave it alone, Chief. Everything has worked out for the best. Don't go stirring up the hornet's nest."

"I am not a council chief, I am a war chief," said Spotted Tongue.

"I ain't surprised," said Old Bill, raising his hand in farewell. "Have yourself a good evening and a good life as long as you can. I don't imagine I'll be around to see the plains change. I have been running from civilization all my life, and I reckon I'll be in my grave before it can catch up to me. I doubt you'll be so lucky." He walked away, his shoulders slumped as an old man's would.

"I don't think I will either," said Spotted Tongue to the wind that came with the setting sun as he turned to walk along the banks of Medicine Lodge Creek toward his lodge.

CHAPTER EIGHTEEN

Let, then, the Indian Peace Commission come to a fair understanding with tribes of Indians, who are in fact mere wards of the government, and let them at the same time devise and recommend a system of dealing with them by which past wrongs shall be avoided and the pledges of the government be faithfully kept.

Excerpt from correspondent Milton H. Reynolds of Lawrence, Kansas, State Journal, October 25, 1867, published by the Missouri Republican of St. Louis, October 27, 1867

Spotted Tongue shivered as he walked back toward his lodge. The air was damp and the wind sharp, heralding the coming of winter. He wished he had his blanket to wrap around his shoulders. Leggings and a breechclout were not enough to keep a warrior warm when not on a hunt or a raid. Then, the blood ran hot with excitement and kept a warrior warm. Otherwise, a Comanche was like any other man; he felt the cold.

"Where have you been?" demanded Green Willow, putting down her needle threaded with sinew. The other women seated in a circle around her looked up from their sewing with bright, curious eyes. Little Flower sat with the other women and was the first to put down her needle and the buffalo skin she was working on to watch him with more than curiosity. She watched him as if she were prepared to flee into the prairie. He sensed both defiance and fear but didn't know why; she had no reason to fear him, but she was always defying him. Why she was defying him now, he didn't know. He hadn't done anything he could think of that would ruffle her fur like an angry cougar's.

His own fur ruffled, Spotted Tongue frowned at his first wife. She shouldn't question him in front of her sewing circle. It was disrespectful. The women should go back to their work of sewing buffalo hides together to make the coverings for lodges. Or maybe they were sewing clothes. At any rate, they had their own tasks to do, even Little Flower, who was still watching him more closely than the other women. He wanted to believe it was because he was a fine-looking warrior, but he doubted it.

"I was about men's business," said Spotted Tongue, snapping off his words as he glared at Green Willow, then at her circle of squaws. The other women immediately looked back at their sewing. They had more respect for a war chief than his own wife did. Little Flower did not look down but continued to watch him as if he was Cannibal Owl preparing to eat her..

Green Willow swallowed and folded up the buffalo skin she was working on. "It is cold, and it looks like rain is coming. Let's put these skins away. We can work on them when we reach our winter camp. We will need to take down the lodges and pack our goods when Father Sun rises again."

"No, you will not need to take down the lodges. The Cheyenne asked that we stay until they come to the council so we might all talk about the treaty."

Green Willow looked at Spotted Tongue as though he had lost what few wits he had left. "Since when do we do what the Cheyenne tell us to do? We have our presents already, and we need to be back in the Comancheria before the Moon When the Frost Covers the Ground. You warriors must have a last buffalo hunt before the snows come, and we squaws need to dry the meat and prepare the buffalo skins for blankets. There is much to be done. We need to be back in the Palo Duro. The ponies have eaten all the grass on the hills above Medicine Lodge Creek. We need to leave here so our ponies can graze on the prairie above the canyon."

The women in the sewing circle looked up at him again, their sewing forgotten. Spotted Tongue felt like a rabbit being stared at by a coyote. "Your husbands left the Council when I did, and I heard Fat Belly say he was hungry," he said, staring at Slow Like a Turtle, the fat warrior's wife. The woman was captured in Mexico by Fat Belly, who made her his first wife. She rolled up her buffalo skin, pushed herself up from the ground, and with a hesitant smile, fled the circle in the direction of her own lodge. She was a smart woman. Spotted Tongue often wondered if she wasn't smarter than Fat Belly.

Spotted Tongue frowned at the other women who hurriedly bundled up their buffalo skins and trotted toward their own lodges, glancing over their shoulders at their husbands' war chief. At least he was obeyed by the other women—until they could tell their husbands that Green Willow dared to argue with Spotted Tongue.

Sometimes squaws were more trouble than the pleasure they provided, thought Spotted Tongue until he felt Little Flower's fingers wrapping around his legs. Her blue eyes held a worried expression along with a little fear, but the defiance was gone..

"Spotted Tongue, we worry when you are gone," said Little Flower in a barely understood Comanche. "Don't be mad."

Spotted Tongue felt as if Father Sun was shining, and his chest was filled with the first real happiness he had felt since he lost his medicine. "Little Flower, you know my tongue!"

Her eyes now held a wary expression along with fear. "Please, go home, Spotted Tongue. I am afraid."

"Don't be afraid of me, Little Flower. I will never hurt you." He pulled her up into his arms and stroked her back. "But we can't go home. I have given my word that we will stay until the Cheyenne come to the Council and touch the feather to the treaty. And I will have time to find Pap Dickerson's killer."

Both women erupted in loud objections, one in mangled Comanche and the other in shrill words that made his ears hurt.

"No!"

"Always in the white man's business! Why do you risk trouble to find this man?"

"Go home, Spotted Tongue! Go home!"

Little Flower's words were more garbled than before, and Spotted Tongue could hear the desperation in her voice.

He stroked her back as he would his favorite pony. "Shush, Little Flower. It is all right; we will go home soon, perhaps in four more sleeps. Go to the lodge and rest. You have lived through a bad day and need to settle your wits." He released her and pushed her toward the lodge. She looked back at him, the fear in her eyes turning to hopelessness.

"She is afraid and desperate about something, Green Willow. Have you punished her for something today?"

Green Willow raised her arms in the air and brought them down to slap her hips in the sign of a woman near the end of patience. "Make it my fault! It always is if your second wife fears something."

"What does she fear? Has someone hurt her besides you?"

"I have not hurt her! She is always sad and refuses everything Comanche."

"But she is afraid of something, too. I see the fear in her eyes," retorted Spotted Tongue.

"I have done nothing and don't plan to. Why don't you ask her now that she speaks our tongue—not very well, but it is better than the nonsense of her own tongue."

Spotted Tongue wondered why he had not thought of that. It must be the shock of learning she could speak his tongue. He had treated her as a slow-witted child, but she wasn't, and now they could talk to each other. There would be no more secrets between them. There would be happiness in his lodge forever.

"I will ask her," he said, stalking toward his lodge and the delicate white woman with eyes the same color as the sky and an attitude as prickly as a cactus. But all would be better now that they could talk.

In what seemed like an endless number of heartbeats, Spotted Tongue crawled out of his lodge, his belly feeling so low he might as well be a worm dragging himself along through the dirt. He pushed himself to his feet, surprised that he could. As a war chief, he had never been defeated; as Little Flower's husband, he was defeated with no idea how it happened.

"Did she tell you?" asked Green Willow, her arms folded across her chest.

"No," he said, sitting down and slumping over like a dead man. "She kept saying she wanted to go home, that the band needed to go home."

"Maybe she is right, Spotted Tongue. Why do the Cheyenne want everyone to stay? What good will talking together by all the tribes do for us? Why do the white men give in to the Cheyenne? The white men will keep their word, or they will not. Talking will not change anything." Green Willow pulled at her hair in frustration. "Unless the Cheyenne want everyone together to plan to go on the warpath."

"No! We will not go on the warpath with the Cheyenne. We will fight if we must, but we will fight beside the Kiowa and the Kiowa-Apache. Too many tribes together will mean we will argue against each other. And who would lead such a fighting band? The Cheyenne Dog Soldiers? The Comanche will not follow the Dog Soldiers. We fight our own way. I don't know what the Cheyenne are planning, but our band will stay to see. I am finished talking."

"You want to stay to put your nose into the white man's business, Spotted Tongue. I don't know you anymore. You never used to care what the white man did as long as he stayed out of the Comancheria. Now, it seems all you care about is the white man's business. The man who bothered Little Flower is dead! It is all over! Someone took his revenge against a white man not worth a handful of buffalo shit, and you want to know who! Why do you want to know?"

"I don't know!" shouted Spotted Tongue. He felt he was being beaten about the head by that question by everyone he saw. He was so, so tired of it.

He wiped his face and felt moisture. He didn't realize that cold dampness, neither mist nor rain, but something in between, had begun to fall over the Comanche camp. The campfires in front of the other lodges appeared to be surrounded by a circle of cold mist, and the sounds of howling dogs and the loud voices of men seemed quieter and further away than they really were. The night that began with such a happy feeling in his belly when he first heard Little Flower speaking his tongue had turned wet, cold, and miserable.

Why did he want to know the answer to the question Phillip McCusker said no one cared about? He only knew he had to, that the earth was uneven, and he must make it level again. He wished he could make medicine again, that his spirit wolf would bring him peace. And an answer to the mystery no one cared about except a Comanche warrior, who no one cared about either, as long as he rode the trail to the reservation to shrivel and die like leaves when the cold kills most things green.

Green Willow shook her head, and Spotted Tongue didn't know if she meant he was wrong or that she had given up trying to understand him.

"Spotted Tongue, I don't know what to say to you. I used to know what thoughts were in your head and what you might decide to do. I don't anymore."

"It is well you do not. My thoughts are not happy ones. Go sleep, Green Willow, you and Little Flower. I will sit by the fire for a while."

He watched his first wife flounce into his lodge like a woman who obeyed while making sure her husband knew how displeased she was. No one did it better than Green Willow.

Spotted Tongue sighed, sank down by the campfire, and picked up a small round stone laying on the ground. The stone was smooth as if it had been tumbled about by Medicine Lodge Creek until the waters rose during the spring rains and left the stone and others like it on the creek banks when the waters quieted after the floods.

He rubbed his thumb over the stone, then placed it on the ground in front of him. "This is Evan Flynn, who shot Pap Dickerson but didn't kill him," he murmured to himself as he picked up another stone and placed it beside the first. "And this is Pap Dickerson who faced him."

"Spotted Tongue! What are you whispering about?" demanded Green Willow, pushing aside the hide flap and poking her head out of the lodge.

Spotted Tongue grimaced. Green Willow had ears like a cougar. Nothing got past her. He got up, leaving his stones by the campfire. "Don't wake up the whole camp with your yelling. I'm coming." He might as well, he thought. There was no thinking with Green Willow's voice in his ears.

CHAPTER NINETEEN

"We are now ready to hear your complaints and take them to Washington that the President and the Council may address them. We do not want war, but we must accept it sometimes, when we cannot get an honorable peace. Some of our bad people mock and scoff at us because we want peace with the red man....Such men on both sides must be cast away because their counsels are black with death."

Remarks by Senator Henderson to the Cheyenne and Arapaho Grand Council at Medicine Lodge Creek, October 28, 1867, as reported by William Fayel to the Missouri Republican of Saint Louis, published November 2, 1867.

The days before the Cheyenne Dog Soldiers rode to Medicine Lodge Creek from their camp on the Cimarron were long with nothing to do but race their ponies, play the games the Comanchero had taught them, and explore the tents of the correspondents and Peace Commissioners. Green Willow had hands full of papers that Phillip McCusker called "used envelopes." Spotted Tongue didn't know what his first wife planned to do with them, but he didn't care. The used envelopes kept her busy and allowed him to wander around the teamsters' camp without her knowing and yelling at him about getting into the white man's business.

Spotted Tongue had watched the children pick up everything in each tent, including knives, clothes, pieces of wood the correspondents used to make marks on paper, tin cups, boots, and the small bottles filled with black water that they often spilled on the dirt floors of the white men's tents, as well as on themselves. The white men often yelled at the children and took away whatever they were playing with but never hit the little ones. The next day, the children would be back, looking and touching everything all over again.

Comanche children, well, any children, were curious, a good trait for a future warrior, and they were as tough as their fathers and older brothers, although Spotted Tongue wondered how they could stand to go about with little or no clothes on. He found the days cold and damp even if it wasn't raining and was glad for his blanket. Little Flower made it, and he was surprised when she gave it to him. Rather, she dropped it on his lap without smiling at him. It was a little stiff and crackled when he wrapped it around his shoulders because she had little skill at working the buffalo hide to soften it. Still, she gave him a gift and learned his tongue, not well, but at least she tried. Gift blankets and learning the Comanche tongue must mean something. But he wasn't sure what. Was Little Flower happy with him now, or was she fooling him for some reason? Thinking about it made his head hurt.

"Little Flower made this blanket for me, Wild Horse. Do you think her heart is softer toward me?"

Fat Belly hooted with laughter like a sick owl before Wild Horse could answer. "More likely, Green Willow tried to teach her how to work the hides into leather, and that was one she gave to you so Green Willow wouldn't find out she hadn't scraped it clean before she tried to make something out of it. I can hear your blanket creaking like limbs of the cottonwood in the wind. Little Flower should stick to what she is good at."

"And what would that be?" asked Spotted Tongue through teeth clenched together so hard, his jaws hurt.

Fat Belly fell onto his back, trying to scoot backward from the campfire while Shaking Hand hastily interrupted. "Fat Belly was just talking about Little Flower's stew. It was very good last time she made a pot."

Spotted Tongue recognized that Shaking Hand was trying to make peace between his war chief and Fat Belly. He wasn't very good at his attempt because everybody knew that Little Flower's last attempt at making stew was fed to the dogs, but Spotted Tongue pretended to accept Shaking Hand's peace-making efforts. He would teach Fat Belly to respect Little Flower when they arrived back at the Palo Duro. It was not good to have fights among The People while at the Peace talks.

But Spotted Tongue wouldn't forget Fat Belly's talk.

"Didn't I hear Slow Like a Turtle calling you, Fat Belly? She must have a pot of stew ready," said Spotted Tongue. Food was always one way to get Fat Belly to leave.

"No, I don't hear her," said Fat Belly, "but here comes that old white teamster. I wonder what he wants tonight."

Spotted Tongue wondered if he would survive the peace talks without grinding his teeth into dust. "Leave!" he shouted. "I would talk to the teamster alone. He has much to tell me about the Peace Commissioners and the Cheyenne."

Shaking Hand and Wild Horse grasped Fat Belly under the arms and hauled him off into the dark. The two warriors knew when Spotted Tongue had reached the end of his patience and was liable to demonstrate his skills at lifting scalps. He had never lifted the hair of one of his own warriors, but there was always a first time.

Spotted Tongue smiled at how fast his three warriors fled for their own lodges. He sat cross-legged close to his own cooking fire, wrapped in Little Flower's gift blanket. It was cold in the Comancheria in the winter, but the air was not damp. Damp was good when Father Sun was hot during the moons of the raids, but this wasn't that time.

"Them Injuns run off like a hungry wolf was chasing them," remarked Old Bill as he sat down across from Spotted Tongue. "They ain't scared of me, are they?"

Spotted Tongue nearly laughed at the idea that Comanche warriors would be afraid of a man near crippled with age. "No, their wives called them. There are cooking pots full of buffalo stew ready for them."

Old Bill looked as if he doubted Spotted Tongue's words but didn't call him out on it. The aged teamster had started dropping by the Comanche war chief's lodge while the whole camp waited for the Cheyenne to show up at the Council. They would talk of this or that: hunts they had been on, trapping beaver along the Arkansas as the teamster had done when he was young, horse trading with Comanchero.

Spotted Tongue envied Old Bill's coat made from buffalo skin with fur on the inside and long sleeves that covered the old man's arms. He said an Arapaho squaw made it for him to replace a cloth coat. He said he wished he had taken that squaw with him when he left her village because she was a fine woman and a good cook.

"When a man gets a little older, what a woman can do outside the blankets is as important as what she does under the blankets, Spotted Tongue," said Old Bill.

Spotted Tongue was glad he wasn't that old yet. Then he wondered if Green Willow would sew him a coat like Old Bill's.

"I hear tell the Dog Soldiers will be riding in sometime tomorrow," said Old Bill. "I heard Black Kettle tell the Peace Commissioners that they would come in all painted up and firing their pistols and for nobody to get scared. The Dog Soldiers aren't going on the warpath, just letting off some steam."

"The Cheyenne Dog Soldiers like to show off," said Spotted Tongue. "I will be glad to see them bury the hatchet and touch the pen to the treaty so I can ride to my winter camp. I thought I could catch Pap Dickerson's killer before I left, but I have failed, and we cannot stay here much longer."

"I saw you skulking around our camp, studying us like you could read guilt on our faces. Hard to learn anything when you don't have our tongue. All you can do is watch, but the other men are getting a little twitchy. They keep patting their heads like they're checking to make sure they still have their scalps. I told them they would know if you lifted their hair. They would feel your knife cut and hear the poppin' sound when you pulled their hair from their head, but I reckon I didn't give them any reassurance. Some of them have taken to sleeping with their long guns, Winchesters if they happen to have one, so you can see a lot of them are really nervous. But Evan Flynn thinks you hung the moon after you got him out of being chained to a wagon wheel."

Spotted Tongue wondered what Old Bill meant. He could not reach the moon to hang it. "I want the man who killed Pap Dickerson more than I want to lift a teamster's hair. I have enough of those already hanging on my lance. Besides, that would just cause trouble for my first wife."

Spotted Tongue leaned closer to the cooking fire, now burning low. "You know his name, don't you, Old Bill? Why don't you tell me?"

"I figure it's not something for me to tell. Let's just say I'm protecting some-one who was protecting you---"

"I don't need to be protected! I'm a Comanche warrior, and I protect other people, the squaws, the children, the old men near to taking the trail beyond

Father Sun. The Mexicans tremble when they hear my name, and the Texans in their wooden lodges fear the sight of me leading my band. Who thinks me so weak that I need protection?"

"You got it all wrong, Spotted Tongue, but I ain't gonna set your feet on the right trail. Some things you need to find out for yourself." The old teamster pushed himself off the ground and stretched the stiff joints that the old must suffer. "I reckon I'll see you tomorrow. I hear you and your warriors are going to put them Dog Soldiers to shame, prove that there ain't no finer horsemen than the Comanche. I'm looking forward to seeing it."

"Ten Bears told the Peace Commissioners that he wanted them to see what good horsemen the Comanche are. We ride before the Dog Soldiers arrive; let everyone see how real warriors ride."

"You're gonna show up the Cheyenne?" asked Old Bill with a grin.

Spotted Tongue shrugged with a grin of his own. "We will ride as we always have. You know the tribes north of the Arkansas do not make war with us. Except for the Arapahos for a little while."

Old Bill studied Spotted Tongue for a moment, a serious expression often seen on the face of the old when they question the young but expect a less-than-truthful answer. "You gonna bring your wives to watch? We all would like to see that second wife of yours give her our regard for being a fine fighter. She just comes up against too big a man and a dirty fighter to boot."

"She is still recovering from her bruises. She will stay in our lodge." No way Spotted Tongue would let Little Flower outside when Father Sun shone from the skies. Even with her haircut and a painted face, she still didn't look much like a Comanche. And then there were her blue eyes. No Comanche had blue eyes. Except for Quanah Parker, and his were more gray than blue. He was different from the ordinary Comanche, and not just because his mother was a Tejano. He was just different.

Spotted Tongue watched old Bill walk away on stiff legs and rounded shoulders. The teamster was nearing the time he would ride beyond the sun, although Spotted Tongue thought white men had different trails to the life that came after they closed their eyes for the last time. He was curious, but he didn't know why. He was curious about many things since he lost his medicine. He guessed he was like the children searching through the goods belonging to the correspondents and the Peace Commissioners: he just wanted to know about the strange white men.

He sighed and scooted to one side of the cooking fire, closer to where his war shield rested in its rawhide covering and propped on a three-legged stand. He touched it with reverence as no squaw was allowed to do. It was convex, stuffed with many layers of paper taken from white men's books during raids, which was best for deflecting lances, arrows and even bullets, provided they weren't from one of those big guns used by buffalo hunters. And some of the long guns that fired many times that had been appearing since the white man's great war.

His shield had magic symbols painted on it, with decorations of animal fur, shells, and scalps from those men who put up a fight. Scalps from men who ran or cowered were not as prized as those from men who fought to the death. And if a warrior happened to take a scalp from a hated Texas Ranger, well, that was the most prized of all.

There was no finer shield in the Comancheria than that of Spotted Tongue.

He would carry it tomorrow when the Comanche would demonstrate their horsemanship. Everyone, white men and Indians alike will admire the Comanche on horseback. There are no warriors to rival them.

Turning away from his war shield, he fingered his collection of stones. He now has as many as there were men and one woman abused by Pap Dickerson. Each stone stood for a person, and Spotted Tongue touched a particular one. "Lizzy, Pap Dickerson's wife, hated him for beating her. How long until a woman takes revenge? Why wait so long? She had many moons, many seasons, to kill him. I think she feared him more than she hated him. I think her fear would hold her back. This murder needed a person strong in his wits, able to take advantage in the time of a heartbeat."

Spotted Tongue reluctantly laid down the stone. "No, I do not think that Lizzy killed her husband. She may have the wits good enough to survive alone, but I do not think her wits are up to seizing the chance to murder when it comes around."

He touched another stone. "Mountain Mike Flynn beat Pap Dickerson, and Dickerson took revenge. But Mountain Mike's brother, Evan Flynn, did not take revenge. He had the opportunity to kill Dickerson but pulled off his aim instead. Just like Evan Flynn said, he is not a killer. No one can fail to shoot a man in the belly when he is standing only a few paces away. Would that he had, so I would not be puzzling over a white man's death."

He picked up another stone, this one small and rough. "This is Pinkie Jones, who lost his fingers when Pap Dickerson hacked them off over a game of cards. But Pinkie could not use his crippled hand to hold a gun and fire it. He could not use his other hand because he was clumsy with that hand. Most men have one clumsy hand and one good hand, and so it is with Pinkie Jones. Who else is left? Old Bill? Yes, he is able. He would kill a man without thinking about it if he thought the man deserved it. But he wouldn't have missed. Old Bill may be old, but he is not a man to take abuse from another. His eyes are still as bright as a young warrior's, so he can still see as well as the eagle that sees a rabbit while flying high and close to the clouds. No, Old Bill didn't kill Pap Dickerson. I am almost sure."

"But who did kill him?" mused Spotted Tongue to himself. "What do I not see?"

"Spotted Tongue! You are whispering again and keeping me awake, and Little Flower is, too. You need to quit playing with stones and sleep. You will fall off your pony when showing the white men how much better you are than the Cheyenne Dog Soldiers."

Green Willow's voice was shrill enough to echo off the bluffs, and Spotted Tongue ground his teeth together as he got up and stalked toward his lodge. One day, Green Willow would push him too far. She had no respect for a war chief.

CHAPTER TWENTY

"…..the Arab of the Prairie—the model of the fabled Thessalian 'Centaur,' half horse, half man, so closely joined and so dexterously managed that it appears but one animal, fleet and furious."

Imaginative Description of the Comanche on Horseback by Homer Thrall in A Pictorial History of Texas, St. Louis, 1879, page 445

Spotted Tongue finished braiding a loop of rope into his pony's mane since he and twelve of his band would be riding without saddles. One of their many maneuvers required a loop slipped over the head and under his arm so that the warrior might hook his leg over the pony's backbone, slide down the animal's side and shoot arrows at the enemy without exposing himself. The pony acted as a shield for the warrior. Other Plains Indians might attempt to perform the trick, but none were as successful as the Comanche, who practiced their tactics over and over again as long as Father Sun ruled the sky.

There were other tactics that the Comanche warrior practiced until he could perform them without thinking. One such tactic was picking up a wounded warrior and swinging him across his pony's back while riding at full speed. It was the most honorable task for a Comanche. Never leave a wounded or dead warrior on the battlefield. Of course, the maneuver was usually performed by two warriors riding side by side, particularly if Fat Belly was the one needing to be carried off. There was a limit to what Spotted Tongue asked his warriors to do. A single warrior picking up Fat Belly was not a task he asked anyone to do.

Spotted Tongue patted his pony's nose and admired the animal's sleek white hide. Most Comanche preferred the spotted ponies, but this animal had been Little Flower's pony she rode to escape capture. He captured both horse and woman. They were now his personal property to use as he saw fit. He claimed the woman and trained the pony he now called White Ghost to obey him as the warriors of his band did.

Actually, White Ghost, being a stallion rather than a gelding and larger than the other ponies, was apt to misbehave at some unforeseen moment.

"Hey, Spotted Tongue, We are ready," yelled Fat Belly from his perch atop his black spotted pony that never looked big enough to carry his rider. "The brush target is ready, and there are two rawhide strips laid out at the end of cleared ground.

As the band formed a line behind Spotted Tongue, each warrior's pony nearly touching the pony in front of it, all waited for their war chief's signal to gallop toward the bush target, slide down the pony's side, and shoot at the target beneath their pony's head. They would begin their show with this stunt.

Finally, Shaking Hand, first behind Spotted Tongue, called to him. "Your warriors are ready, Spotted Tongue!"

Spotted Tongue barely heard his friend over the noise coming from the crowd of Peace Commissioners, soldiers, teamsters, white correspondents, and what seemed like most of the other Indians at the Council. Squaws held on to the younger children lest they dart out in front of the ponies, and he saw the bucks talking excitedly to one another while pointing to one Comanche or the other. The men were betting on the winner of the stunts.

Behind the men, standing on a wagon tongue, was Green Willow, surrounded by the wives of his warriors. But no Little Flower.

Spotted Tongue searched the crowd around Green Willow for a glimpse of his second wife, but she was nowhere to be seen. Had she run away again? Then what was Green Willow doing gawking at his warriors on their ponies? He told her to stay at the lodge and watch Little Flower. Did she not have any respect for him at all that she would disobey him like this?

"I will return her to her father's lodge and demand the ten ponies I paid for her. I swear to Father Sun I will. But first, I---"

"Spotted Tongue! Everyone is waiting. The Cheyenne and Arapahos will begin to laugh at us! Even the Kiowa will laugh."

Spotted Tongue finally heard the urgency in Shaking Hand's voice and raised his hand above his head as he kicked White Ghost, but carefully as the stallion was not well trained yet.

The white stallion galloped toward the target, his hooves raising a cloud of dust behind him. Spotted Tongue slipped the braided loop of rope over his left shoulder and under his right arm and slid down the side of his pony, hooking his heel over White Ghost's backbone. Peering underneath his pony's head, he notched an arrow in his bow and shot it at the target as White Ghost swept past at a gallop.

He heard the shouts of the crowd and knew that he had hit the target in the center. He pulled at the braided loop to turn White Ghost to the left to lead his warriors in a circle behind him. He led his band at a gallop toward two rawhide strips laying ten feet apart. It was a favorite trick of Spotted Tongue's. A rider's pony must stop with all four hooves between the stripes, then reverse to race back to the starting point. Spotted Tongue had won many ponies from the other tribes who would bet against him. He heard the sounds from the crowd and grinned. The correspondents and some other whites applauded. Not most of the soldiers and teamsters. Too many of them had lost battles with the Comanche. As he prepared to pull himself onto Whiter Ghost's back, he took one more glance at the crowd from beneath his pony's head.

"Old Bill," he breathed in shock when he saw the old teamster and his companion, then repeated in a shout. "Old Bill!"

The teamster jerked his head toward Spotted Tongue, then turned to say something to a squaw standing next to him before he pushed her away.

"Little Flower!" Spotted Tongue yelled at the squaw, who hesitated before turning and disappearing into the crowd.

Nearly blind and deaf with rage, Spotted Tongue pulled himself onto White Ghost's back and turned him at a gallop toward Old Bill.

Squaws and children, teamsters, and white correspondents scattered like leaves in autumn when the wind blows. The Peace Commissioners fled toward their lodges except for General Harney, who waved his arms and shouted for the soldiers.

"Stop that Indian! But don't shoot! This is a Peace Council, for God's sake!"

"I'll kick anybody's ass who shoots at that Indian! His horse probably just bolted!"

Spotted Tongue heard Harney but ignored him and whatever he said. He needed to catch Little Flower, take her back to his lodge, and tie her hand and foot so she wouldn't escape again. Then he would come back and teach Old Bill what happens to a man who messes with a Comanche warrior----or his squaw. He felt disgust at himself like a whip across his shoulders. He had *liked* Old Bill. He had been fooled! You could never trust a white man.

Old Bill didn't obey the old general's order. He pulled his revolver and shot several feet above Spotted Tongue's head. "Hold Up, Spotted Tongue," he shouted in Comanche.

At that moment, White Ghost plowed to a stiff-legged stop with all four feet braced against the hard-packed ground. Caught by surprise, Spotted Tongue catapulted between his pony's ears to dangle upside-down by the loop braided into the animal's mane, temporarily blocking White Ghost's vision and sending the horse into a head-shaking panic.

Before Spotted Tongue could free himself from the loop, four soldiers grabbed both his arms and legs while trying to evade being kicked by a confused and angry stallion. Livid with both anger and humiliation, Spotted Tongue fought the soldiers. For a Comanche war chief to lose control of his pony, no matter how poorly trained, is unheard of. To become a prisoner of soldiers is also unheard of. He would never live this down. The story of Spotted Tongue and his wild pony would be told around every cooking fire in the Comancheria.

Seeing Spotted Tongue fighting four soldiers and his own horse, Shaking Hand and the other warriors pulled their horses around and galloped back to surround the soldiers holding their war chief, pointing their lances inches away from the white men's crotches. No one seemed to notice Spotted Tongue was still entangled in the loop and gasping for breath.

"Somebody cut that loop off him before he chokes to death," shouted General Harney. *"But don't cut him by accident or on purpose. By God, anybody cuts him on purpose, and I'll lock that man up myself---soon as we get to a fort that has a stockade! Before I could do that, though, his warriors will geld you. McCusker, this is one of your Comanches! Get over here and calm him down and do it quick! And one of you men, bring that teamster over here. He was shooting at that Indian, trying to kill him the best I could tell."*

Two soldiers grabbed Old Bill by the arms and dragged him in front of the irate general, who was now pacing up and down in front of his soldiers and a flailing Spotted Tongue. He stopped to glare at Old Bill. *"What the hell were you thinking, shooting at that Indian like that? Next thing you know, Comanche will be lifting your hair, and you won't even know it until it's too late. The good Lord save me, but I've had nothing but trouble from you teamsters and the Indians. I ought to lock you all up in the stockade if I can find one big enough."*

"But General Harney, Sir, the Indians were invited to the Peace Council," interrupted Major Elliot. *"I don't think you can lock them up."*

His face was as red as the flames of a cooking fire, the tall, old General whirled on the Major. *"Elliot, you're already on a short leash for letting that damn fool correspondent and some of your boys shoot those buffalo without anyone intending to eat them. Pissed off old Santana like nothing else could have done, so don't be telling me what my duty is. How did you ever make it to major anyway? What I 'ought' to do and what I 'can' do are two different propositions, and I know which is what. McCusker! Where are you?"*

Phillip McCusker, followed by William Fayel, squeezed in front of Major Elliot to face Harney.

"Right here, General Harney. I believe you were right. I think Spotted Tongue's horse must have been scared of something. This horse is a whole lot bigger than a Comanche's horse usually is---they mostly pick spotted horses about 14 hands high or maybe 15---this white devil is at least 17 hands high and doesn't appear to be too well trained. Spotted Tongue is generally the best rider around, but that horse just got away from him. You know how strong a horse this big can be. They're hard to handle."

Harney rubbed his chin and peered suspiciously at Phillip McCusker. *"I've never had trouble with a big horse, McCusker."*

"I'm sure you haven't, General." He turned to William Fayel. *"Haven't I remarked on what a good horseman the General is?"*

"That's enough, McCusker! I'm willing to buy your story, so don't go stretching it too far. Now get your Comanches out of here and back to their lodges, or so help me God, I'll---" the General hesitated as if searching for words *"---You know what*

I'm going to do, McCusker? I got a bottle of fine whisky in my tent, good for settling a man's nerves, and mine need settling. Now get your Indians out of my sight! And don't let them geld my soldiers before they go! I expect I might need them boys in the future. That peace treaty isn't signed yet."

Spotted Tongue didn't understand what McCusker was telling the white chief, but he suspected it was something he wasn't going to like. The white interpreter had that sweet sound in his voice that signaled a lie like the buzzing of flies signaled a dead buffalo lying in the hot sun.

Before General Harney could turn toward his tent and his whiskey, Old Bill shook off the two soldiers holding his arms and spoke to the old army leader. *"That's right, General, that horse was wall-eyed scared, no tellin' why, and I shot off my revolver to stop him runnin' into the crowd and hurtin' the women and children. That horse was tryin' to bolt or ready to kick the devil out of anyone who was standin' between him and the open prairie. It kinda confuses the horse, as gunfire does, but mostly, it makes him want to go in the other direction, away from the gunfire. It makes the horse stop and take his bearings. And it gives time for that Comanche to get control of his pony."*

General Harney glared at Old Bill and sniffed as if he could smell a lie. *"That might work, or that Indian might get himself trampled---what's your name anyway?"*

"My name's Old Bill, General," said the teamster.

"I've been around this territory off and on for a lot of years, Old Bill. Would I know your full name if I heard it?"

"Might do, General, but I ain't gone by nothin' but Old Bill for a coon's age. I ain't sure what my full name is anymore 'cause it's been so long since I needed it."

Harney studied Old Bill and finally shrugged. *"Guess it doesn't amount to a hill of beans anyway. So you swear you shot at this horse to shock him into confusion? You weren't trying to shoot the Indian?"*

"If I had meant to kill the Indian, I would have done. Don't often miss what I aim at, and I wasn't aimin' at him," said Old Bill.

"I reckon you're truthful about that if nothing else. You strike me as more than a teamster, but on the other hand, a lot of teamsters are good with a long gun. Have

to be since they don't have any better sense than to drive across land still claimed by some Indian tribe or the other."

The General sighed loudly, a man feeling put upon by duties he didn't necessarily want or enjoy. He waved his arm toward the crowd of soldiers and Indians, correspondents, teamsters, camp followers, other Indians of various tribes with their squaws and children, and sundry other observers of the scene. *"Show's over, folks, you can go back to your tents or lodges or wherever you lay your heads. I'm going to my tent, where I can hear that whiskey calling my name. Elliot, make yourself useful for a change and move these people out."* The old general sighed loudly again and turned toward his tent, walking faster the closer he came to that bottle of fine whiskey.

The minute the soldiers released him, Spotted Tongue lunged for Old Bill, who ducked aside, while Phillip McCusker and William Fayel lunged for Spotted Tongue. "I don't know how many more times I can talk the soldiers out of shooting you," said Phillip McCusker, trying to hold a wiggling, spitting Comanche war chief who didn't want to be restrained.

"He talked to Little Flower," said Spotted Tongue, "and he gave her something. I must know what he gave her and why she ran when she saw me."

"Did you talk to Spotted Tongue's wife?" Phillip McCusker asked old Bill.

"I talked to a Comanche squaw, gave her a little doo-dad I had that she liked, had some glass beads on it. If she was Spotted Tongue's wife, she never told me so. You're just seeing your wife where she ain't. I saw her with that other squaw. They were watching you and your warriors linin' up to show off."

"It was Little Flower," insisted Spotted Tongue.

"Give it up, Spotted Tongue," said Phillip McCusker. "Go find Green Willow. See if your wife is with her, but for God's sake, get away from this crowd. All these folks are like a horse on loco weed: ready to attack anything that moves."

Spotted Tongue expelled a deep breath and took another. His fury was cooling as doubts crept in. Was it Little Flower or not? He did not see the squaw's face full on, only the side of it, and that was painted. He looked around at his warriors, at Phillip McCusker and Fayel, at soldiers gripping their rifles. Teamsters and camp followers, all staring at him. He felt like a fool.

CHAPTER TWENTY-ONE

As long as the buffalo ranges upon the Plains and we are at peace, we agree that you may chase him as agreed by the treaty of the Little Arkansas, but the herds of buffalo are becoming fewer and fewer every year. You can see this for yourselves, and therefore you must prepare for the day when he will cease to be."

Opening Remarks by Senator Henderson at the Cheyenne-Arapaho Grand Council at Medicine Lodge Creek, Kansas, October 28, 1867, as Reported by William Fayel in The Missouri Republican, November 2, 1867.

Gunshots and war whoops heralded the arrival of the Cheyenne Dog Soldiers. Shaking his head to clear it of his humiliation at the hands of the soldiers and the behavior of his pony, Spotted Tongue leaped again on the back of the white stallion. "If you shame me again, I will cut your throat and give your hide to Green Willow to make me a breechclout. And every time I lose gas, I will think of you."

The horse snickered, and Spotted Tongue suspected the animal was laughing at him, and well, he might because he knew no Comanche would willingly kill a pony without a good reason. Spotted Tongue admitted he would not kill a pony for any reason, not even a misbehaving, poorly trained, mean-tempered, stubborn pony like White Ghost, who either tried to buck him off or bolt to the open prairie---or both.

Spotted Tongue kicked White Ghost gently and took his place in front of his band of warriors beside a group of Kiowa. The two bands took a position on the banks of Medicine Lodge Creek, their lances ready, war shields on their left arms. He only noticed a dozen or so Comanche were in war paint, those who had been in their demonstration that ended in his humiliation. The other Comanche and the Kiowa were called by their chiefs before they could paint their faces.

"Hey, Spotted Tongue. Are you sure you can stay on your pony? Maybe I should lead this band," called Coyote Dung in a voice louder than necessary. Those warriors around him, not many, since Coyote Dung had few friends, laughed at Spotted Tongue.

Spotted Tongue felt his face burn with humiliation. "Perhaps you would like to try to ride White Ghost when he is angry. Make sure you have on a clean breechclout first. White Ghost doesn't like a warrior with a stinky ass."

The laughter was louder and lasted longer. Everyone knew about Coyote Dung's passing gas and leaving a deposit behind.

Spotted Tongue laughed hardest of all while wondering what kind of trick Coyote Dung would play on him in revenge. Just as long as it wasn't something deadly like rattlesnakes in his lodge.

"Ho, Spotted Tongue! It's just the Cheyenne Dog Soldiers showing off," shouted Fat Belly. "Look at those feathered headdresses! How can they fight wearing something like that? It's just looking to be jerked off and your head along with it."

"I don't know, Fat Belly, and I don't care. Since there is no fighting to be done, I'm going back to my lodge to talk to Green Willow. She needs to explain herself."

"Ho, Shaking Hand, Wild Horse! Spotted Tongue is going to 'talk' to Green Willow. I'd rather go watch what Green Willow does to Spotted Tongue than fight with the Cheyenne." Fat Belly laughed until his belly shook, but Wild Horse and Shaking Hand looked at Spotted Tongue and swallowed their laughter.

"Go listen to the Council tomorrow, Fat Belly, and come tell me if the Peace Commissioners tell the Cheyenne anything different from what they told us. Wild Horse, Shaking Hand, go with him. I want to know everything."

"Aren't you coming?" asked Wild Horse. "We might miss something."

"I will be there, but I may be late. I must learn if I am losing my wits and seeing things that are not there or if Green Willow disobeyed me," said Spotted Tongue as he kicked—gently—White Ghost and loped toward his lodge and his untrustworthy first wife.

He pulled White Ghost to a stop in front of his lodge and leaped off. "Green Willow!"

Green Willow poked her head out of the lodge, saw Spotted Tongue and ducked through the lodge's flap. She stood, her hands on her hips in her typical fighting stance. "Well, did you finish showing off for the white men while I had to stay here and watch Little Flower so she wouldn't run off. I was the only wife who had to stay in camp, and I was the War Chief's first wife. I should have been there!"

Spotted Tongue lost his words for a heartbeat before he took a breath. "You were there, Green Willow! I saw you! But you know who I didn't see? Little Flower! Where was she?"

"The same place she is now. Sewing beads on a pair of new moccasins! She finally learned how to do that without ruining the moccasins." Green Willow pulled the lodge flap back. "Look for yourself, Spotted Tongue. Not that it's easy to work with so little light. And hot! This lodge is hot when you make us close the flap. You didn't used to be so mean to me—and Little Flower," she added as an afterthought.

Spotted Tongue ducked into his lodge. Little Flower sat in the back of the lodge, holding a moccasin in one hand and an awl in the other. She looked at him, raising one eyebrow as if asking what he wanted. A bead of sweat rolled down her forehead. "It's hot," she said in his tongue. Or that's what he thought she said. In his confusion, he could hardly understand her.

"But I saw you," he said, looking at Green Willow, "and Little Flower was talking to Old Bill."

"That hairy old man that sits around our cooking fire every night? Why would Little Flower be talking to him? Your wits are confused, Spotted Tongue. That's what comes of sticking your nose in a white man's business. I've told you before that nothing good could come of it. You walk around like you can't see what's in front of you. You nearly walked into the cookfire last night. You could have knocked over the buffalo stew that Little Flower made."

Spotted Tongue thought knocking over Little Flower's stew might not have been a bad idea. At least his belly would not be making noises this morning. And hanging upside down over White Ghost's nose didn't help. And neither did being held down by soldiers. "I just have many thoughts in my mind. I must go to the Peace Council tomorrow, and that will be many more thoughts. The Cheyenne are here, and I must make sure their treaty is the same as that for the Comanche and Kiowa. I can't be worrying about women's complaints. And this lodge is not hot; it's cold. Your temper makes you too hot. You must think sweeter thoughts," he said as he dashed beneath the lodge flap and out into the cold wind to White Ghost, ignoring the screeching of Green Willow.

His obsession with Little Flower confused his senses and disrupted his peaceful life. Listening to the Peace Commissioners tomorrow will be like a calm day after the storm in his lodge.

CHAPTER TWENTY-TWO

"We are willing, when we desire to live as you do, to take your advice about settling down, but until then, we will take our chances."

Cheyenne Chief Buffalo Chief in reply to Senator Henderson's opening remarks at the Cheyenne-Arapaho Peace Council, Medicine Lodge Creek, Kansas, October 28, 1867.

His unease followed him to the arbor and the Peace Commissioner's voices that droned on like the sound of the hopping bugs in the prairie in the hot months. He only paid half his attention to the speeches. The rest was focused on Old Bill and the Comanche woman he spoke to. If it wasn't Little Flower, then who was it? He knew all the squaws in camp. It was someone young because she moved quickly when she disappeared into the crowd. And she was tall, or taller than most of the squaws. Only Slow Like a Turtle, Fat Belly's wife, was as tall as the woman he saw. But Slow Like a Turtle was---slow. It couldn't be her. Besides, for some reason, she believed Fat Belly was the most wonderful warrior among the Comanche. Not everyone agreed with her.

Spotted Tongue thought again of the white man and one woman abused by Pap Dickerson. Old Bill, Lizzy Dickerson, George Carter, Pinkie Jones, Evan Flynn. No, Evan Flynn was innocent, he had proved it himself. Of the others, only Old Bill claimed he was planning to kill Pap Dickerson the first chance he got but that someone else had done it first. The other men abused by Pap Dickerson were reluctant to challenge him. They were not cowards, but all knew Dickerson was a dirty fighter who would do whatever it took to win. The fight between Dickerson and Evan Flynn provided an opportunity to take vengeance without being caught.

Spotted Tongue doubted any of the other men would seize that opportunity. They were too mild of nature. Why did all the teamsters tell him how Pap Dickerson abused them? Just to point a Comanche warrior to a trail that led nowhere?

Spotted Tongue smiled to himself. The teamsters were more clever than he had first believed. The Comanche often did the same thing to mislead an enemy: a few warriors would appear to an enemy and then ride away. The enemy would ride after them, allowing the rest of the band, including the women and children, to get away. The teamsters hinted one of them was guilty so he would not look further. Point the enemy in one direction when he should go in the other.

But it is hard to fool a Comanche. Who else did Dickerson abuse? His daughter? But Old Bill and the other victims knew he would not tell Lesser Chief Elliot the daughter's name. No, they were telling tales to protect the guilty from *him*. They feared he would take his revenge on the guilty.

Spotted Tongue touched a finger for each person abused by Dickerson. Five! But there was another, there had to be, one who the whites would protect from him. He closed his eyes to see each person in his mind, to watch their abuse as if it was happening in front of him: the rattlesnakes in the bedroll, the knife slash across George Carter's face, Old Bill's dead mules, Pinkie's missing fingers, the young daughter abused by her own father. He wondered if Dickerson had attempted to rape his daughter as he had Little Flower. At least Evan Flynn's brother saved the young daughter, as Evan Flynn saved Little Flower. Both Flynns had interfered with Pap Dickerson. That must mean something, but he didn't know what yet, but he would. He could sense the answer hovering just out of his reach. He would think about it.

When the speeches ended, Spotted Tongue mounted White Ghost and rode away from the peace arbor for the last time. The stallion shook his head and snorted. Spotted Tongue patted the pony's neck. "Yes, I feel the same way," he told the pony. "There has been much talk here, some from the white men and some from the Indians, but there is no common tongue, only what the interpreters say each side says. My heart is heavy in my chest with knowing there is no understanding."

He shivered. Even the weather was unsettled. Dried leaves from the elms that surrounded the arbor where the Peace Council met swirled in the restless wind that blew cold over the valley of Medicine Lodge Creek. Dark clouds rolled in from the west, but as yet, the rain held off. Spotted Tongue wished for a buffalo robe and his fur-lined, knee-high boots rather than his plain moccasins. At least he had on his ceremonial leggings that a warrior would wear for meeting a white man to talk of a new treaty. But the air grew colder, the wind stronger, and the sky filled with purple clouds, their undersides painted a dull gold by the late afternoon sun. A storm was coming that would blow all that stood before it. Already, those correspondents and Peace Commissioners were holding their hats on their heads, and the wind was whipping at the loose canvas tops of the ambulances.

Spotted Tongue reined in White Ghost and watched the soldier orderlies packing ambulances with large cook pots, metal spoons, and many other items he did not know the names of while others packed grease into the hubs of wheels. Other soldiers rubbed down the Army horses just as all the tribes were driving their pony herds toward Medicine Lodge Creek. Squaws were taking down lodges, packing travois with presents and such household goods as they had brought with them.

Most of the teamsters had already harnessed their mules, ready to make a late start across the prairie toward Fort Harker. Spotted Tongue saw that Old Bill lingered by his packed wagon but had not harnessed his mules. He must be waiting for Father Sun to rise before driving away toward wherever he decided to go.

At that moment, a white streak of light crossed the sky as if the Great Spirit was tearing the world in two. White Ghost reared up on his back hooves. The mules pulled at their harnesses, and the army horses reared up in fear, pulling on their reins held by the white soldiers. There were hoarse shouts by the soldiers and the teamsters. Spotted Tongue didn't need Phillip McCusker to translate. The teamsters and soldiers were calling animals many names, none of them kind. Most men, whether white or Comanche, would do the same.

The white man called the streak of fire a comet.

Spotted Tongue called it an omen.

His warriors surrounded him on their trembling ponies. "What is that fire in the sky, Spotted Tongue?" cried Wild Horse. "What is the Great Spirit saying?"

"He is saying tell your war chief what you heard at the Council," said Spotted Tongue.

"But what of the fire in the sky?" asked Wild Horse.

"You have seen such fire in the sky many times, Wild Horse. It comes in a bad storm, and this night will be a bad storm that will frighten the ponies and the whiter soldiers and teamsters, but not Comanche warriors. Isn't that true, Shaking Hand?" he asked. "You must be strong warriors before the squaws and children, so they might not shiver with fear. And you do not want to show fear before the white men. A Comanche warrior must be brave and fearless."

Spotted Tongue leaned over in his saddle and stroked White Ghost's neck to calm him. Now, tell me what you heard at Council?"

"The white chief tells the Cheyenne and the Arapaho the same thing he told us, Spotted Tongue, that the buffalo will die off and that the Peace Commission will save us from starving by sending us to reservations. But there are as many buffalo as lights in the sky. The white man is trying to trick us!" said Fat Belly in a loud bellow. Shaking Hand and Wild Horse, riding beside their fat brother, silently nod their agreement.

Spotted Tongue didn't doubt that the white man would trick the Comanche as well as the other tribes, but not about the buffalo. The white hunters were killing and skinning the buffalo, leaving the flesh to rot, and soon, there would be too few to feed the People. Unless the Peace Commissioners stopped the hunters, and he didn't see any signs that was happening or would happen. No, the white hunters would swarm over the prairie like locusts, killing every buffalo they saw.

He didn't know what to tell Fat Belly except what he had said before. "We will hunt the buffalo as our fathers and their fathers have done. What will come, will come."

He saw Wild Horse frowning at him and shrugged his shoulders. Wild Horse had always had better wits than Fat Belly. He wasn't sure that the other warriors agreed that the Comanche should live as they always had. Perhaps Shaking Hand also wondered at his answer to Fat Belly, but what else might he say? The buffalo will all disappear from the Comancheria, and the People, starving and sick, will take the trail beyond Father Sun? Or ride the Reservation Trail to be a beggar, to lose themselves to what the white man calls civilization? Spotted Tongue knew much of what might happen given certain circumstances: dark clouds mean heavy rains, Father Sun burns hot for two or more moons, the streams dry up, and the People go without water.

But he did not see everything that might happen, so until he could, he would live as he always had. He had no magic to stop bad luck for the Comanche, so each warrior must decide for himself: to fight or to surrender. Spotted Tongue saw no third trail for the Comanche. He had already decided. He would not take the Reservation Trail.

"Spotted Tongue, that is not all," said Wild Horse. "The Cheyenne war chief, Little Man, accused the Kiowa and Comanche of saying bad things about the Cheyenne. He said we were spreading rumors that the Cheyenne were going to attack the Peace camp, and that's not all," he finished in a loud voice.

Spotted Tongue wished it was. He had already heard enough about Little Man and his words to last him until he took the trail beyond Father Sun. "I know, Wild Horse. Little Man also said all the alarms about the Cheyenne were caused by us. His tongue is twisted. All those things were done by the Arapahos. Do we want to fight Cheyenne over his false words or let them disappear like the morning mist in Father Sun's light? I say Little Man's words are not worth the sweat off my pony's back."

"So we do nothing?" asked Fat Belly, his large stomach quivering with indignation as he rocked back and forth on his pony's back.

"We do nothing," agreed Spotted Tongue. "There will be fights to come. We will not waste our blood on Chief Little Man and his Cheyenne. Instead, let us sharpen our weapons, do our war dances, practice our death songs, and watch for our true enemies."

"The Tonkawa," shouted Fat Belly. "Those man-eaters! They are lower than snakes that crawl on their bellies!"

"Yes, Fat Belly, the Tonkawa deserve to lose their hair and be stripped of their skin by Comanche knives in revenge for their treachery against us, but they are worms to be stepped on. Let us save ourselves for a greater enemy."

"The soldiers," said Wild Horse in a flat voice. "You believe the soldiers will hunt us."

Spotted Tongue hesitated. He did not know without any doubt, but yes, he did believe the soldiers would come for those who did not ride the Reservation Trail. But what should he tell his warriors? The truth or a lie? He might possibly be wrong, so should he burden men who were more like his brothers than only his warriors with the dark thoughts that stole his sleep at night. Or should he let them live as they always had, with no thoughts of the blue coats riding over the Comancheria? Let them enjoy the last happy days of the People, he decided.

"I cannot see what happens the next moon or the next season," said Spotted Tongue. "Perhaps we can kill the white hunters and save the buffalo. Then we will follow the herds as before, and the white government cannot force us on the reservation because the buffalo are not gone."

"See, Wild Horse, it will be as Spotted Tongue says," said Fat Belly, raising his war lance in jubilation.

Fat Belly would believe that all was well or would be if Spotted Tongue used his medicine. "Would that I could," whispered Spotted Tongue to himself.

His dark thoughts and the questions from his three warriors were drowned by the singing and shouts of a large group of Arapahos, who rode toward the Peace Commissioners' camp. Some wore long headdresses and beaded shirts, and most had their faces painted in bright colors. As a group, they dismounted, formed a large circle, and began to dance, shaking bone rattles and blowing on buffalo horn whistles. Spotted Tongue thought Santana's bugle made a better sound.

Shaking Hand, Fat Belly and Wild Horse stopped to watch, but Spotted Tongue looked toward the south, where lightning had set fire to the prairie. "Forget the Arapahos! Ride to our camp!" he shouted toward his three warriors. "Tell the women not to take down the lodges. There will be a terrible storm soon, and we must have shelter. Bring the presents and our goods into the lodges, so they will not be ruined by the rains. Hurry! I will follow."

He watched his warriors kick their ponies' sides and ride toward their camps, then turned White Ghost toward the nearly empty teamsters' camp.

CHAPTER TWENTY-THREE

"The storm worsens, the lightening turning the clouds to fire. The wind blows down the white man's tents and the Indians' tipis. It is an omen of what is to come. War between the Comanche and Kiowa and the white man will erupt again, setting the prairies on fire as the lightening sets fire to the clouds."

Comments by War Chief Spotted Tongue to Interpreter Phillip McCusker at the end of The Medicine Lodge Creek Peace Council on the evening of October 28, 1867.

Intermittent flashes of lightening lit up scenes of dancing Arapahos, their face paint beginning to streak in the light rain; white men clutching their hats in the rising wind; tent ropes bulled loose from their pegs; and canvas ripping free of the loaded ambulances. Trees swayed back and forth, with branches broken by the storm crashing to the ground and high winds sending dead leaves whirling in the air.

Spotted Tongue peered through the increasingly heavy rain, finally shading his eyes with his hand to keep the rain from blinding him. He reached the teamsters' camp, although few teamsters remained. Most were foolish enough to leave between the end of the Council and the beginning of the storm, abandoning what shelter the camp provided for the dangers of a storm on the open prairie. But Old Bill remained, huddling against his wagon under a buffalo robe, hide outward to deflect the rain.

He was waiting, Spotted Tongue knew, waiting for him.

"Now, exactly why are we out in the driving rain to talk to an old teamster, Spotted Tongue?" asked Phillip McCusker, swiping his sleeve against his face in an effort to keep the rain off his face.

"We must ask the Great Father to send even more rain, rain enough to make it hard to breathe without drowning. The rain is not heavy enough yet to put out the prairie fire. Look, Phillip McCusker, the flames are near the other side of Medicine Lodge Creek. The Cheyenne and Arapahos are trying to drive their ponies to this side of the creek so they will be safe from the fire. They should have done it earlier instead of staying to grab all the presents their arms could carry. Only witless Indians do not believe a bad, bad storm was coming."

"You're being a little hard on the Cheyenne and Arapaho, Spotted Tongue," said Phillip McCusker. "You can't expect every Indian to be as prophetic as you. And you didn't answer my question. Why are we talking to that old teamster?"

Spotted Tongue wondered what the English word 'prophetic' meant. He wished Phillip McCusker would not mix his tongue with the Comanche tongue. "Old Bill knows who killed Pap Dickerson…"

"…For God's sake, Spotted Tongue, if I had known you were going to chew over that old question, I would have stayed back in my lodge out of the rain."

"Rain is pouring through the smoke hole in the top of your tipi. Might as well come with me to interpret what Old Bill says. He speaks our tongue very badly."

Phillip McCusker stopped as if turned to stone, then stepped in front of Spotted Tongue, forcing him to stop. "That old man speaks the Comanche tongue? Then you don't need me. I'm going back to my lodge. I can't get any wetter than standing out here in the rain."

"He speaks well enough for talking around the cookfire in front of my lodge, but I must be sure I understand what he says. The Peace Commissioners did not understand the Indians, and the Indians did not understand the Peace Commissioners. Each side only understood what the interpreters said, and the interpreters, sometimes even you, Phillip McCusker, did not always understand what the Indians meant, only what their words said. The same word can mean many things."

"Are you saying I didn't interpret every word of the Comanche tongue as it was spoken? It isn't my fault the Peace Commissioners heard other words than what I said. I did the best I could, but I couldn't explain to them what the buffalo meant to the Comanche, the Kiowa and the other Plains Indians. To the white man, the buffalo is just something to eat to keep from starving, and any other animal will serve as well. They don't understand that The People's whole life revolves around the buffalo and hunting and war. These white men don't live like the Comanche, so they don't understand why you live like you do. All the white men see are dark-skinned men wearing feathers and animal hides, torturing, and scalping their captives, and living in buffalo hide tents. They don't see how much alike the white man and Indian are. Well, some of them do." Phillip McCusker stopped to take a breath before continuing, like a man running a race he knew he was going to lose but giving it his all anyway. "But you don't understand the white man either, Spotted Tongue. You don't understand why white men live in wooden lodges on the same piece of ground season after season and plant crops when the buffalo are so plentiful and good eating. You don't understand why they kill buffalo, strip the hide, and leave the flesh to rot. You don't understand the white man needs those hides to operate the machinery that makes their factories run. You don't understand what I'm talking about. You've never been out of the Comancheria. You've never seen the white man's world, but many of the chiefs who signed the treaties have. They believe the treaties are the only way to save the Plains Indians from extinction. Otherwise, it is General Sherman and the Army, and few of you will survive. I don't see either white man or Indian understanding each other and finding another solution."

"I understand the white men want to kill the buffalo and drive The People onto the reservation like a herd of sick ponies," said Spotted Tongue, his voice sounding bitter to his own ears. He didn't understand much of what Phillip McCusker said, but that was nothing new. "You can't always understand the Comanche even though you are kin through your wife and speak our tongue. You are still a white man, and sometimes, that side of you hides your understanding of the Comanche. But come, I need you to listen, and I will listen, and the two of us will learn not only what Old Bill says but what he means."

Phillip McCusker studied his face, but what he hoped to find, Spotted Tongue had no idea. Finally, the interpreter sighed, a man who knew he was fighting a losing battle. "If it scratches that itch you have about who killed that worthless teamster and shut you up about it, I'll go. I still don't know why you're so hellbent on knowing the name of the killer when you have so much more you need to worry about."

"I know the name, but what is the meaning behind the name? There is much more I would know, and Old Bill can tell me."

Phillip McCusker stopped and stared at Spotted Tongue, his mouth gaping open before he could find the words to say. "You know? How long have you known?"

"Just today—when I realized Old Bill and the teamsters were protecting the killer from me, not from Lesser Chief Elliot or Big Chief Harney."

"Why? You weren't going to turn over the killer to the army, and you weren't going to lift his hair for taking his revenge before you could take yours. You weren't, were you, Spotted Tongue? Whoever killed that teamster did you a favor. If you had sent a lance through his belly, the soldiers would have put paid to you, and General Sherman would have spit on your grave."

"That is another reason why someone killed Pap Dickerson; they did it to protect me."

"Hey, McCusker, Spotted Tongue! Wait up!"

Spotted Tongue turned to see the wet figure of William Fayel sloshing toward them, holding his sodden hat on his head. He ground his teeth in frustration. He didn't want the correspondent to listen to what Old Bill might say. He was afraid of what William Fayel might do that would endanger The People and, more importantly, Little Flower.

"Get rid of him, Phillip McCusker. What Old Bill has to say is only for my ears," said Spotted Tongue urgently.

"What are you and Spotted Tongue doing out in the rain? I tried to catch you after the Peace Council adjourned, but I had to wait for any final comments the Cheyenne and Arapaho might have to say. So where are you going? Have you solved the mystery yet, Spotted Tongue, and do you have any comments about the Great Treaty Council?" asked William Fayel.

Spotted Tongue turned to Phillip McCusker. "What did he say?"

"He wants to know if you found your killer and what you thought of the Peace Council?" said Phillip McCusker. "I take it you don't want to tell him who the killer is. I don't know why, but I reckon you have your reasons. So tell him what you think about the Council. That ought to satisfy him."

Spotted Tongue looked up at the deep purple clouds, felt the heavy rain now falling at a slant, and heard the thunder as loud as the big guns on wheels that the white soldiers fired. He felt light-headed as he did when he felt a vision coming on. A streak of lightning lit up a cloud, and he saw the shape of a wolf for a heartbeat. Then it was gone as if it had never been, and he knew he would never see it again. His spirit animal confirmed what he knew was coming. A mood darker than the storm clouds covered him as he realized he didn't need his spirit animal anymore. He could already see what came next to The People, and no magic could change it.

"Tell William Fayel this, Phillip McCusker. Let him make marks upon paper so the white men far away may know what Spotted Tongue sees. The storm worsens, the lightning turns the clouds to fire...."

Spotted Tongue listened while Phillip McCusker turned his words into the correspondent's tongue. William Fayel looked at him, then finally lifted his hat and nodded before turning to the interpreter. *"McCusker, I may have met a noble red man, or close to it, if you ignore the odd scalping or two. At least I've met an eloquent one. Tell him I am sorry for the end of the Comanche. Would that this will not happen. But it will."*

The lanky correspondent turned and disappeared into a sheet of rain.

Old Bill rose from a crouch to meet the two men. "Spotted Tongue, I figured you'd be along to talk to me. I'd invite you to sit a spell, you and McCusker, but I've got no tent, so unless you want to sit in the mud underneath my wagon, we best say what we got to say and find some pitiful excuse for dry shelter."

"Why did you hide the gun the morning of the shooting?" Spotted Tongue asked.

"I wasn't sure, but what you might think you were shamed, her killing Dickerson in your place, and I sure didn't want nobody seeing her with a smoking gun, so I took it. If the army found out about her, well, General Sherman plans on coming down hard on tribes that hold white captives, wipe them out likely, and I didn't want no part of that. See, I know what kind of man Sherman is, and I wanted to know what kind of man you were before I said anything. So I'd go down to your lodge of an evening and jaw a little. By the way, I don't think your squaw likes me much."

Spotted Tongue wasn't surprised; Green Willow didn't like many people. "So you wanted to see if I was better than this big chief? What did you decide?"

Old Bill gazed at him, then wiped the rain off his face. "To get on with my story. I gave the gun back to her that morning you tried to run your pony over me, so she could put it back where she got it. She said you would figure it out eventually but that it was her right to get her own back from Dickerson and that you would understand. Anyhow, I asked her if I could take her back to her folks, but she said she didn't have any, just you and your squaw, and no home to go to but your camp with you. I didn't like her answer, still don't, but I figure she earned the right to make up her own mind."

Old Bill grinned at Spotted Tongue. "She's quite a woman, but you better keep her hidden until you get back to the Comancheria. It wouldn't do to have word get out that you have a white captive. Me and the other boys, the ones Old Pap Dickerson abused, ain't gonna say anything, so you don't have to worry about us."

The old teamster shook Spotted Tongue's hand. "I don't reckon we'll meet again, so you stay well, War Chief Spotted Tongue. Your people will need you when all this is over. Mr. McCusker, you take care, too. You're a man of two loyalties, and that can tear a man apart. Good luck to you, and do your best for Spotted Tongue when the time comes." The old man looked at both, then turned away to climb on his wagon and huddle under his buffalo robe.

Phillip McCusker turned to Spotted Tongue and opened and closed his mouth several times before he found his voice. "Your second wife killed Pap Dickerson, and she's WHITE! You brought a white captive to the Peace Council disguised as a Comanche! If old Sherman finds out, you're a dead man. You know that, don't you?"

"I do now. Old Bill just told me."

"This is not funny, Spotted Tongue! That redheaded devil is going to want to know why the principal Comanche interpreter didn't know about this and tell him. My God, you dropped me in the shit pile."

"What will you do?" asked Spotted Tongue. He didn't want to kill Phillip McCusker, but he would if it meant keeping Little Flower as his second wife.

Phillip McCusker walked a circle around Spotted Tongue, then reversed to circle him again. He wiped the rain off his chin and took a deep breath. "Well,

Hell, Spotted Tongue, I guess I better get used to being in the shit pile if I'm going to keep company with you. Now, suppose you tell me how you knew your second wife was a killer."

Spotted Tongue wasn't sure he liked Phillip McCusker calling Little Flower a killer. She wasn't....exactly. "When I realized that the teamsters were protecting the killer from me. Why would they do that? I already told them I wouldn't say anything, and I wouldn't kill anyone for taking away my vengeance. But they didn't know if I had honor enough to keep my word. Old Bill must have told the teamsters that I had honor. Still, they protected her. Why? Because they knew captives were less than Comanche. I might punish a captive woman for shaming me. While the teamsters were protecting Little Flower, I was thinking of all Pap Dickerson had abused. None had the fire in the belly to kill except Old Bill, and I believed him when he said someone else had killed the man first."

Spotted Tongue shivered in the rain, now heavy enough to quench the flames from the prairie fire. Buffalo hide lodge covers blew away, and he saw squaws with babies and older children huddling under buffalo robes while the lodge poles were blown down by the wind. The campgrounds where lodges and all manner of goods had been were now a morass of ankle-deep mud.

"Damn it, Spotted Tongue, how did you decide it was Little Flower?" demanded Phillip McCusker.

"Whoever killed Pap Dickerson had been abused by him. I knew all those who were abused, and they were innocent. That meant there was another who was abused, someone the teamsters didn't tell me about. Once I used my wits, I knew of one more abused victim."

"Little Flower!" exclaimed Phillip McCusker.

Spotted Tongue nodded. "Little Flower. And she has the fire in her belly to kill a man for revenge. Now, I will go to my lodge if it is still standing and confront my wives. We will be leaving tomorrow for the Comancheria, and we may not see you again."

"You believe what you said about war coming, Spotted Tongue? What will you do?" asked Phillip McCusker.

"The war will destroy the lodges of the People, but a man fights until he is without pony, without lance, without chance to win. I will lead my band to join Quanah Parker's people to the Staked Plains, the last refuge of the Comanche, and there we will live until we can fight no longer."

Leaving Phillip McCusker standing in the rain and staring after him, Spotted Tongue ducked under the flap of his lodge. Green Willow might be a woman who will drive a man to lose his wits, but she knew how to set up a lodge that the wind could not blow away.

His two wives huddled at the back of the lodge to stay out of the rain pouring in a steady stream through the smoke hole. Green Willow stared at the mud that coated the floor of the lodge so she couldn't meet his eyes. Green Willow never avoided a fight with him, so Spotted Tongue knew she was guilty of disobeying him and then lying about it. For once, she was afraid of what he might do to punish her. That had never happened before, so he enjoyed the moment. Knowing Green Willow, it wouldn't last long.

Unlike Green Willow, Little Flower sat up straight and looked at him with defiant eyes. She pulled up her skirt to show him the scabbed furrows on her thighs. She pointed to the partly healed wounds and slapped her fist against her chest. "He did that, the filthy, lice-ridden teamster. He wanted to rape me, Spotted Tongue! No one abuses me like that. I killed him, and Old Bill helped cover it up. I avenged myself as is a Comanche's right. I didn't need a man to do it for me. Tell everyone in the Comancheria that I am a squaw to be feared!"

Spotted Tongue watched tears roll down her cheeks, leaving streaks of her face paint, but he knew the tears didn't mean Little Flower was sorry for what she did. No, she was fearful that he might be angry at her. "Yes, you are a Comanche, and vengeance is your right."

He turned to Green Willow. "Little Flower told you what she had done, and you helped her, too. You were both there to watch the warriors show off. You let her meet Old Bill so he could give her back my gun. You ran back to the lodge when you realized I saw you. I should have known when I saw sweat on Little Flower's face. The lodge wasn't hot as you kept saying, Green Willow; it was cold."

Green Willow looked up at him, swallowed loudly and opened her mouth. Spotted Tongue shook his head and folded his arms. "Not a word, Green Willow, and don't ever lie to me again. A Comanche woman must never lie to her husband. It is disrespectful. Another thing, woman, when you take down the lodge tomorrow and pack our goods on the travois, make sure Little Flower can't get a gun or knife. I will sleep better at night."

SUGGESTED READING LIST

These are only a few of the books and articles I consulted while writing MUR-DER IN THE MOON WHEN THE LEAVES FALL, but the reader will find them most informative without being onerously scholarly. In particular, I highly recommend Douglas C. Jones for a meticulous physical description of the Medicine Lodge Creek Treaty Council right down to what the seating was like for the Indians, the Peace Commissioner, and the correspondents, as well as a dissection of the correspondents themselves, their reporting styles, and their accuracies and inaccuracies. THE TREATY OF MEDICINE LODGE: THE STORY OF THE GREAT TREATY COUNCIL AS TOLD BY EYEWITNESSES is required reading for anyone interested in the Great Peace Council of Medicine Lodge.

The other book that covers the Treaty Council almost hour by hour is MY EARLY TRAVELS AND ADVENTURES IN AMERICA AND ASIA BY HENRY M. STANLEY. The book contains some errors, such as Stanley's mis-naming Phillip McCusker as McCloskey and assigning some of the council chiefs to the wrong tribes, but reading it is like eavesdropping on all the participants. FYI: don't expect a warm and fuzzy opinion of the Indians from Stanley, although he does credit them with great oratory.

Among the scholarly books in the following bibliography, I would particularly recommend COMANCHES: THE DESTRUCTION OF A PEOPLE BY T.R. FEHRENBACH and THE COMANCHES: A HISTORY 1700 – 1875 BY THOMAS W. KAVANAGH.

Published books and articles about the Comanche and the Indian wars number in the hundreds, perhaps the thousands. Unless the reader is obsessed with the subject, those published works I have included should satisfy the mildly curious. If not, check the individual bibliographies for more titles. There are often errors, inconsistencies, and contradictions between the titles listed. I picked the facts that best suited my plot so individual authorities may disagree with me. It is their prerogative to criticize and my prerogative to ignore their criticism in the pursuit of a good story. May civility rule each endeavor.

D. R. Meredith

Amarillo, Texas

November, 2023

Berry, Gerald, *Comanche Society: Before the Reservation.* College Station, Texas: Texas A&M University Press, 2002.

Language and Cultural Preservation Committee, *TAA NUMU TEKWAPU?HA TUBOOPU (Our Comanche Dictionary).* Elgin, Oklahoma: Comanche Language and Cultural Preservation Committee, 2nd Printing, June, 2003.

Dary, David A., *The Buffalo Book: The Saga of an American Symbol.* New York: Avon Books, 1974

Ewers, John C. *Plains Indian History and Culture: Essays on Continuity and Change.* Norman: University of Oklahoma Press, 1997.

Fehrenbach, T. R., *Comanches: The Destruction of a People.* New York: Alfred A. Knopf, 1974.

Gwynne, S. C., *Empire of the Summer Moon: Quanah Parker and the Rise and Fall of the Comanches, The Most Powerful Indian Tribe in American History.* New York: Scribner, 2010.

Jones, Douglas C., *The Treaty of Medicine Lodge: The Story of the Great Treaty Council as Told by Eyewitnesses.* Norman: University of Oklahoma Press, 1966.

Kavanagh, Thomas W., *The Comanches: A History, 1706 – 1875.* Lincoln: University of Nebraska Press, 1999.

Lee, Nelson, *Three Years Among the Comanches: The Narrative of Nelson Lee, Texas Ranger.* Guilford, Connecticut: The Globe Pequot Press, 2004

Lehmann, Herman, *9 Years Among the Indians, 1870 – 1879, Edited by J. Marvin Hunter.* Albuquerque: University of New Mexico Press, 1993.

McHugh, Tom, *The Time of the Buffalo.* Lincoln: University of Nebraska Press, 1972.

Michno, Gregory and Susan, *A Fate Worse Than Death: Indian Captivities in the West, 1830 – 1885*. Caldwell, Idaho: Caxton Press, 2007.

Meadows, William C, *Kiowa, Apache, and Comanche Military Societies*. Austin: University of Texas Press, First Paperback Edition, 2002.

Moore, Stephen L., *Taming Texas: Captain William T. Sadler's Lone Star Service*. Austin: State House Press, 2000.

Neeley, Bill, *The Last Comanche Chief: The Life and Times of Quanah Parker*. New York: John Wiley & Sons, Inc., 1995.

Rathjen, Frederick W., *The Texas Panhandle Frontier*. Austin: University of Texas Press, 1973.

Smith, F. Todd, *From Dominance to Disappearance: The Indians of Texas and the Near Southwest, 1786 – 1859*. Lincoln: University of Nebraska Press, 2005.

Stanley, Henry M., *My Early Travels and Adventures in America and Asia*. London: Gerald Duckworth & Co. Ltd., 2001.

Wallace, Ernest, and E. Adamson Hoebel, *The Comanches: Lords of the South Plains*. Norman: University of Oklahoma Press, 1986.

Wilbarger, J. W., *Indian Depredations in Texas: Reliable Accounts of Battles, Wars. Adventures, Forays, Murders, Massacres, etc.., Together with Biographical Sketches of Many of the Most Noted Indians Fighters and Frontiersmen of Texas*. Austin: Statehouse Press, 1985.

Wistrand-Robinson, Lila, and James Armagost, *Comanche Dictionary and Grammar*. Arlington,. Texas: SIL International and The University of Texas at Arlington, 1990.

Worcester, Donald E., Editor, *Forked Tongues and Broken Treaties*. Caldwell, Idaho: The Caxton Printers, LTD., 1975.

Zesch, Scott, *The Captured: A True Story of Abductions by Indians on the Texas Frontier*. New York: St. Martin's Press, 2004.

ARTICLES

Benson, Bruce C.: "The 19<sup> Century Comanche: A Legal System Based on Individual Rights," PERC *REPORTS:* *http://www.perc.org/perc.php?subsection=5&id=806.*

Lipscomb, Carol A., "Comanche Indians, "*https://www.tshaonline.org/about/people/carol-lipscomb.*

Oman, Kerry R., "The Beginning of the End: The Indian Peace Commission of 1867 – 1868,"

DigitalCommons@University of Nebraska – Lincoln, (winter, 2002).

Robinson, W. Stitt, Editor, "The Kiowa and Comanche Campaign of 1860 as Recorded in the Personal Diary of Lt. J. E. B. Stuart," *Kansas State Quarterly, Winter, 1957 (Vol. XXIII, No. 4).*

Kavanagh, Thomas W., "Domestic Architecture at the Comanche Village on Medicine Creek, Indian Territory, Winter, 1873, "*http://php.indiana.edu/~tkavanag/asoule.html.*

Wynkoop, Christopher H., The before, during, and after of the Great Treaty Council at Medicine Lodge Creek, Kansas, October, 1867, in numerous articles online *http://freepages.genealogy.rootsweb.com/~wynkoop/index.htm.*

MISCELLANEOUS ARTICLES WITH WEBSITES

Comanche Timeline, *http://www.comanchelanguage.org/Comanche%20Timeline.htm*.

Comanche History: Part One, *http://www.tolatsga.org/ComancheOne.html*

Comanche History: Part Two*: http://www.dickshovel.com/ComancheTwo.html*

Comanche History: Part Three, *http://www.dickshovel.com/ComancheThree.html*

The Handbook of Texas Online, "Blanco Canyon, Battle of:" *http://www.tsha.utexas.edu/handbook/online/articles/BB/qfb2.html*

The Handbook of Texas Online, "Yellow House Canyon, Battle Of:" h*ttp://www.tsha.utexas.edu/handbook/online/articles/YY/qfy1.html*

Indian Affairs: Laws and Treaties, Vol. II, Treaties: Treaty with the Kiowa and Comanche, 1867, Compiled and Edited by Charles J. Kappler. Washington: Government Printing Office *http://digital.library.okstate.edu/kappler/Vol2/kio0977.htm*

Wikipedia, "William S. Harney:" https://en.wikipedia.org/wiki/William-S-Harney

Texas Indian Reservations: A Legacy of Failure, 1854 – 1859, *http://www.texashistory.com/history.html*

Native American Relations in Texas, List of Persons Killed and Wounded in Parker County, June 9, 1867. *Texas Indian Papers Volume 4, #148, Archives and Information Services Division, Texas State Library and Archives Commission.*

Native American Relations in Texas, Mark Walker to Chauncy McKeever, May 14, 1867, *Texas Indian Papers Volume 4, #140, Archives and Informational Services Division, Texas State Library and Archives Commission. Original in the Records in the Department of Interior, Office of Indian Affairs, Letters Received, Kiowa, 1867.*

NEWSPAPERS

Missouri Republican of St. Louis, William Fayel, correspondent. Fayel included a column on a Comanche's quest for vengeance for a wrong done. Published October 24, 1867. *St. Louis: Missouri History Museum, Reference Department.*

The New York Times, "Peace Commissioners: A Treaty of Peace Signed with the Comanche and Kiowa Indians---Other Tribes Willing to Make Treaties." *Published: October 26, 1867.*

Chicago Tribune, S. F. Hall, Correspondent. The Indians: The Visit to the Southwestern Tribes." Short article covering the fight between two teamsters: *Published: October 24, 1867.*